HUDSON RIVER HOMICIDES

MEMENTO MORI: BOOK FOUR

C.S. POE

Hudson River Homicides

Published by Emporium Press
https://www.cspoe.com
contact@cspoe.com

Cover Art by Reese Dante
Cover content is for illustrative purposes only and any person depicted on the cover is a model.

Edited by Tricia Kristufek
Copyedited by Andrea Zimmerman
Proofread by Lyrical Lines

Published 2025.
Printed in the United States of America

Trade Paperback ISBN: 978-1-952133-56-5
Digital eBook ISBN: 978-1-952133-52-7

For Nic.

Thank you for your patience, support, and belief while this book took on far too many iterations before getting here.

MEMENTO MORI

Remember that you must die.

CHAPTER ONE

It was Thursday, July 9, 11:07 p.m., and there was a body in a fridge.

Everett Larkin stood in a pool of tungsten lamplight on Pier 34, brackish wind running invisible fingers through his ash-blond hair. The choppy currents of the Hudson River were capped white from the glow of several strategically placed mobile lighting units, while members of Port Authority and the NYPD's Harbor Unit worked in tandem near the pile fields. Directly ahead, the black framework of downtown skyscrapers stood out against an even blacker night sky, their illuminated windows like monsters with a thousand teeth or a thousand eyes. Law enforcement had parked alongside the deserted bike lane of West Street to the left of the pier—a mix of patrol cars with flashing red and blue lights, as well as vans from the Crime Scene Unit and Office of Chief Medical Examiner. Just beyond those were parked news vehicles, members of the press being kept outside a wall of yellow crime tape.

Homicide detective Ray O'Halloran—the bulky Irishman with strawberry blond hair, a ruddy complexion, and a personality not unlike that of a schoolyard bully—was approaching from the throng of uniformed officers and PPE-wearing scientists, skirting a truck-mounted crane with its boom extended beyond the guardrail and into the water. "That you, Grim?" he called over the crane's engine. O'Halloran dipped in and out of the overhead light before coming to a stop at Larkin's side. "Almost didn't see you in that Funeral Director Special."

Larkin wore his usual uniform of a charcoal-gray suit, crisp white shirt, pink tie, artfully arranged paisley pocket square of white and gray, and mint-green derbies. He diverted his gaze from the aquatic recovery effort to level his reaper-gray stare on O'Halloran.

O'Halloran pointed and said, "I guess I shoulda just looked to the shoes for confirmation."

Larkin quoted, "One does want a hint of color."

O'Halloran's brows scrunched together.

"Albert Goldman," Larkin stated. "*The Birdcage*. You called me in the middle of date night."

"Your idea of date night is Nathan Lane in drag?"

"You're lucky it wasn't a Marilyn Monroe film—otherwise, I'd have not picked up at all. Why have you called me to an active crime scene."

As if in answer to Larkin's inquiry, someone from the water shouted the go-ahead, which was echoed by another individual, and then the crane began to retract and hoist a secured refrigerator from the river. Water gushed from the bottom panel as the unit was lifted high enough overhead to get it over the pier railing. It gradually rotated midair to face Larkin and O'Halloran, and scrawled across the door in all caps with what was likely permanent black Sharpie was the message: *PIN ME TO DETECTIVE LARKIN.*

"Port Authority called it in," O'Halloran explained. "Asked if we had a Larkin on the force. Considering you've become something of a household name… didn't take Dispatch long to confirm." O'Halloran looked over his shoulder and pointed toward the news vans. "Your fan club must have been listening to the scanner."

At that, Larkin said in a clipped tone, "I'm not interested in giving them material for another write-up that compares my real-life detective skills to that of a century-old fictional character."

"So sayeth the cop with enough commendations to rival the damn commissioner."

A man with the recovery effort jogged onto the pier, approached the suspended kitchen appliance, and gave the crane operator a series of hand gestures until the white, Marcom brand refrigerator—standard in every typical New York rental—was laid on its condenser on a tarp that'd been set out in advance.

"I take it that your presence is a formality," Larkin stated, watching as the slings were removed from the fridge.

"It's being treated as a homicide," O'Halloran confirmed. "If you want it, you gotta play ball."

"It's incredible, the asinine amount of red tape justice must contend with."

A third voice interrupted the two. "That you, Larkin?"

Larkin sidestepped O'Halloran. Approaching the scene, wearing a shapeless PPE jumpsuit, with a black Pelican case in one hand and a camera strapped around his neck, was Neil Millett—the perpetually cynical and sharp-tongued detective with the Crime Scene Unit who Larkin had worked alongside of on three cases since Monday, March 30. Millett was several inches taller and a few years older than Larkin, with honey-brown hair and a pulse on fashionable attire—although he shied away from Larkin's more extreme color combinations.

Walking beside Millett and hastily pulling on a navy-blue windbreaker with the emblem of the OCME on the left breast was Dr. Lawrence Baxter. Given the number of years a forensic pathologist dedicated to schooling, residency, and fellowship alone, Larkin logically knew that the good doctor had to be *at least* his own age of thirty-five. But when taking in Baxter's slight frame, coppery red hair done up in a classic James Dean quiff, those retro browline glasses, and a solid skincare regiment, it all had a way of aging him like a particularly vague autopsy report: *Decedent is between twenty and fifty years of age.*

Millett came to a stop on the opposite side of the fridge and set his kit down on the cement walkway. "I'd say it's nice to see you again, but a crime scene is hardly the place for such platitudes."

Larkin's mouth twitched.

Baxter said, "I don't attend scenes for just anyone, you know. Where's your hunky forensic artist for me to ogle?"

"Contrary to what my recent caseload would suggest, Detective Doyle is not typically at my side in an official capacity," Larkin answered.

"What about unofficial?" Baxter countered.

"All right, all right," O'Halloran started. "Before someone starts crying 'always the bridesmaid, never the bride.'"

Larkin replied, "In a 2015 report presented at the Annual Meeting of the American Sociological Association, a six-year study that followed the same 2,262 heterosexual couples—aged nineteen to ninety-four—found that women initiated sixty-nine percent of all divorces and consistently reported lower levels of relationship quality than their male counterparts. A particularly interesting takeaway from this research was that, among the *unmarried* heterosexual couples who broke up, there was no statistically significant difference between who initiated the split, suggesting that nonmarital relationships are more equal, flexible, and adaptable to the rapid-fire changes of today's society."

"Good fucking God," O'Halloran said under his breath while pinching the bridge of his nose.

"So the takeaway is, don't get married," Millett said, collecting a pair of latex gloves, safety glasses, and N95 mask from his kit.

Baxter countered, "I think the takeaway is actually, don't be straight." He was smiling to himself as he watched Millett finish donning his PPE, but as the CSU detective began to snap a series of rapid photographs—collecting visuals of the fridge from various angles and distances, including the aggressively scrawled message addressed to Larkin—Baxter's smile faded. Rather solemnly, he asked, "This isn't normal, is it?"

Funny, Larkin thought, how desperate humans were to anthropomorphize something as lawless as the universe, to find order in its chaos, to find sense in its senselessness, to accuse man of deviating from the norm—*living*—when there was nothing true of human design except for the inevitability of *death*—but *this* should be viewed as abnormal. Nietzsche's aphorism 109 warned: *Let us be on our guard against ascribing to it heartlessness and unreason, or their opposites; it is neither perfect, nor beautiful, nor noble; nor does it seek to be anything of the kind, it does not at all attempt to imitate man! It is altogether unaffected by our aesthetic and moral judgments!*

Man would always give birth.

Man would always raise his hand against the weak, the opposite, the other.

Man would always die.

And the world would never stop turning. It was *unaffected*.

It was only through man's ability to theorize, to conceptualize, to empathize that he could assign meaning—*morality*—to a word such as "normal."

A cool breeze skimmed uptown along the river's surface as Larkin said, "'There is nothing either good or bad, but thinking makes it so.' Hamlet believed Denmark a prison, and so it was. Rosencrantz and Guildenstern believed it not, and so it wasn't."

Baxter raised an eyebrow.

"Humanity despairs for *reason*, doctor," Larkin continued. "From belief in the divine to chaos theory to existentialism. No matter how fraught with uncertainty, mankind yearns for purpose. Murder is not normal because you believe it so."

"You don't?"

"What I believe won't change anything."

"And yet, here you are," Baxter said, gesturing at the crime scene surrounding them.

"Yearning for purpose," Larkin concluded.

O'Halloran heaved a sigh strong enough to move mountains. "A regular fucking conversation just isn't possible when you three idiots are involved…."

Larkin glanced sideways at O'Halloran. "We can discuss the career of Pete Alonso at a later date."

"*Sure*," O'Halloran said with a disbelieving snort.

"I've become quite adept at the ins and outs of baseball over the last few months."

O'Halloran's expression shifted to that of wary curiosity. "Yeah?"

Larkin turned to watch as Baxter busied himself with his own safety gear. He continued in his usual monotone, "My Mets statistics are more a regurgitation of facts, but I'm certain you can use your limited imagination to pretend you're discussing the current season with someone who appreciates sabermetrics."

"Asshole."

Millett lowered his camera. "Now that we've covered the American trifecta of divorce, death, and baseball… can we have Dr. Baxter examine the contents?"

"Please," Larkin answered.

Millett reached across the fridge, gripped the door handle, and yanked it backward.

A pungent odor immediately wafted out, acrid and overwhelming, like bleach and cat piss and human decomposition had all been mixed together in the same vat and was left to bake in the summer sun.

"Jesus H. Christ and his twelve fucking apostles!" O'Halloran swore. He took a step back and put a hand over his nose and mouth. "I've been working Homicide nearly fifteen years and never smelled a body this rancid."

Millett had immediately gone to his kit and collected additional PPE. He gave the fridge a wide berth and approached O'Halloran and Larkin with the offerings.

O'Halloran held up his other hand in defense and asked Larkin, "Grim, you want the case, right?"

"Of course."

To Millett, O'Halloran made a gesture of wiping his hands and said, "Best of luck with your acid bath."

"Ammonia is an alkaline," Larkin replied in an almost absent manner. He'd accepted Millett's PPE and was adjusting the mask on his face.

"Anyone ever tell you that you've got a nasty habit of always getting in the last word?"

"Frequently."

Another snort. "Good luck."

"Thank you."

Millett watched O'Halloran cross the pier and make for the cordoned-off street before saying offhandedly, "That asshole was practically pleasant tonight."

Larkin didn't comment as he put on the safety glasses, approached the fridge, and peered inside. The contents didn't look any better than they smelled: a murky brown, almost black water—the Hudson's natural, sediment-heavy color— mixed with the internal fluids from a melting body. The shelves had been removed and the victim, entirely nude, first appeared to have been placed into a cramped sitting position, but upon closer inspection, Larkin realized it was actually a pile of dismembered body parts. The victim's forehead rested against a pair of raised knees, short blond hair plastered to the sides of their face. The back of the neck showed off where they'd been decapitated—the tool brutal, violent, with serrated teeth. All over the skin that wasn't submerged in the sludgy water was a waxy gray substance.

"Sure hope they were dead before the hacking began," Millett muttered, seemingly to himself, before he raised his camera and started taking pictures.

Baxter said to Larkin matter-of-factly, "That smell is the by-product of anaerobic bacterial hydrolysis of body fat. Ever hear of adipocere?"

Larkin glanced up from the decomposing mess. "Corpse wax."

"The body underwent saponification?" Millett interrupted.

"Sure did," Baxter answered. "That's what this gray substance is. If left alone, its texture will eventually harden and can preserve the identification of a body. It's not mummification, although it displays similar attributes. The Soap Lady in Philadelphia is an incredible example of nineteenth-century saponification and preservation."

"I've never heard of adipocere developing on a dismembered body," Larkin said.

"Anything is possible when presented with the ideal conditions."

"And what would those be," Larkin asked.

"Hmm… a mild alkaline pH level, moisture, lack of oxygen, and a consistently warm temperature."

Larkin glanced at the gray, greasy skin a second time. "According to Hudson River Park, the water quality typically measures at just above neutral. And the airtight seal on the fridge would significantly reduce oxygen levels while also preventing blowflies from laying eggs."

"Summer's been hot as shit too," Baxter added.

"Not the technical term I'd use, but yes, this season has been notedly warmer," Larkin replied.

"Textbook conditions," Baxter concluded.

"How much time is required for this process."

"I've seen a case where it occurred within three weeks of time of death," Baxter answered. "But it more often develops after about two or three months."

"A rough estimate of sometime between April 9 to June 18. What else can you tell me about the victim."

"Nothing," Baxter answered. "Adipocere tends to develop more often on female bodies since it requires the breakdown of body fat—of which females have about ten percent more of on average. The victim appears to be a white female, but beyond that, I can't give you age or cause of death until I do the autopsy." Baxter peeled his latex gloves off as he took a step back. "If you gentlemen don't mind, I need to speak with my team and figure out how we're moving the decedent to the morgue."

"Sure thing," Millett answered distractedly, now crouched beside his open kit.

Larkin acknowledged the doctor's exit by returning his attention to the body parts in the fridge. He reached into his pocket, removed his phone, and turned on the flashlight app. Larkin bent his knees and tilted his head, studying what little of the victim's face was visible from where it was pressed into their raised knees. "She has something in her mouth."

"What?" Millett dropped his supplies and hastily stood.

Larkin indicated with the light on his phone. "Her tongue is pushing it out."

Millett got close, angled the camera still strapped around his neck, and took several photos, asking in between the flashes, "How'd you even catch that?"

"I looked for it," Larkin answered.

Millett shot him an irritated glare.

"Tuesday, May 19, you provided me with a picture reminiscent of nineteenth-century mourning photography with the phrase, 'Deliver me to Detective Larkin,' written on the back side," Larkin explained. "Then on Wednesday, June 10, after unknowingly recovering fabric that was once used in a period mourning costume, I was supplied a VHS tape with another handwritten note reading, 'Watch me, Detective Larkin.'

"Now we're at a scene featuring a much more blatant attempt at communication—from whom I have to presume is the same unknown sender—'Pin me to Detective Larkin.' And since at-home electric refrigerators weren't popularized until after the first World War, and as far as I'm aware, have no connection to outdated mourning practices, I simply suspected there was some other item needing to be found."

Millett lowered his camera. "I didn't know there was a VHS tape on the last case."

"It was delivered to my home."

"That's brazen." Millett reached into the fridge and carefully tilted the head back to rest face up, revealing a bullet hole in the middle of the woman's forehead. "Found the cause of death," he stated.

Larkin's eyes widened. "I know her," he said on impulse.

"What?"

Despite the bloating, decomposition, adipocere, and third eye, Larkin would always recognize those pinched features, that Machiavellianism complex. He said, "Matilde Wagner."

"The Angel of Death?" Millett asked. And when Larkin narrowed his eyes, he protested, "Hey, I didn't name her. I just read the papers."

"Wagner was the mastermind behind the deaths of Broadway sex workers. Her husband, Earl, was present—was the bait—and an accomplice to over forty years of killings," Larkin explained. "But on June 12, Matilde murdered Earl."

Millett observed with a touch of detachment, "Dead men tell no secrets."

"The dead always speak. You just have to be willing to listen."

"I guess that's why O'Halloran calls you the Grim Reaper," Millett said before tugging his mask down and shouting toward the street where Baxter stood speaking with OCME staff, "Doc! Come back—we got a probable ID!" He shoved his mask back onto his nose and then reached into Matilde Wagner's mouth to remove the protruding object.

Larkin said, "She outsourced an attempt on Detective Doyle's life to her brother, Sal Costa, before going on the lam."

"Precinct gossip was—shit, hang on, it's got a pin pierced through her tongue… there we go—the gossip was that Costa almost killed *you*."

"That's correct."

Millett glanced sideways. "That was stupid."

"And I'd do it again."

The item popped free from Wagner's mouth, and Millett straightened his posture while extending a gloved hand. Despite the viscous body fluids, Larkin could easily make out a brooch with an antiquated clasp. It was made of black stone, seed pearls, and cut glass that housed delicate strands of braided human hair.

"You say she's been on the lam the past month?" Millett asked, shifting the brooch this way and that in the pier light. "Looks like the wrong person found her."

CHAPTER TWO

The second-floor bullpen of Precinct 19—the home away from home of the Cold Case Squad members—was empty at 12:34 a.m. Rows of industrial desks meant to withstand heavy use and abuse were all of the same faux wood surface and battered metal frame, like the department had done a single bulk purchase of office furniture when Larkin was still in grade school and called it done. It was in the desktop bric-a-brac where person-alities became apparent: Baker's cluttered mess of pilfered office supplies and outdated photos of her son; Porter's collec-tion of unwashed coffee mugs and half-empty clamshell containers of generic grocery store cookies; Miyamoto's stress balls and desk plate reading: Assistant to the Regional Manager; Ulmer's deluge of Post-it reminders; even Larkin's cup of Lisa Frank pencils and the recent addition of a small succulent— these mementos spoke of who the ten elite detectives were in the precious hours they spent elsewhere, away from the banks of fluorescent overheads, citrus-scented bathrooms, and pragmatic discussions of the city's forgotten dead.

Pulling out his computer chair, Larkin draped his suit coat over the back, adjusted the shoulder holster strapped to his right side, then took a seat. He typed up an initial report on the recovered body—an official ID would need to wait on fingerprints and a DNA test to legally confirm what Larkin already knew: the victim was Matilde Wagner and she'd been murdered to protect the secrets of the sender's decades-old criminal enterprise.

Larkin had theorized that his and Doyle's last three cases hadn't been isolated events of brutality, overlooked throughout the years due to the cleverness of a perpetrator and incompetence of law enforcement, but instead they'd been part of a tangle, a snarl, a literal spider's web of bribery, blackmail, corruption, extortion, rape, and murder—all of it connected via a once-mutualistic relationship with a single person.

The sender.

Adam Worth.

During an interview at the Tombs, Sal Costa had fearfully whispered this name, as if the walls might be listening—and maybe they were. Larkin had investigated the moniker, borrowing a book from the New York Public Library entitled *Before Moriarty: The Life of Adam Worth.* Now little more than a footnote in history, Worth had been a class of criminal so renowned throughout the nineteenth century that he'd garnered the respect of not only some of New York's greatest crooks and fences, such as Sophie Lyons and Marm Mandelbaum, but also the country's most renowned detective agency: the Pinkertons.

Worth had been born to a poor immigrant family, grown to be a man of slight stature who'd served in the Civil War, and became known for his aversion to violence just as much as his obsession with wealth and status. He'd built an organization that was so much more than the territorial disputes, bloodshed, and hierarchies of gangs seen both then and now in the twenty-first century. Worth had built a business out of stealing, and as its sole proprietor, he'd organized and funded the jobs committed by others, thereby keeping his hands clean and pockets full. The American thief had lived a prosperous double life as a British gentleman, all while evading the law and pulling the puppet strings of his underlings from New York to London, Paris to South Africa. He was the Napoleon of Crime, the inspiration for the machinations of Professor James Moriarty, archenemy of virtuoso detective, Sherlock Holmes.

After the events of the Niederman case, the *Times* had written a glowing review of Larkin's policework, including one assessment he hadn't been particularly fond of: *The NYPD's been hiding their very own Sherlock Holmes within a small, forgotten team known as the Cold Case Squad.* It'd been about his ego in the beginning—being compared to a fictional character when Larkin and his powers of deduction were very much real—but after Costa's slip of the sender's name….

Larkin stopped typing his report, looked at the books set neatly on the corner of his desk, then leaned to his right and grabbed the hefty tome of the complete collection of Sherlock Holmes. He'd been steadily re-reading the sometimes compelling, other times eye-rolling detective shorts whenever he remembered to take a lunch break, and just that afternoon had finished *The Adventure of the Final Problem*. Holmes, describing his nemesis to Watson—and thereby the reader— spoke gravely of an organization: *Again and again in cases of the most varying sorts*, and that he'd deduced Professor Moriarty to be at the center of a great spider web. *He does little himself. He only plans. The central power is never caught—never so much as suspected.*

Thumbing through the worn pages read by a thousand patrons before him, Larkin had to wonder if this entire game of cat and mouse had been orchestrated by the sender not because he had been bored, had been aroused by the thrill of the hunt, but because the sender had so easily gleaned the sort of man *Larkin* was. The sender had understood how puzzles were a sort of pleasurable distraction from the atrocities of life, and he'd seen how Larkin yearned for mental stimulation of a certain caliber in the same way a dying man might thirst for water. Sherlock Holmes had realized, with a sort of somber glee, that he had at last met an antagonist who was his intellectual equal—but his fight with Moriarty was only a work of fiction, and Holmes's obsessive desire to outsmart the professor hadn't put a target on Watson's back. Larkin understood the sender had chosen to reference Adam Worth for that very reason—to be an ever-constant reminder that this was the real world, with real consequences.

And unlike Holmes, if Larkin made the wrong move, he wasn't coming back from Reichenbach Falls.

Larkin grabbed the receiver of his desk phone and dialed a number.

The line was picked up after three rings and a gruff, sleep-logged voice answered, "O'Halloran."

"It's Everett Larkin."

"Hang on." Bedding rustled in the background, followed by a door clicking shut. O'Halloran grumbled, "This better be good, or I'm gonna wring your dapper little neck."

"We have a tentative ID on the Hudson River body."

Amid a yawn, O'Halloran asked, "Jimmy Hoffa?"

"What. No. Matilde Wagner."

"*Sonofabitch*." O'Halloran was awake now. "Are you sure?"

"As sure as I can be with DNA results pending," Larkin said.

O'Halloran swore under his breath before saying, "Did you know a man experiences unbridled joy only three times in his life?"

Larkin leaned back in his chair and rested his free hand against the back of his head. "Cite your source."

But O'Halloran continued, "When he gets married, when his first child is born, and when he sees the look on Matilde Wagner's face as the judge hands down a verdict of half a dozen consecutive life sentences."

Larkin rolled his eyes to the ceiling.

Since his near-fatal brawl in the shabby apartment on East Third, Larkin had been actively searching the thousands of unsolved cold cases for records that would be possible matches to Wagner's twenty-two alleged victims. But without names, faces, bodies, without knowing if any of those women had been reported as missing by friends or family, if their deaths had been investigated or deemed NHI by original responding officers, it'd been an exercise in futility for the last twenty-seven days. While Larkin had been lost in the past, O'Halloran had been presiding in the here and now—leading the search for Wagner, who was wanted not only for the premeditated murder of her husband, Earl, but also for conspiracy to commit murder— specifically that of law enforcement officer Ira Doyle. It wasn't anything personal. O'Halloran barely tolerated Larkin and, frankly, didn't even know Doyle, but he stood by the code of: You attack one of us, you attack all of us. O'Halloran had been determined to make the conspiracy charge stick, so his target winding up dead threw a serious wrench into the works.

Larkin was accustomed to the disappointment of being unable to see perpetrators stand trial; so often they were already dead themselves by the time their victim's case reached his desk—but Wagner was different. She'd been the cipher to understanding, to discovering who the sender was. She'd been the first person Larkin could confirm had been in direct communication with the mysterious Adam Worth, and losing the opportunity to question that relationship—never mind holding her accountable for the Broadway killings or for planning to take the life of a man who meant *everything* to him—it was absolutely criminal.

As for O'Halloran, who was very quietly cussing up a storm because it was clear his family was asleep and perhaps he'd disturbed them once already when he'd returned home less than an hour ago—Larkin suspected he wasn't nearly as familiar with the injustice that dominated these occasions.

Larkin asked, "Is there anything you can tell me about your search for Wagner."

"Like where she's been hiding out? If I knew that, I'd have had her ass in the cell across from her shithead brother already."

"No."

"What do you mean, *no*?"

Larkin explained, "The ME says her body underwent saponification inside the refrigerator, which, from my understanding, takes a minimum of three weeks to develop after being placed in an ideal environment."

"She poisons Earl right under my fuckin' nose," O'Halloran began, "gives ol' Sally-Boy the go-ahead to off your buddy, hightails it to Queens or Jersey or *wherever*, and then it turns out she's been dead for almost as long as she's been MIA?"

"That is most likely the case, yes."

O'Halloran blew out a breath, which briefly distorted over the phone line. "Look, I'll see if I can sit down with Costa in the next day or so—have a little chat. With his sister out of the picture, he's got no secrets worth protecting."

"Please call me when you have an update."

"Sure. Hey, Grim?"

"What."

"You couldn't wait until a more respectable hour to drop this bomb? It's one in the morning. I'm in my underwear, for Christ's sake."

"I suppose I could have. But then again, you had no reason to call me to an active crime scene and interrupt my date night, did you."

"Fuck you," O'Halloran said, but more with exhaustion and less with malice.

"Sleep well." Larkin hung up.

A ballast buzzed in one of the fluorescent overheads.

The public school-style clock on the far wall behind Ulmer's and Miyamoto's desks ticked.

A conversation between two uniformed officers in the lobby drifted upward:

"Hey, man, how was the date?"

"Awful. Said she moved to New York to live her *Sex and the City* era."

"Be for real."

"Pretty sure she was doing coke in the bathroom."

Sounds were louder at night. They bounced off the precinct walls and vaulted ceiling like ping-pong balls without the swell of motion, of bodies, of life, to absorb them. Larkin hadn't ever liked making personal calls from his desk—had been especially wary of nosy neighbors during the last year of his marriage, when it'd gotten rather volatile between him and Noah—but the officer downstairs, still regaling his buddy with his misadventure starring Miss Bradshaw, was a reminder that the building's museum-like quality at one o'clock would basically broadcast anything he said.

Larkin stood and headed back downstairs.

The heels of his derbies loudly clipped the tile floor. The two men in uniform stood near the front desk. They stopped talking, waiting until Larkin had walked past, pushed open the front door, and stepped into the night. Their shared laughter was abruptly cut off by the closing door.

The sweltering heatwave that'd been blanketing the city for the last three days wasn't supposed to break until tomorrow, so the night was punctuated with the steady hum of window units from surrounding buildings on the block. The air was thicker here than it'd been along the Hudson, and the heaviness pressing against Larkin's chest felt like the promise of a summer storm.

He pulled his cell from his pocket. The home screen illuminated, displaying the time and temperature against a backdrop of Ira Doyle's sunshiny face. Larkin had snapped the photo while on their walk last weekend. Doyle wore his beloved Mets cap backward and offered the camera his trademark, suck-up-all-the-surrounding-oxygen smile. Green vegetation and gold sunshine made his skin glow bronze and brown eyes sparkle.

The screen timed out.

Larkin tapped the power button a second time.

He didn't want to make a call this late when Doyle had to work in the morning like everyone else, but after the events of June 12, Larkin was haunted—truly haunted—by the memory of Sal Costa holding a Maglite to Doyle's throat, trying to crush his windpipe, ready to beat Doyle to death, to crack open his skull and let free all that trauma and love and grief and joy because someone calling themselves Adam Worth had commanded it so. The event had caused Larkin's already erratic sleep to get worse, and he'd recently gotten into the habit of pacing at night, falling into bed only when he'd exhausted his body beyond its means, never telling Doyle he counted his boyfriend's breaths in bed like they were talismans to keep evil at bay.

Doyle had been under the impression that Larkin was struggling to adjust to his new medication.

But the Prozac wasn't the problem.

In fact, the Prozac was pretty good. Larkin was surviving the detox and withdrawal from Xanax, and had been feeling more levelheaded, more who he'd been before the benzos had further complicated his already perpetually fucked-up life.

It really was just that goddamn Maglite.

"We have to be a team from the onset or this won't work."

The growing complexity of the investigation, as well as his and Doyle's positions within it, had allowed for paranoia to take root, like an invasive species, in Larkin's brain. How was he supposed to translate this wordless dread that kept him awake into something rational for another cop to understand—another detective—the very man who'd been instrumental in solving the previous three cases? How was Larkin supposed to keep his partner both involved and out of reach from danger when Doyle represented what a partner was both on *and* off the clock?

Larkin knew that if he begged Doyle to step aside, to let him handle the case on his own, the request would blow up in his face. This was his job, his career—Larkin could practically hear Doyle's words, hear the upset but never the raised voice—that one threat wasn't going to scare him away, that he was armed too, and Larkin just couldn't find it in himself to tell Doyle that his weapon wasn't a gun, it was a pencil. That he was hope, he was happiness, he was so gentle, and someone—Adam Worth—was going to take advantage of him. But Doyle had been fighting for years to be taken seriously as an investigator, to be seen as more than a middleman struggling with burnout, and if Larkin chose to once again not disclose certain particulars he felt were too sensitive to Doyle's well-being, it'd be seen as a betrayal and nothing more.

No matter how noble his intention.

Everett Larkin was one of sixty known individuals worldwide with Highly Superior Autobiographical Memory, and of those, the medical community regarded his condition to be in the top percentile—the textbook definition by which all others were to be diagnosed. As such, Larkin's long-term memory was nearly infallible. He could recall the total layout of a room he'd only been inside of once, right down to the number of unused tealight candles collecting dust on the mantel, and he was able to recite entire conversations with the accuracy of a court transcript. Larkin's brain was a Rolodex stuffed beyond capacity, every trivial detail, every significant event, all of them analyzed and memorized, his mind a battlefield of the unforgotten—the good, the bad, the violent, the cruel—roiling waves of grief eroding his sanity bit by bit, always one association away from a freshly broken heart.

For his entire adult life, Larkin had had to forge a path alone in a world that didn't understand him, that laughed and mocked and became frustrated with him because his personality was too abrasive, his words too curt, his stare too intense. None of them understood what it cost to get out of bed some days, what it took to function while just under the surface, Larkin was reliving an assault that had taken his identity— memories as intense and vivid as if it were all happening for the first time.

His parents were embarrassed by his trauma.

His doctor was fascinated.

His ex-husband was disgusted.

And then on March 30, Larkin had met Doyle, and for the first time since August 2, 2002, he'd felt different.

He'd felt *better*.

Larkin tried to swallow the wedge of emotion stuck in his throat. He tried to breathe through it, but he felt like he'd stepped on a landmine. Adam Worth, that psychopath, thought he could touch even one errant hair on Doyle's head?

No.

Fuck no.

—pacing the night, identifying and cataloguing every creak, every groan, every sigh indicative of a hundred-year-old walk-up, waiting for the whisper that didn't align, waiting to put a bullet between Adam Worth's eyes, and then glass breaking on the street below, his sleep-deprived brain hearing

instead a clap of thunder, Doyle's face transposed over Patrick's—dead in the mud, haloed by his own brains and blood—the baseball bat coming down on Larkin, and then his knees cracking as he dropped to the tile floor in the dark bathroom, vomiting into the toilet—

Larkin shook himself hard, like a dog coming in from the rain. He thumped his chest, coughed, dislodged the painful knot, and took a few shaky breaths. He couldn't afford to get overwhelmed now, not when his night's work had only just begun.

Count to ten, Doyle would say.

At six, Larkin was able to admit that from a policing standpoint, it'd be a huge misstep to not continue requesting Doyle's assistance on these cases. Seven, Doyle possessed the artistic skills, mourning knowledge, and gut instinct that Larkin didn't. Eight, Doyle knew when to ask questions and how to redirect a conversation. Nine, Doyle knew how to handle people.

He knew how to handle Larkin.

Ten.

Until Worth and his verifiable army of miscreants were caught, Larkin would just have to remain armed at all times. He'd require constant check-ins from Doyle, would watch over him while he slept, but most important of all, Larkin would have to take every terrifying nightmare his damaged brain could envision happening without complaint. He'd throw up, rinse his mouth, then return to his safeguarding of the man he loved beyond words, beyond comprehension, because what other choice did he have?

Every compulsive behavior.

Every debilitating association.

Every fucked-up, neurotic, intrusive thought.

He could handle them. They'd been a part of life every day for eighteen years, after all.

Adam Worth would not beat Larkin.

COME FIND ME

Larkin whispered, "I intend to." He tapped Doyle's name in his list of contacts before putting the phone to his ear.

Doyle answered on the second ring. He sounded sleepy. "Hey."

"Hi. I'm so sorry to wake you."

"That's okay." The bedsheets rustled and Doyle bumped something—probably the alarm clock—before saying, "I take it you're not calling because you're on your way home?"

"Unfortunately not. Listen… there's been—" Larkin faltered, tripped over the words. There was no coming back from this.

"What's wrong?" Doyle sounded more alert.

"A body was found at Pier 34. It's Matilde Wagner."

"Holy shit."

"There was a message, as well as an artifact found on her body. It's Adam Worth—the sender."

"I'll get dressed."

Larkin shook his head and said, "No, that's not necessary."

"Evie—"

"I'm neck-deep in paperwork. There's no reason to forgo sleep just so you can watch me cross t's and dot i's. I felt it was necessary to tell you now because of out-in-the-field rule five. That's all."

Doyle's smoky baritone was like a balm as he said, "I appreciate that."

Larkin studied his shoes for one, two, three seconds, then raised his gaze to the murky black sky. There weren't any stars visible in Manhattan. "Did you lock the door."

"Yeah."

"Including the chain lock."

"How're you supposed to get back in?"

Larkin knew he wouldn't be seeing a bed tonight. "Ira."

Doyle sighed. "Sometimes investigations are marathons, not sprints."

"I know…." Larkin lingered a moment longer, then said into the quiet, "I'll let you go."

"Be safe."

"Sleep well." Larkin ended the call. He pocketed the phone and started to turn, but something—movement?—from within a double-parked blue Honda caught his eye. For a split-second, Larkin thought it was Doyle's car. But of course not. His boyfriend was in a bed over fifty blocks south of there, falling asleep this very minute with his face pressed into his pillow, like he always did. As far as associations went, this one was harmless. But as Larkin studied the vehicle, tried to determine in the dirty glow of surrounding streetlights if the model was indeed a Civic or perhaps an Accord, he considered: had it been there this whole time or had it parked during his call?

Larkin couldn't be sure.

He'd been a little distracted, a little worked up when he'd exited the building.

It was an odd place, though, to perform a traffic violation—in front of a police precinct.

Larkin took the steps down to the sidewalk, but as he approached the car, the Honda's engine suddenly turned over and the headlights flashed the high beam. He instinctively raised a hand to shield his eyes, and from between the black spots in his vision, watched as the Honda sped off.

It was 3:48 a.m. and Larkin stood at the breakroom counter, his hands resting on its laminated top as he waited for a fresh pot of coffee to finish brewing. He tapped his bare ring finger to the steady *drip, drip, drip*, and when the water reservoir gurgled and the machine beeped, Larkin took the carafe by the handle and refilled his mug.

He took a sip. It tasted like the coffee maker needed to be cleaned.

The printer in the bullpen had been left unsupervised to spit out the preliminary crime scene report and accompanying photographs, and all those moving components had a way of sounding louder during the witching hour, as if the spirit bound to that particular case were trying to break free of where the veil was most thin. So when Larkin heard quiet footsteps intermingled with the tired buzzes and whirrs of inkjet and paper, for a heartbeat he imagined Matilde Wagner pacing the rows of unoccupied desks, still bleeding from the bullet hole in the middle of her forehead.

Larkin stepped out of the breakroom, rounded the corner, and was both relieved and confused by the sight of— "Ira."

Doyle turned around from where he stood at Larkin's desk, and his smile breathed a sense of life into the empty space. "There you are." He pulled the strap of his portfolio bag over his head before resting the bag against the side of the desk. Doyle's chocolate-brown hair had that usual appearance of having been finger-combed before leaving the house, and while Larkin gave him a hard time about the ever-present stubble, he'd also become so accustomed to Doyle's whiskers, their grit and rasp against his own skin, that Larkin found pictures of his partner when younger and clean-shaven to be like looking at a doppelganger—almost, but not *quite* right.

Doyle was wearing a light-gray suit—a shade he didn't typically favor—but in Larkin's opinion, as a card-carrying gay man, the color really complemented Doyle's physical blessings. He'd paired it with a powder-blue button-down and a navy tie with the knot just the slightest bit askew.

"It's the middle of the night," Larkin stated before crossing the bullpen. "Why're you here."

"I couldn't sleep," Doyle answered as he shrugged out of his suit coat. "It didn't seem fair—not when you're here working on the same case I'll inevitably be a part of by midmorning."

"Who said I had any intention of having you assigned."

Doyle paused as he made to drape his coat over one of the many molded plastic chairs that migrated around the bullpen. He looked at Larkin in blatant confusion—thick eyebrows raised, mouth slightly ajar.

"I'm joking," Larkin said, cracking a smile.

Doyle's laugh was tinged with relief. "I thought we were about to have it out."

"I've already emailed Bailey."

"Thanks."

"But you should have told me you were coming in."

"Would it have made a difference?" Doyle asked. He unbuttoned the cuffs of his shirt and began to roll back the sleeves.

Yes, Larkin wanted to say. *Because what if it happens in the dead of night, when I have no reason to suspect you're anywhere but your bed. The sender leaves you bleeding out on the sidewalk until the early-morning hours, the hospital calls me because I'm your emergency contact, and they say: I'm very sorry, Mr. Larkin, and then you're simply* gone—

Larkin shoved his thumb into the corner of his left eye, pressed hard, and said, "Never mind. Would you like some coffee." He about-faced and returned to the breakroom without waiting for an answer. Larkin set his own mug down with a clatter, coffee sloshing over the edge and onto the counter. He snapped the hair tie around his left wrist hard.

Again.

And again.

Larkin only stopped when he heard Doyle's heels echo on the high-traffic linoleum at his back. His wrist stung as he reached overhead and selected a mug at random from the cupboard. "I'm sorry about date night," he began, going to the fridge for cream and adding a splash to the cup.

"It's not your fault," Doyle answered.

Larkin had cooked chicken Milanese for dinner, which had paired wonderfully with Doyle's arugula salad and delicious blood orange and tonic water mocktails, and the evening had quickly become one of good food and even better company. In fact, it had been shaping up to be one of the best stay-in dates Larkin had had in years—and then O'Halloran had phoned.

Larkin topped the mug with freshly brewed coffee, picked up his own a second time, and turned. "I'd like to make it up to you."

Doyle met Larkin halfway, accepting the extended cup. He glanced at the red mark on Larkin's wrist, but somehow, he seemed to know when it wasn't about *what* was bothering Larkin, so much as *how* it was bothering him. Doyle had become rather exceptional at redirecting intrusive thoughts and quieting the endlessly repetitive bullshit that haunted Larkin day in and day out, and he did so without the expectation that he was now privy to the finer details of such horrors. All he said was, "It's a date," and then he leaned down and kissed Larkin.

This close, Larkin could smell Doyle's warm, freshly scrubbed skin, as well as the neroli and sandalwood and cardamom of his cologne. He was so alive and so vibrant, and Larkin couldn't resist deepening the kiss, shocking his partner with a hint of unexpected tongue.

"*Mm*—gon' make me spill coffee," Doyle murmured before reluctantly breaking the kiss. He licked his lower lip and blinked a few times. "Are you standing on your toes?"

"What. No." Larkin set his feet flat on the floor.

"Oh my God, you were." Doyle leaned back and took Larkin in as a grin spread across his face. "Do you do that a lot? Have I never noticed?"

"No, I don't do it a lot," Larkin admonished. "Only when you… don't lean down far enough." He was quick to add,

"Five foot nine is the average for American men, Ira. My proportions are—"

"Perfect?"

"I was going to say, within norm. In fact, I'm taller than the world average, which for men, is five foot seven."

"Hm-hm, but you see, I've been getting this crick in my neck," Doyle said as they left the breakroom. He gave his nape a rub for good measure. "From being so tall, you know?"

"Jesus Christ."

"I think you'll need to stand on your toes for a kiss more often."

"It creases my shoes," Larkin answered. He strode across the bullpen, collected his paperwork from the printer, and then motioned for Doyle to follow. "I'd like to show you some of the photos CSU just sent me."

They walked past Connor's closed and unoccupied office, two interview rooms, and down the hall to the Fuck It. The room was sometimes used by detectives seeking a bit of solitude, when the only other spot in the precinct that promised one could remain undisturbed for a minute or two was inside a toilet stall, but mostly, the Fuck It was the squad's dumping ground for a hodgepodge collection of garbage. The piles of worn-out furniture and obsolete technology were shadows in the dark room, faintly outlined in orange from the streetlights outside that came in through the blinds on the far side of the room that someone had left partially open.

Larkin turned on the overhead light and started for the right side of the room. He set his mug down, pushed two towers of bankers boxes, stacked five and six tall respectively, to one side, and revealed a large bulletin board still installed on the wall. It was discolored from sun exposure, darker squares but memories of once-important documentation now lost to time. There were bits of cork missing throughout, and what remained was heavily riddled with leftover staples.

He began to tack the photos up while saying, "A refrigerator was found caught up in the pile fields of Pier 34. On the door, written in permanent marker, was this message: Pin me to Detective Larkin. Inside were the dismembered remains of who I've been able to tentatively ID as Matilde Wagner."

Doyle came to stand beside him. "What the hell is she covered in?"

"Adipocere," Larkin said. "More commonly known as corpse wax."

"Gross."

"According to Dr. Baxter, for the adipocere to form, her body would need to be placed in ideal conditions no later than mid-June."

"And when was Wagner last seen alive?"

"June 12." Larkin pinned the photo of Wagner's face to the board. Her third eye was stark against the pallor of her greasy skin. "To use an idiom suitable for a killer nurse," he began, "I believe she got a taste of her own medicine." He picked up his mug and took a sip of the now-lukewarm coffee. "Autopsy report is pending. If Dr. Baxter was serious about my cases having priority, perhaps we'll hear from him come morning. Until then, I can't be sure of the caliber bullet or tool used for dismemberment."

"This is going to be exactly like the Niederman case," Doyle said.

"Not exactly. We already know the victim."

"I mean, it's going to be difficult to muster giving a shit, you know?" Doyle's brows were drawn together. "Wagner murdered a lot of innocent women, including a teenage girl."

"Her victims deserve justice and remembrance in a court of law," Larkin added, while motioning to the photo of the dismembered body, "I suspect Matilde Wagner ended up like a game of Operation gone wrong to keep her from talking about the relationship she had with Adam Worth. Because of

Sal Costa's admission, we know she was in business with him."

"You think the sender offed Wagner?"

"Not him, specifically. Remember the ants and the aphids," Larkin said. "Worth makes his clients' crimes a reality, but when the relationship is no longer beneficial, he uses what they've done as blackmail, turning a mutualistic relationship parasitic. Earl Wagner murdered Charlie Stolle. Matilde murdered Earl."

"Worth pits them against each other?"

"Yes. He's hands-off—always."

Doyle sipped his coffee, thoughtful. "I guess that logic applies to Alfred Niederman as well. Worth egged Noel Hernandez into a physical confrontation. It was only bad luck that Megan York got involved." He leaned in to more closely study the photographs, rubbing the stubble on his chin with his index and pointer fingers.

"What," Larkin asked.

Doyle tapped the image of the fridge door. "What if Worth does the same thing with the messages? Stolle admitted to having written that ridiculous fax, as well as the note on the back of the postmortem photograph, but that still leaves the VHS tape from last month, which I don't think he's responsible for."

"Why don't you think so."

"Because there's only so much one person can do to alter their penmanship, and we saw that his technique for doing so was using his nondominant hand."

Larkin turned to the bulletin board and considered. "Worth blackmails his clients, they write the correspondence, which muddies the waters and keeps his own penmanship a mystery, thereby rendering it an unreliable clue."

"Worth is personally responsible for the notes you've gotten, though," Doyle added. "The ones with the cut-out letters."

"Oh, absolutely," Larkin agreed without hesitation. He took one more sip of coffee before setting the mug aside. "He can't resist making it personal. Those letters are his special touch."

"And unless one of his clients is ambidextrous," Doyle continued, "I'd say we're looking at two different people for the VHS tape and *this*." He tapped the photo of the fridge a second time.

"That's always a possibility," Larkin said. "I'm ambidextrous and my lefthanded penmanship is distinctly unique from my right."

"How many people are truly ambidextrous?" Doyle countered.

"One percent of the human population—around seventy-eight million. Statistically, if we consider the thirteen thousand criminals convicted of violent felonies in New York City last year, one hundred and thirty of them are likely to be ambidextrous."

"That's very impressive," Doyle said. "But do you believe it?"

"It's mathematics, not ideology. But I understand your point." Even though the bullpen was empty, the building was not, and Larkin found himself double-checking the open door of the Fuck It before saying, quieter, "We both know, whether my lieutenant wants to believe it or not, that Worth has a connection to law enforcement—Detective Stolle was proof of that. And if prison bars won't stop him, Sal Costa and Harry Regmore might be involved in a limited capacity."

"It's like going after a hydra…."

Larkin nodded before tacking another photo to the board. "This is where you come in. I believe the message 'Pin me to Detective Larkin' is in direct reference to a brooch we found inside Wagner's mouth—pierced through her tongue, to be exact. To me, it looks like costume jewelry, but this many cases in, it would be remiss to make such an assumption."

Doyle was shaking his head as Larkin spoke. "Not costume," he confirmed. "That's mourning jewelry—hair jewelry, to be specific. The braided lock would have belonged to the deceased and the brooch would've been worn by the mourner—typically a family member. This was probably designed for a mother, wife, maybe a sister."

"Interesting," Larkin murmured, still staring at the photograph.

"It probably belonged to a parure," Doyle continued thoughtfully. "In nineteenth-century Western mourning, jewelry sets for a woman of means would have also included a pair of earrings, necklace, and bracelet. Do you have any photos of the back side?"

Larkin glanced down at the remaining printouts in his hands, shuffled through them, then pinned another photograph.

"Yeah, see that? It's an inscription. The mourner might have only worn this for the designated period of time, in regards to their relationship with the deceased—"

"Wives mourned husbands for up to three years," Larkin interrupted. "That's what you told me."

Doyle nodded. "That's right. But jewelry was easier to maintain than the strict clothing guidelines. Some mourners wore these pieces for the rest of their lives. Do you see how faded the inscription is? It rubbed against clothing for a long time."

"What might it have said."

"It's typically the name and death date of the deceased," Doyle confirmed. "But I'd need to see it to be certain."

"It's at the lab in Queens."

"Whaddya think the brooch has to do with Wagner?" Doyle asked. "I mean, could it have belonged to her? Like a family heirloom?"

"Speculation without the introduction of evidence allows for anything to be a possibility," Larkin replied, and when he didn't get an immediate response, when he instead felt eyes on him, Larkin turned his head.

Doyle's expression had gone soft, almost dreamy, around the edges. Every minute of every day, he had this way of looking at Larkin, like being in his presence was akin to having been struck by a lightning bolt—just three hundred million volts of attraction and affection coursing through his body—and all of that sentiment portrayed in the smallest of gestures, like the way his eyes drew a little half-lidded whenever he listened to Larkin speak.

Larkin had been with other men, loved other men, had been married to another man, but in the last eighteen years, not one of those men, not even Noah, had been *smitten* with Larkin's brand of sarcasm and humor, wrapped up and delivered in a monotone package.

Doyle touched a bit of hair that'd fallen free from Larkin's side part and curled against his forehead. He gently combed it back into place before suggesting, "This whole thing has an uncanny resemblance to the subway events… it mirrors how Alfred Niederman was found."

Larkin crossed his arms and studied the brooch again—the way the camera flash had picked up the viscous fluid covering it. He said, "Serial killers who opt to take a trophy have utilized a number of different personal effects—undergarments, driver's licenses, the victim's internal organs, even—but jewelry is by far the most commonly found cache. Rodney Alcala, the Dating Game Killer, kept the earrings of several of his victims. DNA from some found in a storage locker was later used in his conviction."

"I sense a 'but.'"

"But we know what Wagner kept as a trophy: scraps of clothing from her victims. She had sewn them together—a mourning veil by another name."

"Somebody did a sweep of the Wagners' apartment, right?" Doyle asked.

"O'Halloran," Larkin confirmed. "Last month, after Sal Costa was arrested."

—the sour taste of the handsewn rag stuffed in his mouth, the weight of the gun barrel against his forehead, the gurgle and choke of the Maglite crushing Doyle's windpipe—

Larkin flinched.

He wanted to spit.

Instead, he took a swig of cold coffee.

Doyle's reaction, always subdued where Larkin's was visceral, was in his tone of voice. "We should go back."

Larkin set his hands on his hips, index finger *tap, tap, tap*ping as he considered. After a moment, he asked, "What does a toothpick have to do with the Hudson River."

"What do you mean?"

Larkin glanced up. "The first letter included a transit token. Forty-eight days later, Alfred Niederman is found dead in the subway. The second letter had a ticket stub. Nineteen days later, Mia Ramos—"

"Is found on Broadway," Doyle finished.

"So, what does a toothpick have to do with the Hudson," Larkin asked again.

"I don't know."

Larkin blew out a breath. He checked his watch. "Would you like to take a night drive."

CHAPTER THREE

It was 4:42 a.m. and Larkin sat behind the wheel of his Audi, driving downtown on Second Avenue. It was still dark and traffic was negligible, an assortment of trucks making early deliveries to businesses, taxis looking for a fare, and the poor bastards commuting into the city from Jersey or Brooklyn before the crack of dawn. The sidewalks were quiet, but not empty, and the smattering of joggers in reflective gear, dogs taking their morning constitutional, or folks descending stairs down to the subway was proof that Manhattan might have gotten sleepy, but it never truly slept.

The glow of streetlamps bounced off the windshield, interposed with traffic lights that, if Larkin pressed on the gas just so, he could cruise for several blocks before a red light managed to interrupt his nightly meditation. He glanced at the dashboard—the temperature read eighty degrees, and already before the glass and steel and asphalt of the city had a chance to bake under the sun's summer rays. Larkin adjusted the AC's settings and hoped the heatwave would actually break as predicted.

Doyle sat in the passenger seat—which existed in a near permanent state of being adjusted as far back as it'd go in order to accommodate his legs—and he looked so comfortably poured into the seat that he reminded Larkin of when you pick up a housecat and they turn into a noodle. Doyle had his right arm resting on the door and would turn his head occasionally, studying a sign or bit of architecture as the city passed them by. Doyle was typically quiet whenever he accompanied Larkin on night drives. He seemed to understand that this was one of Larkin's few tricks for centering himself without falling back on the dependency of pharmaceuticals, but also, there was a kind of bliss in their shared silence that Larkin was certain Doyle appreciated as much as he did.

It was a shame this wasn't a drive intended for the sake of that peace.

Larkin turned left onto East Fourth Street, continued on toward Avenue A, and entered Alphabet City. It was a well-lived-in neighborhood, with a resiliency that could be read in the weathered façades and oxidized fire escapes of century-old walk-ups, and the mom-and-pop shops that catered to the practical needs of a working-class community holding on by their fingernails: bodegas, laundromats, and barber shops, as well as independently owned pharmacies and groceries. Graffiti freckled the area—spray-painted on security gates rolled down over business fronts, splashed across the sides of the double-parked interborough delivery trucks, even overhead in the nooks and crannies between brick tenements. Alphabet City had survived a lot of drugs, a lot of crime, and had been a haven for immigrant families and artists priced out of the Village. But now, like so many other neighborhoods, it was fighting for its life against the real estate industry desperate to raze old character to the ground in order to construct luxury high rises none of the locals could afford.

Larkin had to make a bit of a U-turn at Avenue D and pulled onto the one-way East Third Street. That was when Doyle finally spoke.

"How's Jessica Lopez doing?"

Jessica Lopez, the best friend and former roommate of Andrew Gorman—the very case that had brought Doyle into Larkin's orbit—had been instrumental in helping them reconstruct the face of a long-lost person of interest, which had led to the abrupt end of Harry Regmore's murderous rampage. She'd been shot by Harry's cousin and accomplice, Ricky Goulding, and would have most certainly died if Larkin and Doyle hadn't still been within a stone's throw of her apartment, which was only three blocks north of their current location.

Larkin parallel parked behind an orange Kia—one of those box cars that'd been all the rage when he'd been in high school—with the ease and finesse of a man long practiced. He turned off the engine and unbuckled his seat belt. "Physical recovery always outpaces the mental," he answered. "But she's still in agreement to testify for the prosecution when Gorman's murder finally goes to trial."

"Glad to hear it."

They climbed out of the Audi and were hit by a wall of warm humidity. Larkin grumbled under his breath as he crossed the empty street alongside Doyle. As they approached two rundown multiuses standing side-by-side—the ground floor businesses Chinese takeout and dry cleaning, respectively— Larkin had thought he'd been allowed enough time, between their decision back in the Fuck It and having to drive all the way downtown, to fortify himself for the associations sure to come from entering the dilapidated apartments overhead.

—the stink of dirty laundry and cooked meat, worn linoleum underneath, the pounding, pounding, pounding *in his head, and Doyle fighting to breathe—*

Larkin came to an abrupt stop before the familiar blue door.

—the Maglite choking him—

He winced hard enough that the gesture was comical.

But there was nothing funny about the memory of having almost lost Doyle to a frustrated Adam Worth and a rabid Sal Costa. Larkin could taste that rag again, and this time, he *did* spit. He could feel the duct tape pulling on his skin, could feel that undiluted fury that'd been burning in his soul when Costa shot and lunged at Doyle. Had Larkin's hands not been literally tied, he'd have committed murder on June 12.

Without question, without hesitation, Larkin would have killed Sal Costa.

The realization that he wasn't immune to the most depraved and base human behaviors shook him so abruptly, so profoundly, that Larkin's Rolodex memory spun wildly, cards scattering—

—*removing the handles, retainer nuts, and cylinders on the bathroom sink, installing new parts while Noah leaned in the open doorway to watch, saying Larkin's decision to fix the leak himself when the Super had failed to address the issue was a little dramatic because you couldn't even hear the* drip, drip, ick—

—tick, tick *of his wristwatch on the bedside stand as night after night after night Larkin lay awake, listening to every second slip away like a grain of sand falling in an hourglass, unable to stop the obsessive daydreams of death befalling his partner, his heartbeat an erratic* thump, thump, ump—

—bump, bump *coming from inside the apartment, finding Doyle surrounded by parts to an unassembled shelving unit and open tool kit, saying he'd meant to have it built before Larkin got home, to surprise him with a place to keep his recently acquired houseplants, but that the delivery had been a little late*—

"Larkin?"

Larkin blinked a few times. He began to mentally retrieve all his spilled Rolodex cards, tuck them away, and pretend that homicide wasn't among them. He grabbed the door handle and pulled it open.

They stepped into the tiny vestibule with its mismatched tile floor and low wattage overhead light. There wasn't any abandoned junk mail this time but for a scattering of the usual business cards advertising locksmiths and pest control, and an outlier for a Midtown detox center called Butt Baths. Larkin grabbed the knob of the interior door—residents had once again taped the latch so it couldn't automatically lock behind them. Stepping through, they quietly took the old stairs to the second floor and walked toward the door of 2A. The NYPD had slapped a neon green door seal at eye level and a key lockbox around the knob. Larkin took a moment to put in the code, retrieved the house key from inside, used it to rip the sticker, then unlocked and pushed open the apartment door to Earl and Matilde Wagner's former residence.

Larkin stepped inside first, listening to Doyle follow and shut the door, briefly enclosing them in total blackness. The grimy overhead light flicked on, and Larkin watched a massive roach quickly scurry along the living room baseboard. The apartment had a musty, closed-up smell that tickled his nose, and the lack of circulating air was already making him sweat. He brushed aside the blackout curtain at the window overlooking East Third, but there was no AC unit installed. Larkin shrugged out of his suit coat and then hesitated over where to set it.

The home wasn't filthy, or even messy, but there was this general sense of malaise—an evil and vile sickness that seemed to permeate the very air, that would embed itself into the fibers of his clothes, a stink that Larkin would never be able to wash away. The closet beside the front door opened and Larkin turned. Doyle was pushing aside several hanging articles before he motioned for Larkin's coat. He hung both of theirs inside but left the door open, like he too could sense the peculiar illness that Matilde had left on the world and wanted their clothing to be able to breathe a little.

Doyle pulled two pairs of latex gloves from the front pocket of his coat before joining Larkin and offering him a set. Larkin accepted, yanking them on with a snap as he examined the room he'd only seen once before in shadow. The love seat against the wall was upholstered in brown corduroy, something designers were undoubtably trying to bring back as modern chic but that should have been left behind in the '70s where it belonged. A pill-covered flannel blanket had been thrown haphazardly over the back of its cushions. The recliner to the right looked a bit like a La-Z-Boy knockoff that the Wagners had tried to match to the love seat's color, but it was just different enough to look tacky. The television on the left side of the room was one of those behemoth box sets that'd take two men to lift. It sat on a blond faux-wood stand with a VCR shoved into the compartment beneath, a handful of VHS tapes stacked atop, and a pull-out drawer on the bottom that undoubtably held more. There was nothing by way of wall decoration but for a vintage, twelve-inch wooden crucifix with a gold Jesus hanging over the love seat.

Doyle's voice broke the quiet. "What if I'm wrong?" He rested his gloved hands on his hips. "What if the brooch isn't Wagner's personal property *or* a trophy?"

Larkin motioned for Doyle to continue.

"The brooch was obviously planted by the person who killed Wagner," Doyle explained, "so what if it belonged to them too, and we're just spinning our wheels by digging through a serial killer's sock drawer before the sun's up?"

"The memento in past cases has always connected the initial investigation with another cold case. Whether the brooch was Wagner's or not, we need to learn how it fits into her murder, and this is our best starting point until the OCME has caught up."

Doyle said, "You could have come home, Evie. You could have slept."

"I wouldn't have been able to sleep."

"Why?"

"Can we please focus on the task at hand."

Doyle's critical look was a promise that Larkin hadn't heard the end of this, that the divulging of his truth—love came at the cost of rest, of *sleep*—was nigh. He silently motioned toward the bedroom on his left, just past the television.

"Thank you." Larkin took a few steps in that direction before stopping. He backtracked and stared down at the VHS cassettes on top of the VCR.

"What is it?" Doyle asked.

"There's no doubt that Matilde was the manipulator and abuser in their Machiavellian relationship," Larkin said as he crouched before the entertainment stand. "But Earl had something of his own to hide."

"Bad taste in movies?" Doyle asked as Larkin picked through the VHS tapes still in their worn and tattered cardboard sleeves: *Free Willy*, *Rocky V*, *Batman & Robin*....

"I kinda liked the original *Ninja Turtles*."

Larkin looked over his shoulder.

"Cowabunga."

"I meant, blackmail material," Larkin corrected. He slid the cassette free, and the center label that should have advertised the movie in hand as *Barb Wire* was absent. He set it aside and did the same with the rest of the tapes, showing Doyle that all of them were blank, like those sold for home use.

Doyle's eyes lit up. "There're still twenty-two alleged and unknown victims of the Wagners. You think they're on these tapes?"

"I don't think the tape we have in evidence of Esther Haycox was a one-off," Larkin replied. He stacked the VHS tapes in an orderly pile on the floor before opening the bottom drawer and retrieving even more.

"Why didn't O'Halloran take these into evidence?"

"Because Ray isn't a genius." Larkin stood, said, "We'll have CSU come by to collect these," then started again for the next room.

"Earl could have told Niederman about those tapes while they were in prison together," Doyle said thoughtfully, following close behind. "It'd explain how the sender came to learn about them—use them to force Earl to murder Stolle…."

"Exactly what I was thinking," Larkin confirmed. He tapped the wall switch in the bedroom.

More of the same low-watt tungsten light lit up the room. It had the same blackout curtains pulled taut across the window on the far right wall. The space was big enough for an unmade queen bed, which might have been due to the Wagners' housekeeping, but Larkin suspected it was more likely from CSU's investigation last month. There was a laminated particleboard nightstand on the left side that had a hideous yellow lamp with a white pleated shade atop, a vintage wicker dresser across from the foot of the bed that was painted in an off-white and covered in fingerprint powder, and a water radiator beside that. Someone had installed a decorative hood over the painted pipes and turned it into a makeshift shelf now cluttered with an assortment of personal knickknacks that meant little to outsiders but everything to the collector.

Larkin moved away from the concentration of furniture to stand before an open closet on the left side of the room.

Doyle, however, made a beeline for the radiator shelf, asking, "Is this too obvious?"

Larkin looked to see Doyle had a gloved hand resting on what was clearly a jewelry box. "Matilde Wagner was cunning but not arrogant," he answered, reaching to feel along the overhead shelf in the closet. "An organized killer like her is going to intentionally place an object."

"What do you mean?" Doyle asked. He opened the case and could be heard sifting through the contents.

"It's when an individual makes a deliberate attempt to hide an item. Valuables—jewelry, cash—documents—passport, legal—or contraband—drugs, pornography—by choosing a location that isn't logical for the item. Humans have a persistent belief that the more distinct the site, the more it affords us memorability." Larkin made a *tsk* sound, grabbed the shelf with both hands, and hoisted himself up to get a look. Finding nothing, he dropped back to the floor.

"You could have asked me to check that." But when Larkin turned, Doyle held his hands up in mock-surrender and parroted, "Five nine is perfectly average."

"The problem is prewar tenements with their nine- or ten-foot ceilings that make storage space like this inaccessible."

Doyle shut the lid on the jewelry box. "Nothing in here but for some tarnished junk."

"Like I said, she's going to hide it, not flaunt it."

"What sort of irrational hiding place would she pick?"

"That's the crux of the issue with intentional placement," Larkin replied. He shoved aside hanging clothes, pressed his hands against the wall, and began knocking here and there. "When we choose a location that isn't logical to the item—such as hiding money in a sack of flour versus a wallet—we lose the ability to associate one with the other." Satisfied there were no false walls, Larkin pivoted on his heel and crouched before the nightstand. "It's also why we are twenty-five to thirty percent more likely to misplace an intentionally placed item—there was no conscious attempt to first encode the memory and create an association between object and location."

Yanking open the drawer, Larkin found several bottles of lotion, lube, and three Fleshlights, including one that was neon green with anatomy that he was pretty sure was *supposed* to look alien. Larkin listened as Doyle opened one of the wicker drawers and began to dig through what was likely socks and underwear before saying, "The worst part of searching a suspect's home is the constant reminder that monsters are human." Larkin shut the drawer on Earl's masturbation paraphernalia and got to his feet. "With the same needs as the rest of us."

"Physiological, maybe," Doyle agreed, his back still to Larkin. "Food, sleep, sex… but the rest of it?" He closed the top drawer and moved onto the second. "Killers warp and twist the intricacies of what makes humanity so complex and beautiful. The way that you and I yearn for safety and love and esteem—to be protected, to feel as if we belong, to have a sense of self-worth—a serial killer turns those evolved concepts upside down." Doyle closed the drawer and turned to face Larkin. "It's just primitive anger, thrill-seeking, and sexual gratification. There's no respect for life, no realistic perception of reality, certainly no exploration of the human condition."

"Maslow's hierarchy of needs."

"Monsters are human, but they have no humanity."

"In a remarkable scholar, one not infrequently finds a mediocre man; and often, even in a mediocre artist, one finds a very remarkable man," Larkin quoted before adding, "Not that I am, in any way, implying your art is mediocre. Only that artists—you—are remarkable."

Doyle scratched the tip of his nose bashfully, leaving behind a smudge of fingerprint dust. "Nietzsche?"

"I am rather predictable," Larkin agreed, stepping close enough to wipe Doyle's nose clean. "But Nietzsche *did* propose that the pursuit of aesthetic beauty justified the depressions and joys of living, and Maslow puts creativity in the top tier of his pyramid."

"Speaking of art," Doyle began.

Larkin raised both brows.

"Have you noticed these walls?"

"Are you being rhetorical."

"I mean, there's nothing on them," Doyle explained. "*Nothing*. Not a single family photo, no artwork, movie poster, magazine clipping… just the last rites crucifix in the other room, which is actually a weird place to put it."

"What do you mean."

"In Catholicism, it's hung over the bed," Doyle explained. "Grandma had one. It's got a hidden compartment for—" He stopped abruptly.

Larkin immediately walked out of the bedroom, saying over his shoulder, "Matilde Wagner was pharisaic." He came to a stop in front of the love seat and studied the crucifix. As Doyle joined him, he asked, "What's the purpose of the compartment."

"Nothing nefarious. You store candles and holy water inside—tools of the trade when performing last rites for the dying."

Larkin reached forward, gently lifted the crucifix from its nail, and then turned it around a few times.

"Here, let me show you." Doyle took the crucifix in both hands and easily popped the front free, revealing an empty slot inside. "Well, that's anticlimactic," he murmured.

But Larkin immediately grabbed the back cushions on the love seat and tossed them to the floor.

"What're you doing?"

"Have you ever lost a nail in the cushions while trying to hang a picture frame over the couch."

"Actually, yes."

Larkin felt along the bottom cushions on either side before something dull poked him. Pinched between thumb and index finger, Larkin carefully retrieved a dangly earring. It was made of black stone—the top portion unadorned but for a single seed pearl and the bottom featuring glass housing to protect delicately braided strands of human hair.

Standing straight and turning to Doyle, he said, "Wagner had no intentions of returning home after silencing Earl—before he had a chance to spill everything to O'Halloran. But she also had the sender to contend with. She had no opportunity to plan, to be methodical. In a rush, she took with her what mattered, what was important. Adrenaline pumping, hands shaking, she came over here, grabbed the crucifix, and removed the contents, accidentally dropping one piece in her haste." Larkin set the earring into Doyle's open hand. "Wagner didn't worship Jesus. She worshipped Death."

Doyle pulled out the chrome and red cushioned chair across from Larkin at the retro diner table for two. He took a seat while saying, "Sorry. When's the last time you saw a cash-only restaurant?"

"I could have paid," Larkin murmured, not looking up from studying the earring inside a plastic evidence bag.

"Nah, I got it."

"Did you find an ATM."

"Yeah. There was one across the street."

Good Enough was a diner on the corner of East Third and First Avenue that catered exclusively to breakfast eaters—whether that was the tried and true 6:00 a.m. crowd, or just the sort who had a particular craving for pancakes and sausage at three in the afternoon. The restaurant was small, with half a dozen two-tops and a bar with five stools upholstered in the same bright red as the seats, a décor that *screamed* secondhand—Larkin was certain the framed crying clowns, weathered Alphonse Mucha prints, and movie poster of *Taxi Driver* were, in fact, from the thrift shop next door—and a handwritten menu on bright poster board behind the register, which, at the very bottom, in all caps, read: CA$H ONLY.

Two guys working the griddle were visible through the pass window, and a third was pouring coffee for a middle-aged woman seated at the counter with her back turned. Larkin and Doyle were the only other customers in the diner, and while the radio was playing, it was localized to the kitchen and sounded like a mundane morning talk show. Good Enough was a little too sloppy for Larkin's liking, but they had an A grade in the window, so he figured the lived-in feel probably meant they'd been a neighborhood staple for decades.

Doyle reached across the table. "Can I see?"

Larkin handed the evidence over. He picked up his cup of coffee and took a sip. Grubby or not, no caffeine hit quite like that slung at a New York diner.

Doyle studied the earring. "This is a day-to-night earring."

"Forgive my ignorance, but what does that mean."

"It was popular during the nineteenth century. Proper etiquette was to wear studs in daytime and dangly earrings at night when attending social affairs like banquets or parties. This style earring was devised—see this loop at the top?—so you can remove or add the lower portion without having to change out earrings entirely."

"Does the braided hair identify this as mourning jewelry."

"Yeah, definitely."

"And you're certain it's not a reproduction piece," Larkin asked.

"I'm certain," Doyle agreed. "The hook is accurate for being of the same time period that mourning jewelry was most extensively worn. Women gradually stopped piercing their ears by the turn of the century, and that's when screw-back earrings became popular."

"I see."

"There's also the engraving on the back," Doyle continued, flipping the bag over. "It's done by hand, not machine."

"Would that be the name of the deceased."

"Very likely. But because there's less surface space on an earring, the jeweler chose to only engrave the initials: C.L.F. If they're the same as the name on the brooch, though, we've got a partial set."

"Possibly," Larkin corrected. "Once is chance, twice is coincidence. Only three times demonstrates a pattern."

The guy from the counter appeared at their side just then, holding two big white plates absolutely stacked with food. He put them down and motioned to their mugs, but Larkin indicated they were fine and he left without a word.

Doyle had been the one to suggest they stop for some breakfast before heading back to Precinct 19, which Larkin instinctively wanted to protest—he didn't like slowing down, didn't like having to shift gears to something so mundane as eggs over easy when he had an unhinged killer freely roaming the streets of the city he called home, but Doyle had been uncompromising on the matter since day one, and Larkin wasn't about to change his partner's mind on day one hundred and two.

"Look at this bacon," Doyle said. He took a bite, his groan bordering on obscene.

Larkin arched an eyebrow, his fork poised over his eggs. "I think we need a new out-in-the-field rule."

"About what?" Doyle took another bite.

"You can't make the same sound for when I've got you by the hips and kiss you a little too hard as you do for eating bacon."

Doyle snorted. He glanced toward the counter before murmuring, "It's got a really good crunch, though."

Larkin made a disbelieving "hm-hm" in the back of his throat.

Doyle made a sign of the cross over his heart with what was left of the bacon strip. "Promise." Then he popped it in his mouth and pointedly didn't make a sound.

Larkin rolled his eyes before cutting his eggs with the side of his fork. He shoveled it onto his toast and took a bite.

"Oh. I almost forgot. I watered your peperomia before I left."

Larkin asked midchew, with uncharacteristic concern, "The watermelon or abricos?"

"Abricos."

His shoulders relaxed.

"I know better than to touch your baby," Doyle said, peeling back the foil top on a container of corn syrup masquerading as maple syrup before drizzling it over his french toast.

"The watermelon isn't my baby," Larkin answered. "You're not supposed to pick favorites. It was watered Wednesday morning, is all."

Doyle gave him an indulgent smile.

After a minute, Larkin leaned forward and hissed, "*Yes, it's my baby.*"

Doyle laughed.

The woman at the counter stood from her seat, knocked back the rest of her coffee, then walked to the door, passing behind Doyle. She wore the familiar blue uniform and standing eagle patch of a postal carrier, although Larkin thought she was a bit old to still be schlepping mail—late fifties, at least—but maybe she was looking to hit a certain service benchmark for retirement incentives.

The bell jangled overhead as she stepped out, and a waft of what smelled an awful lot like an original Djarum Black, despite flavored cigarettes having been banned since 2009, lingered in her wake. That distinct scent of spicy burning clove made Larkin think of the boy who'd sat in front of him in AP English. He'd gotten reprimanded for writing poetry about other boys and had had a voice like a shovel dragging over loose gravel. Larkin hadn't thought of him in nineteen years.

Olfactory memory was funny like that.

Doyle must have noticed the smell too, because his nose wrinkled and he said, mostly to himself, "Smells like every music venue I snuck into as a kid."

Larkin redirected his attention. "You snuck into music venues?"

Doyle glanced up. "Oh, yeah, all the time. Well—it wasn't really sneaking, I guess. They let me in." He took a bite of breakfast. "Punk venues in the '90s weren't big into carding. That, and I was already six feet by fourteen."

"Had your voice dropped."

Doyle thought for a minute. "Around sixteen, I think. But by then, I was six four." He gave his chin a quick rub and added, "Couldn't grow a beard until grad school, though."

Larkin's mouth tugged to one side. "If you sounded like this at sixteen, I doubt anyone noticed your patchy whiskers." He sopped up runny yolk with more toast. "I'm sorry I can't share in your musical interests."

"That's all right."

"It's not even because of associations," Larkin continued. "Not really. Music overstimulates me. And your tastes are... very fast."

"System of a Down."

"And loud."

"Bikini Kill."

"Although I am intrigued by the concept of queercore."

"Pansy Division," Doyle laughed. "It's not for everyone. Did you listen to music when you were younger?"

Larkin shrugged. "Showtunes."

"That's just a different kind of queercore."

Larkin smiled at that. "I do listen to Marilyn Monroe when I'm alone."

"I didn't realize you liked her so much."

Larkin set his fork aside. He rubbed his palms up and down his thighs a few times. His heart did an uncomfortable lurch before feeling as if it'd missed a beat, like a roller coaster stalled on the tracks just before the big drop. "Did you know she had a stutter."

"I had no idea."

"When Patrick—" Larkin stopped. He looked down at his lap, then toward the empty counter, then back to Doyle. He cleared his throat and tried again. "My TBI resulted in, among other things, a very bad stutter. Not only did I have to relearn how to walk and write prior to entering college, but all through-out I required continuous neurological rehabilitation. It's why I talk like this: flat, no inflection, no emotional prosody. That innate articulation of emotion—I've never been able to fully regain it, not while having to be consciously aware of my breathing, projection, enunciation. It's a sort of defense mech-anism, I suppose. I've read that's why Marilyn had such a distinct, breathy delivery. It was a tool to work around her stutter. I'm no biographer, I can't say how true it might be, but… I've felt a sort of… kinship with her since learning of that."

Larkin could never predict Doyle's response in these moments of honest intimacy, and yet, he'd been coming full-circle to appreciating the same unknown that used to devastate and isolate him from the rest of the world. Because Doyle was so different from them—from a population who'd proven time and again they didn't want to know, didn't want to listen, because grass was always greener if you chose to believe the atrocities of man could never sink to such levels of depravity as beating a teenage boy to near death with a baseball bat because he'd sat on the dock that summer afternoon with his toes skimming the water's surface and his lips touching Patrick's own.

Larkin could never predict what Doyle would say.

But he at least knew it would always be kind.

"What's your favorite song of hers?"

Larkin's brows rose. "Oh… um…." He smiled a little self-consciously and, leaning forward, whisper-sang in his usual monotone the title and subsequent opening line, "I wanna be loved by you."

"This is even better than when you sang that one line from Sesame Street. I'm serious. You should belt them out more often."

"I can't sing," Larkin answered.

"Says who?"

"I just explained—"

"Marilyn still sang," Doyle pointed out.

Larkin hesitated, and his split-second of doubt allowed Doyle to smile triumphantly.

Larkin's phone rang.

He leaned to one side and retrieved it from his pocket. The ID flashed Det. Ray O'Halloran. Larkin accepted the call and brought the cell to his ear. "Good morning, O'Halloran. Are you waiting for Costa to finish combing his chest hair before sitting down to your interview."

But O'Halloran didn't answer with his usual bluster, and instead said, "Grim, we've got a problem."

"What."

"Sal Costa is dead."

CHAPTER FOUR

On East Twenty-Sixth Street was the Office of the Chief Medical Examiner, and in the basement of this uninspiring government facility was the autopsy suite where forensic pathologists and their team of unflinching medicolegals, mortuary technicians, toxicologists, anthropologists, and consulting dentists interviewed the dead of New York City. It was the responsibility of this century-old institution to investigate any number of deaths throughout the five boroughs, including, but not limited to: criminal violence, accident, suicide, or suspicious manner. The OCME also held jurisdiction over deaths occurring inside correctional facilities, which was why Larkin and Doyle got off the wobbly elevator that opened onto the lower level and hurried down the stark white hallway heavy with the smell of industrial disinfectant.

Larkin came to a stop outside a set of double doors and paused long enough to peer through the window into the theater beyond, with its low-hanging ceiling, exposed HVAC system, and fluorescent overhead lighting. Of the eight stainless steel autopsy tables, only one was occupied, and all of the room's living were hovered around the decedent still dressed in an orange jumpsuit. The rest of the layout was more or less unchanged from their previous visit on Thursday, June 11. The right wall was still lined with sinks and tubing, cutting boards and scales, and the left with PPE and evidence collection bags, formalin and sample containers.

Larkin pushed the doors open.

Five people turned around.

The decedent remained spread out on the table like a specimen in a high school lab class.

Larkin asked, "What the hell happened."

Among the attendees was Dr. Lawrence Baxter, wearing a set of navy scrubs and a white lab coat, his retro glasses pulled back to rest atop his head, and without the frames, he looked younger, and definitely more tired and irritated than was his typical disposition. There was an older woman in a pair of purple scrubs and plastic apron—likely a technician—a uniformed corrections officer, an OCME driver, and Ray O'Halloran, who seemed hastily put together in a brown suit, white button-down shirt, poorly matching striped tie, and with his hair looking a bit flat on one side, likely from having slept on it while damp.

"There are *too many living people* in my autopsy suite," Baxter announced. "Marsha, you stay," he said to the tech. "Hot artist, you stay too," he said, turning and pointing at Doyle. "The rest of you, fight among yourselves."

O'Halloran said a few words to the corrections officer, who nodded and headed for the door without argument. The driver trailed after him, both stepping past Larkin and Doyle, and after the double doors swung shut on their exit, O'Halloran said to Baxter, "Is that better, your majesty?"

"Watch it, Straight and Narrow," Baxter warned, pointing up at O'Halloran with an accusatory finger. "Because out of the two of you, Detective Larkin will tell me I'm cute if I ask for it."

"*Doctor*," Larkin snapped. "That is an unprofessional and inaccurate assumption."

"You're right, I'm sorry," Baxter said. "I'm an adult. I've been trained in mass fatality management. If I want to be called cute, I'll just order one of the residents to say so."

Marsha tittered.

Baxter yanked his glasses down and then reached into a box on the counter for latex gloves. "It's just, I was here all night piecing your Angel of Death jigsaw puzzle back together," he explained. "Look at my hair. Does it have that sexy, tousled, bedhead thing Doyle's got going on?"

"I comb my hair," Doyle protested, hand automatically going to his head.

Larkin pursed his lips.

Baxter continued. "I got about an hour's sleep before this meathead—" He pointed at O'Halloran before course-correcting with "Y'know, there're thirty of us MEs in the city. I know I'm charming to be around, but you Homicide boys—"

"Cold Cases," Larkin corrected.

"I'm not the only one with a telephone," Baxter growled.

"Doesn't the Chief want you on Detective Larkin's investigations?" Marsha asked sincerely, her voice not quite a whisper.

"I'm trying to make a point, Marsha," Baxter murmured.

O'Halloran puffed his chest out and plastered on his best schoolyard bully smirk, clearly considering himself on the winning end of this argument, even if it meant hitching his wagon to Larkin's name. He pivoted on his heel and said to Larkin, "Happened just after six this morning. Inmates were coming out of their cells, lining up to head to the chow hall. He got jumped and shanked."

Larkin and Doyle crossed the remaining distance to the autopsy table and looked down at the bodily remains of Sal Costa. His cropped white hair was in disarray, goatee a little overgrown, the chain of his religious medallion visible in the thick pelt of chest hair poking out at the collar of his jail-wear.

He looked like he'd put on some weight—nothing to do and all day to do it—and his chubby face was twisted into a grotesque mask of horror.

"*Sonofabitch*," Larkin whispered.

"What'd they use?" Doyle asked O'Halloran, who stood a foot or so from the head of the table.

"A sharpened toothbrush."

Baxter carefully lifted the tattered and bloody shirt. "I'm not speaking officially, but a stabbing certainly seems to be the case. His abdomen looks like steak tartare. Marsha, you might as well start taking external photos."

"I can't fucking believe this," O'Halloran growled. "Coulda had Wagner on two dozen counts of first-degree murder. Coulda had them *both* on conspiracy charges. This was a slam-dunk promotion, a raise—" He looked at Larkin and motioned between them. "—a goddamn federal holiday in our honor."

"That last one is simply not true," Larkin replied. "Did you get the name of the inmate who attacked Costa."

O'Halloran grit his jaw like he *wanted* to crack a tooth. He reached inside his suit coat, retrieved a small notepad, and flipped through the pages. "Tony Vargas," he eventually said.

—twenty-five pounds of gear weighing down the utility belt cinched tight to his slender waist, sweat prickling under the standard-issue ballistic vest and heavy winter patrol coat, boots in need of new insoles, adjusting the eight-point cap on his head to keep his hand in a ready position as the belliger-ent neighbor of 2F got closer, spouting bullshit: "Vargas sellin' pills ain't no different than Big Pharma pushin' a new drug every commercial break. He ain't no millionaire, man, just a guy tryin'na eat, tryin'na take care of his girl!" before a scream from the crime scene at his back spurred him into action—

The weight of Larkin's old uniform pulled at him, the bite of gunpowder hung heavy in the air, that howl of pain echoed in his ears like the reverb of a cymbal. January 3, 2013, was seven years ago, seven months ago, seven days ago, seven seconds ago.

He had been dispatched for crowd control.

Larkin had been arguing with the neighbor defending Anthony Vargas's decision to sell ten thousand pills to an undercover cop. An associate of Vargas's had entered the apartment as the deal had gone down, had somehow identified the officer to be active law enforcement, and shot. The officer fired back in self-defense.

Larkin had been there for crowd control.

In the ensuing chaos, first responders hadn't properly secured the apartment, and Vargas's girlfriend had been hiding in the closet as it turned into a crime scene. She'd come out screaming like a banshee and stabbed an OCME driver in the leg. The on-site medicolegal had a panic attack afterward, and Larkin had driven the van back to the office.

He had just been there for crowd control.

What were the odds of *this* Tony Vargas being the very same Anthony Vargas of Larkin's patrol days? The probability of coincidence could be calculated by studying the base rate of two independent events. The act of Larkin, of all available officers, having been assigned to that specific crime scene was 1 in 35,000, and the number of busts involving pharmaceutical drugs in 2013—fuck, Larkin wasn't sure. He hardly ever had reason to interact with the Narcotics Division.

He asked, "What was Vargas doing time for."

"I don't know."

"O'Halloran."

"Do I look like his fuckin' CO?" O'Halloran shot back.

"I know it's early and we're all tired," Doyle said cooly, "but shouting isn't—Larkin, where're you going?"

Larkin was already at the double doors, shoving them open, stepping into the hall. He looked toward the elevator at the far end before calling, "Wait!" and jogging toward the correctional officer just as he was stepping inside the car.

Stumbling back, the officer put a hand on the door to keep it from closing. "Something wrong, sir?"

As Larkin drew close, he took in and promptly filed away the usual details: a big guy who was a little soft around the waist, shaved head, dark eyes, name tag reading: Rodriguez. "Detective Everett Larkin with the Cold Case Squad," he said. "Do you know the perpetrator of this crime."

"Of…?" He pointed toward the autopsy suite before saying, "We caught Anthony Vargas in the act."

"How long have you known Vargas."

He shrugged. "Few years, I guess."

"What is he serving time for."

The elevator beeped loudly.

Rodriguez said, "I don't make it a habit of reading inmates' paperwork. Makes the job easier, not knowing who might've murdered a grandmother."

"But you can find out."

The elevator beeped again.

Larkin reached into his pocket, retrieved his wallet, and removed a business card. He held it out. "As soon as possible."

Rodriguez looked at the card. He looked at Larkin. Then he halfheartedly plucked it from between Larkin's fingers and boarded the elevator without a word.

Larkin narrowed his eyes, frowning as the elevator doors slid shut. There typically wasn't much, if any, serious discourse between their two departments—not in the way Larkin had heard such animosity could exist in smaller towns, with prison guards reporting that patrol treated them like mall cops who couldn't handle the "real job." Larkin had a more complicated relationship with Vice, Homicide—hell, his own team—than he ever had with Corrections.

Maybe Rodrigeuz had been nearing the end of a grueling twelve-hour shift when the attack happened.

Maybe Rodriguez resented having to do any kind of paperwork for outside departments.

Maybe Rodriguez just hated his job.

But still, Larkin took a step forward, reached for the call panel on the wall—

"Larkin?" Doyle had moved into the hall. He held one of the swinging doors open with his foot and had his hands in his pockets, looking relaxed but not at ease. "Everything okay?" he called.

Larkin gave the elevator one final consideration before slowly walking back the way he'd come. The heels of his mint-green derbies echoed loudly against the concrete floor. "Costa was our only other connection to Adam Worth," he said, just loud enough to be heard by Doyle.

"There's no chance in hell his murder was a coincidence—not when his sister's remains were found less than twelve hours ago."

Larkin opened his mouth to remind Doyle of Anthony Vargas, a story he had shared in this very hallway only twenty-nine days ago, but then Baxter stepped out of the open suite and looked between them expectantly.

Prompted by his appearance, Doyle smiled politely and said, "Dr. Baxter's offered to give us an overview of Wagner's autopsy."

"Since you're already here," Baxter added with a shrug. "I'll email you the report later this afternoon."

"Thank you," Larkin said, hoping it didn't sound as stressed as it'd felt to him. He called to O'Halloran, still inside and standing at the table, likely in Marsha's way as she took photographs of their dead man, "We have to speak with Vargas." Larkin waited for an acknowledgment, then said, louder, "*Ray.*"

"I heard you," O'Halloran answered, not looking away from Costa. He shook his head, slapped the notepad against his open palm a few times, then repeated, sounding a little defeated, "I heard you."

Baxter ushered Larkin and Doyle deeper into the bowels of the OCME, saying over his shoulder, "I take it this whole fiasco isn't good for one of your investigations?"

"Sal Costa was Matilde Wagner's brother," Larkin reluctantly explained, walking behind the doctor with Doyle taking up the rear.

"Angel of Death, Matilde Wagner?"

"Yes."

Baxter glanced at Larkin a second time. "Didn't she have something to do with last month's mummy, too?"

Again, Larkin only said, "Yes."

"Huh. And now here you are," Baxter concluded thoughtfully. "Yearning for purpose, right?" He didn't wait for an answer, instead pushed open another set of double doors and stepped into the dark space beyond before flicking on the overheads.

The harsh fluorescents illuminated a rather small, windowless room, furnished with nothing but half a dozen stainless steel gurneys haphazardly shoved into one corner. Opposite the herd was a bank of refrigerated doors along the wall, each with a stenciled number. The linoleum floor had a drain in the center, and the chemical smell that'd permeated the basement was strongest here. Larkin suspected something had been poured down there, and he unbuttoned the front of his suit, lifted his tie, and held the end to his mouth and nose.

"It's been a busy summer," Baxter explained, taking out a fresh pair of latex gloves from his coat pocket and putting them on. "Our walk-in morgue is already at capacity, so we're in the overflow—oh, sorry about the smell. The plumbing is sensitive. When I was hired at the start of the year, I asked why they didn't just *fix* the problem. One and done, right? But I guess it's more in-line with city budget to pay the custodial crew to pour hazardous chemicals down there once a week until we all asphyxiate on the fumes. I don't even notice the smell anymore." Baxter yanked open door number five and pulled out the retractable gurney from within.

Doyle leaned to the side, enough to whisper in Larkin's ear, "I know you said not to smell you at work, but do you think I can get a pass this one time?"

Larkin's cell rang before he could respond. He lowered his tie while retrieving the phone from his pocket and checking the ID.

Noah Rider.

He promptly sent his ex-husband to voicemail, pocketed the cell, then approached the gurney as Baxter unzipped the white body bag and exposed the carefully reassembled limbs.

Doyle swore quietly, and Baxter looked between the two before asking Larkin, "Did you not warn him?"

"No, no," Doyle said, "I saw the crime scene photos."

"Nothing like the real deal, huh?" Baxter pointed to the decapitated head, now sporting a roughly sutured incision across its crown. "The weapon was held point-blank against her forehead. The wound diameter is approximately 9.1mm. I was able to recover the bullet from her brain, and that's been submitted to ballistics for identification."

Larkin made a sound of acknowledgment in the back of his throat. His phone vibrated and he retrieved it a second time to see he had a voicemail notification. He tucked it away.

Baxter said, "As for the extensive bodily damage… there're two distinct wound patterns. Look here, see how the first cut through the bone is relatively clean?" He held a gloved hand over one of Wagner's lobbed-off arms. "But near the bottom, the skin and muscle are torn?"

"Like they went from hacking to sawing?" Doyle asked.

"Exactly," Baxter replied. "Someone stood over her front and changed tools midway through. The blade's approximately seven inches. It's got a slight curve as well. Honestly, it reminds me of a meat cleaver. Which makes sense, since the other blade is about eight inches—"

"A serrated bread knife," Larkin interjected. "She was dismembered with kitchen utensils and then tossed in a fridge."

Changes in the barometric pressure didn't seem to affect Doyle.

Or rather, if they did, he never vocalized it.

The morning humidity had gotten even worse, and Larkin could feel the impending storm throughout his whole body. It was a physical mechanism he'd become more aware of as an adult—as if the heavy sensation was a warning to isolate himself before the first clap of thunder, before he sat on the dock again, touched Patrick's sun-kissed skin again. He had wanted relief from the heatwave as much as the next person, but he hadn't realized that reprieve would come hot on the heels of a new Adam Worth case. And after opting to work through the night, Larkin didn't have the mental or emotional stamina to deal with a thunderstorm.

He stood just underneath the overhanging roof of the OCME, the front doors falling shut behind him and taking with it the last wisps of cool air, but at least he wasn't breathing in chemicals anymore. Larkin looked out over the concrete courtyard. It was empty—too early in the morning to justify a smoke break—and the flag hung limp from its pole overhead.

Doyle stood beside him, wiping the lenses of his tortoiseshell sunglasses on a cleaning cloth.

"Do you recall my story about Anthony Vargas."

Doyle paused and looked sideways.

Larkin prompted, "He was caught selling pharmaceutical drugs to an undercover cop."

"And the OCME driver got stabbed," Doyle said, snapping his fingers as the memory resurfaced. "Wait." He turned to stare at the front doors, then said, "Is he the same Vargas as…?"

"I've asked the CO to check his paperwork and call me." Larkin watched Doyle tuck the cloth away and put his sunglasses on. "What does your instinct say."

"I thought you didn't trust your gut without evidence?"

"That's why I'm asking you."

A smile flittered across Doyle's face, but he said seriously, "My instinct says Worth's been playing a particular game of wits and intellect with you, and he's, I don't know, trying to get in your head—trying to make you doubt yourself, maybe."

Larkin arched one eyebrow. "Please expound."

Doyle ran a hand through his hair a few times. "It's little things. Like, during Niederman's case, the clues pointed us toward St. Jude's Church—the same church where you got married."

"The events surrounding that case could have easily—"

"Yeah, but they didn't," Doyle interrupted. "We found those clues just as the sender wanted us to find them. And what about Wagner and Costa trying to get me to walk through that apartment door first?"

"These two examples are night and day, Ira. Your safety is not a 'little thing.'"

Doyle frowned. He rubbed the stubble on his jaw for a long moment, like he could tell this was territory that'd lead to discourse, before saying cautiously, "Your memory is your greatest asset and he seems to know it. Worth is poking and prodding, looking for any weak spots. If he can throw you off-kilter just enough that you make a mistake, he'll have bested the NYPD's greatest detective. My gut says there's no way in hell the guy who murdered Costa this morning isn't the same Anthony Vargas from your patrol days, which… considering it wasn't even your case back then?"

"I was there for crowd control," Larkin answered somberly.

"Going forward," Doyle said. "We need to question *everything*."

CHAPTER FIVE

It was 7:48 a.m. and the second-floor bullpen of Precinct 19 was now alive with the competing personalities of the Cold Case Squad. Larkin and Doyle reached the landing and took a moment to survey the familiar chaos: Byron Ulmer with his shaved head and villain goatee, a certifiable linebacker in a suit, paced back and forth behind his desk—as far as the phone cord would allow him, anyway—while arguing with the poor sap on the other end of the call. Aiko Miyamoto, a punk personality in a sales rack special, tall and rail-thin, with a bob of shiny black hair, lingered at Jim Porter's desk while holding a flat, green-and-white box in both hands. And Porter— one of the squad's veteran detectives—short and stocky, middle-aged, with a receding hairline, leaned far back in his desk chair as Miyamoto shouted at him.

"James David Porter, the cake batter isn't for you!"

"Grim ain't even here!"

"Yes, I am."

Porter jostled in his chair and abruptly spun toward Larkin.

"Thank God," Miyamoto muttered. She wriggled open the box top and revealed half a dozen fresh Krispy Kreme donuts. "I've been fending this animal off for the last ten minutes. Take your cake batter."

"Thank you," Larkin said, but started for his desk instead. "I'll eat it later." He shrugged out of his coat and draped it over his chair before realizing both Miyamoto and Porter were staring at him. "What."

"You'll eat a donut *later*?" Porter repeated.

Miyamoto closed the box and shot Doyle an accusatory look. "You fed him, didn't you?"

"Ain't you a peach," Porter added with a sly smirk.

Miyamoto stalked off to the breakroom without another word.

Larkin picked up the receiver of his desk phone and dialed voicemail to listen to his missed messages.

Doyle pulled the strap of his portfolio bag over his head, saying to Porter, "I didn't realize runny eggs would put me on a watch list."

Porter snorted. He leaned back in his chair again, picked up his coffee mug, and asked, "Where'd you guys go?"

"Good Enough," Doyle said as he propped his bag against Larkin's desk. "Down in Alphabet City."

"Hmm. Great coffee," Porter said by way of approval. To Larkin, he added, "It's a good thing I ain't into men or you'd have some competition."

Larkin furrowed his brow in response. He leaned to one side and hit a button for the next message.

Doyle slid his hands into his pockets and countered good-naturedly, "I've always been weak for blonds, Jim. But thank you."

"You can afford to be choosy. I bet guys line up around the block for you."

"You think?"

"With an ass that Delta would consider checked luggage? C'mon."

Doyle turned back to Larkin with a huge smile.

Larkin finished with the voicemail and set the receiver back on the cradle before saying, "I'd prefer we not discuss during business hours what God gave my partner."

Thankfully, before the conversation had the opportunity to go completely off the rails, Lieutenant Mike Connor appeared in the open doorway of his office and called, "Grim!"

"Yes, sir."

Connor pointed at Doyle. "Monet."

"Good morning, Lieutenant."

"Both of you get in here."

"Are we in trouble?" Doyle whispered, following close behind Larkin.

"I think he's missed you," Larkin corrected. He ushered Doyle into the office first, shut the door, and turned as Connor shook Doyle's hand.

"How's life at 1PP?" Connor asked, taking a seat. A fifth-generation officer of the NYPD, Connor told anyone who'd listen about how he'd gotten his start as a patrolman, worked his way up the ladder, and was eventually promoted to lieutenant of the elite but woefully understaffed Cold Case Squad. He was a formidable Irishman, with a booming voice and build that rivaled doorframes. A smattering of freckles across his face and forearms was all that tempered his grizzly bear appearance.

"Never a dull moment," Doyle confirmed, mirroring Connor and sitting across from him in one of the two chairs positioned before the desk.

"They keeping you busy?"

"Unfortunately."

"I'd say that having you uptown is a breath of fresh air—"

As Larkin approached, he really had to marvel at Doyle's innate likeability. Not one, but *two* middle-aged straight men had professed their undeniable affection for his partner that morning, and Doyle hadn't even rolled back his shirtsleeves yet.

"—but seeing you here, and after O'Halloran requested Grim at Pier 34 last night, you're probably not delivering a cookie bouquet, eh?"

Larkin took a seat, crossed his legs, and settled his hands in his lap. He said, "Miyamoto brought in donuts."

Connor made a face and *tsk*'d. "'Course she did… when my doc told me Monday I need to start watching my sugar." He made a "what can you do" gesture before asking Larkin, "So what happened?"

"A refrigerator got caught up in the pile fields," Larkin began. "Inside was the dismembered remains of Matilde Wagner."

Connor's face took on a distinct red hue. "You've got to be kidding me."

"I'm aware that my delivery is often stifled by my tone of voice, but I assure you, this is not a joke. We just returned from a meeting with the ME," Larkin continued, motioning to Doyle. "Wagner was shot point-blank in the head and taken apart with what was likely a meat cleaver and possibly a bread knife."

"And Sal Costa's dead," Doyle added.

"He's what?"

"He was jumped at morning roll call," Larkin explained. "Stabbed to death with a sharpened toothbrush by another inmate."

"What the *absolute fuck*."

"O'Halloran called last night because of the message left at the crime scene," Larkin said. "Written on the refrigerator door was 'Pin me to Detective Larkin.'" And when Connor cocked his head to one side, he added, "Wagner had an antique brooch pierced through her tongue."

"That explains you," Connor said, sharp eyes cutting toward Doyle.

"Yes, sir. It's mourning jewelry—hair jewelry. Larkin had the idea to return to the Wagners' apartment—"

"Doyle did," Larkin corrected.

Connor raised both hands and said, "You both had the same damn idea and the accolades will be split accordingly. Why'd you go back?"

Doyle said, "There was a question of provenance, I suppose, for the brooch. The thing about mourning jewelry is not only are they often found in a parure—"

"It's French," Larkin interjected. "It means *set*."

Doyle continued, "—but they're typically inscribed with the name of the individual who's passed. Did the brooch belong to the perpetrator who murdered Wagner? Was it a family heirloom of hers? Or was it possibly a long-kept trophy of yet another victim? We might be able to trace ownership via the name and death date."

Connor had leaned forward a little, his elbows propped on the desktop.

Doyle reached inside his suit coat and held up the evidence bag with the earring. "We found another piece of the set."

"That is speculation until we can get the brooch back from the lab and make a comparison," Larkin corrected.

"I know you've got this thing about patterns and coincidences," Connor said, accepting the bag, "but if Hieronymus Bosch here is the expert on art and mourning and the reason I'm gonna have to expense additional office furniture for an unofficial eleventh member of my squad, let's give him the benefit of the doubt." Connor stared at the earring. "Where's the rest of the set?"

"I believe Wagner took it with her, prior to her disappearance," Larkin said. "It meant something to her. *What*, specifically, it's too soon to say."

"So whoever offed her has the other pieces?" Connor asked.

"That's a reasonable assumption."

Connor returned the bag to Doyle before saying in a low voice, "The sender is back."

"Yes," Larkin said.

"And will this be like the other investigations? A case from our unsolved stacks becoming relevant the same way the Garcia boy and Baby Hope did?"

Larkin said, "In theory. Unfortunately, the circumstances of each past discovery have not availed themselves to any sort of predictable pattern, so it's impossible to say which cold case might become relevant. The discovery of Andrew Gorman's body led to Regmore's murdered sex workers in a fairly straightforward manner, but Niederman was already dead, which forced us to work backward in order to link him to the murders of the kids living in the subway system and their relationship to Marco Garcia. Esther Haycox's murder caught Matilde Wagner and inadvertently led us back to Niederman's first victim: the mother of Baby Hope, Mia Ramos."

"Just like the little Russian nesting dolls or whatever," Connor concluded.

"*Mise en abyme*," Larkin corrected. "Adam Worth—the *real* Adam Worth—lived a very effective double life, and the sender is doing a considerable job in mimicking that success. By day, he's an unsuspecting cog in the wheel of society. By night, he plies a very particular sort of trade: he offers means by which the criminal class can fulfill their most depraved desires. And when that mutualistic relationship has run its inevitable course, when the sender has reaped all there is of ill-gotten gains, he turns that money, that information, that *power* back onto the offender. He becomes a parasite. Murder within murder. Duality within duality."

Connor looked from Larkin, to Doyle, then said abruptly, "Give us a minute alone."

Doyle was a little taken aback, a surprised, "Oh," escaping his lips. But he nodded, stood, and exited the office without a word of protest.

Connor waited until the door closed before he said to Larkin, "I know there was some concern over him being targeted last month…. If you're worried the sender might lean that way a second time, I'll put in a call to his boss and clip his wings."

"That's not necessary."

"If it's about needing an artist," Connor continued into the disquiet, "That unit has two other guys."

"It's not only about composite sketches and facial reconstructions," Larkin answered. "It's about grief and mourning and remembrance, and Doyle's professional credentials make him uniquely qualified." Even though this was a surefire way to keep Doyle out of reach from the madman he called Adam Worth, Larkin *knew*, even if the decision were framed as a direct order from Connor, it would come at the cost of everything he'd been building with Doyle: trust, understanding, even love. Larkin took a breath and said evenly, "I don't have to worry when I have Doyle at my back. And I don't need to wonder who has his."

"If you insist."

"I do."

"All right. And Grim? If the media finds out our manhunt for Wagner ended in half a dozen pieces off the bank of the Hudson, they're gonna be champing at the bit for all the gruesome gossip we've got. I don't need some plucky muckraker coming in and connecting the same dots you have. If a story on the sender gets published before we're able to grab him, we're screwed seven ways to Sunday." He pointed a meaty finger at Larkin. "You say, *no comment*, and send 'em my way."

"Yes, sir."

"Good."

Larkin got to his feet.

"You aren't on any of those dating apps, are you?"

"Dating apps?"

Connor shrugged and leaned back in his chair. "People don't realize how much information they pack into those online profiles. A good journalist with an inkling of which app you might be on—you being gay isn't a secret—casts a net with enough generic 'preferences' to include you in the results and *bam*. One of those reverse image searches of a profile picture might connect to your social media accounts or identify your neighborhood from a visual landmark in the background. A little more digging might expose some not-so-safe-for-work kinks, and wouldn't the subway rags just love—"

Larkin interrupted, "I'm in a relationship."

Connor scratched the back of his head somewhat self-consciously. He then pointed at his office door, indicating Doyle without saying as much.

"That's correct."

"So it's serious?"

Larkin answered, "I've never used dating apps, I'm not on social media, and what goes on in my bedroom is private."

Connor held his hands up in surrender. "You're a consummate professional, Grim. I know that. But the news has been salivating over you these last few months, and I don't want some fucking mouth-breather desperate for a scoop to stoop to an invasive level, you know?"

"The concern is appreciated but unwarranted." He started for the door but stopped and turned. "You're very up-to-date with armchair sleuthing techniques."

"My teenage daughter," Connor answered. "That kid signs off from family chats with 'yeed my last haw,' but give the girl a Wi-Fi connection and fifteen minutes, and she can tell you a guy's shoe size, blood type, and credit score." Shaking his head, Connor muttered, "Keeps me awake at night."

"Perhaps one day her generation will put us all out of work."

"It's enough to make a jaded man start praying."

Larkin's mouth twitched in a smile before he exited. He left the door open because Connor was a bit of a microman-ager and preferred having eyes and ears on the bullpen whenever possible. He approached Doyle, who was resting his backside against the ever-absent Baker's desk, his legs stretched across the aisle toward Larkin's desk, with Baker's desk phone to one ear. Larkin touched his partner's shoulder before stepping over his legs.

"Hey." Doyle turned the mouthpiece away and asked, "What'd Connor not want to say in front of me?"

Larkin took a seat in his chair. Telling the full story, he decided, would only cultivate a situation where Doyle would feel as if he had something to prove, which was atypical to his character, yes, but Doyle had an ego as much as the next man, and it'd undoubtably be bruised if he knew both Larkin and Connor felt iffy on his continued involvement in the Worth cases. Larkin said, "He was voicing concern over the media catching wind of this case."

Doyle's brows rose a little, a prompting, like he knew there was more to it.

"He asked if I was on any dating apps."

Doyle grinned at that. "Are you?"

Larkin ignored the tease and added, "His daughter seems to have introduced him to that particular hellscape, and he doesn't want some journalist finding out my preferred sexual positions."

"Which is?"

"Which is what."

"Your preferred position."

"Who're you on the phone with."

"I'm on hold with the lab," Doyle answered. He leaned forward. "I like missionary. It's not *vanilla*, it's romantic. Plus, I don't have to be a contortionist."

Larkin spun in his chair to collect the manila folder of photographs they'd gone over that morning.

"So?" Doyle pressed.

"Missionary is fine," Larkin said, not looking up as he flipped to a few closeup snapshots of the fridge.

"You don't like it."

"I didn't say that. I prefer having a partner on top, is all."

"You mean, like cowgirl?"

Larkin turned in the chair. "Shouldn't you be talking to someone."

"I'm still on hold," Doyle protested with a laugh.

Larkin checked the nearby desks before leaning closer and saying, quiet but firm, "I enjoy the privilege of watching my significant other take control of their own pleasure."

"That's a very eloquent way to say you like a power bottom, Evie."

"You woke up and chose violence today, didn't you."

Doyle was grinning ear-to-ear as he said into the phone with a voice so smooth, a bartender would charge premium prices, "Good morning, this is Detective Ira Doyle with the Forensic Artists Unit."

The morning ended up being a flurry of phone calls, as was the very *un*sexy reality of working cold cases. A completely smitten lab tech informed Doyle that they'd have the brooch couriered to 1PP no later than noon, while a far less besotted receptionist at the Tombs told Larkin that yes, they had an officer Rodriguez—Devon or Juan?—and after describing the CO to her, he was told that Devon had already clocked out for the day and Larkin would have to call again at 7:00 p.m. if he wanted to follow-up on any conversation they'd had earlier.

While Doyle, now comfortably seated in Baker's chair, spoke with someone on the Crime Scene Unit about picking up all the VHS tapes from the Wagners' apartment, Larkin stood at his own desk, absently stretching his back while listening to the same thirty second sound bite of hold music that was so profoundly awful, he'd have preferred chewing on aluminum foil instead. He moved the phone from one ear to the other, keeping it wedged in place with his shoulder, when his cell, resting beside the computer keyboard, lit up with an incoming call.

Noah Rider.

"Marcom Refrigeration Systems, Parts and Services, this is Ben. How may I help you?" Ben spoke with an easygoing and decidedly rural North Carolina accent.

Larkin promptly sent Noah to voicemail a second time and said to Ben, "Good morning. My name is Everett Larkin and I'm a detective with the NYPD's Cold Case Squad. I have a model and serial number for a refrigerator that I'd like to obtain some manufacturing information on."

"NYPD?" Ben repeated.

"That's correct."

"Well, how's that for a Friday morning? Not a call about a replacement water filter or a broken hinge pin. No, sir, I get a call about a *bonafide homicide*. I know that's what cold cases are—I've watched those true crime shows."

"Yes, sir," Larkin said, like he hadn't just sat through thirteen excruciating minutes of overly compressed electronic free-form jazz and now needed a Tylenol.

"And a New York City detective to boot! No one's gonna believe this phone call…. You read those numbers to me," Ben directed excitedly.

Leaning over the desk, Larkin picked up a photograph and read aloud the model and serial from the back of the unit.

"Wooboy—that puppy sounds old," Ben murmured. "423 means the year ends with a four and the twenty-third week would make that… June. So that's when this particular unit was built. But the year… might be 2014, 2004, might be *1994*. It's not the best system, I admit. I'm gonna put you on hold while I look up that model number, okay?"

"No, please don't—"

The jazz-like music started playing again.

Larkin turned away, held the receiver down at his thigh, and briefly let his chin dip to his chest. He considered whether another coffee from the breakroom would help, but that'd be cup number five since last night, and Larkin had no desire for a self-induced heart attack or for shitting himself, so he opted to count silently and hoped it would alleviate his edginess. He'd reached thirty-seven when he heard the whine of distorted music come to an end.

Ben was already saying, as he brought the receiver back to his ear, "—top freezer style that we offered in 'apartment size' was eleven cubic feet in total. Did you know the average family of four requires a fridge with twelve to sixteen cubic feet? And that don't include the freezer, which is usually another six to—"

"Mister…." Larkin faltered. "Ben."

"Brooks, sir."

"Mr. Brooks. I'm not actually in the market for a new kitchen appliance."

Ben laughed readily. "No, sir, sorry about that. I'm not even sales, just live and breathe refrigerators! Like I was saying, this unit was offered in either white or cream, weighed a hundred and seventy pounds, and was manufactured between 1992 and 1999. We still got that model, but it's more energy efficient now. Also available in brushed steel—hides fingerprints real well. Folks like that modern look. This model you got here is more like what my granddaddy had in his garage.

He kept drinks in there for us kids during the summer. Y'all got Cheerwine in New York City?"

"Mr. Brooks, can you tell me where this refrigerator might have been sold."

"Like, what retailer we might'a shipped to?"

"Yes."

"We don't have a database to track what serial goes where, I'm afraid. Maybe individual shops keep a record like that for themselves, but I can't imagine anyone'd be holding on to sales receipts from the '90s."

Larkin tapped the desktop irritably before asking, "Do you have record of this unit having gone in for repair."

Ben drew out his words in a thoughtful manner, saying, "You know what… it's old, but that don't mean it's down and out. Hang on just a second."

"Don't—" The hold music returned, and Larkin held the receiver at arm's length, shouting, "—make me listen to one more goddamn second of this shit!"

"Anyone ever tell you, Grim, that you sound like one of those rubber chickens when it's stepped on?" Ulmer asked from across the bullpen. He peered around his computer monitor and made an exaggerated *O* face.

"Anyone ever tell you that that face makes you look like a truck stop gloryhole," Larkin snapped back.

Ulmer's complexion darkened. "You would know, faggot."

"Just remember, deep-throating isn't for beginners and lockjaw is very real." The jazz music cut and he promptly raised the receiver to his ear again.

Ben was saying, "—one entry for you, detective. That fridge had its condenser fan replaced under warranty way the heck back in 1997."

"Was a technician sent to do a home repair."

"Yes, sir, that's what usually happens."

"Do you still have an address on file."

"I do… but it's over twenty years old."

"That doesn't matter, Mr. Brooks," Larkin answered, picking up a pen and leaning over the open case file, poised to transcribe.

"Marcom company policy prohibits me from sharing customer details," Ben said apologetically.

Larkin set his pen down with exaggerated calmness. "I'll obtain a search warrant."

"It's not that I want to be a pain in your backside, but the bigwigs will be madder than a wet hen if I break protocol, even in good faith."

"I understand," Larkin replied, curbing his irritation, because it wasn't Ben's fault that Marcom's hold music had drilled a hole in his brain, or that Ulmer was a dickhead, or that a perfectly reasonable company policy would mean just *one more* phone call in Larkin's immediate future. "Thank you for your assistance."

"No problem!" Ben answered brightly. "And when you get your paperwork in order, you just tell them I was the one you spoke with and I'll help you get your man, detective."

Larkin muttered a goodbye before hanging up. He turned to see that Doyle was staring at him. "What does the expression 'madder than a wet hen' actually mean."

Doyle pushed up from Baker's chair as he said, "I think it's a reference to an old southern farming trick—dunk a hen in cold water to break them out of their brooding."

"I can't see how that would work."

"It's probably why the hen gets mad," Doyle concluded. He stretched his arms overhead before saying, "Let's take a walk."

"I don't need a walk."

"I do."

"I know what you're doing."

"What am I doing?"

Larkin carefully scrutinized his partner. Doyle had gotten pretty good at hiding any of his tells when it came to this sort of… reverse psychology tactic. He'd make a perfectly reasonable request for himself—candy break, a walk—and ask Larkin join him, when in reality, Doyle was availing *Larkin* a few minutes to decompress without embarrassment, under the guise of a believable excuse.

Because Doyle knew how to handle Larkin.

Larkin narrowed his eyes, but when Doyle only smiled, he grabbed his cell and started for the stairs. He'd barely reached the bustling ground floor when it rang in his hand. "Jesus Christ," he swore.

"What's wrong?"

"Noah has called me *twice* so far today."

"Would you like me to answer it?" Doyle didn't sound particularly thrilled with the idea, and Larkin couldn't blame him, but ever the gentleman, he'd still offered to lessen some of Larkin's burden.

"No, I—" Larkin trailed off, staring at the screen as the phone continued to ring.

"Larkin?"

Larkin's thumb shook a little as he swiped to accept the call. He put the cell to his ear and said, "Mom?"

CHAPTER SIX

On the corner of Fifty-Seventh and Fifth, nestled among the surrounding luxury of Tiffany, Louis Vuitton, Gucci, and Prada, was La Boîte Dorée—a lounge and coveted place of respite among shoppers with substantial credit lines. Inspired by the culinary prestige of France, the class of England, and the debauchery of America, La Boîte was known for their finger sandwiches, pastries, caviar, and champagne available at all hours. It was, in Larkin's opinion, a haughty and ostentatious café in the throes of an identity crisis.

In the time it'd taken to drive to Midtown and park the Audi in a garage half a block west, the morning had finally given way to gray overcast. It was hot, hazy, sticky, and Larkin had been pacing back and forth in front of La Boîte for the last forty-six seconds. Doyle stood off to the side, saying nothing as he smartly let Larkin work through the myriad of emotions all vying for dominance.

But then abruptly, Larkin came to a stop a few steps short of Doyle and in a rush, said, "She has the audacity to demand that I drop what I'm doing—like I don't have a day job, like what I do is of no importance—because she absolutely must speak with me about Noah. Never mind that on April 13, when

I needed her and had hoped she'd behave like a mother—just once—I was told not to get a divorce because what would *her friends* think. And now this, *this* is where she is? My mother knows I don't like busy dine-in settings. But God *fucking forbid* Jacqueline Larkin has to pour her own champagne."

So calm, Doyle asked, "Do you want to leave?"

Larkin scoffed.

"I know I'm not familiar with your family dynamics, Evie, but you don't owe anyone your time or energy if the relationship is this toxic."

Larkin's throat worked and his left eye began to twitch, like a compulsive tic, until he jabbed his thumb into the corner and pressed hard.

Chaotic stimuli of the tourist-heavy neighborhood bore down on Larkin like an oncoming freight train—the two women striding past them while laughing and talking animatedly, the shrill whistle of an officer directing traffic, a ConEd crew dragging a manhole cover across asphalt—all of it sent sharp, white-hot sparks up his spine and through his brain, and he'd have given anything for a Xanax right then.

Doyle's smoky-smooth baritone broke through the clamor. "Is it all right if I touch you?"

Eyes still closed, Larkin shook his head.

"Okay." His brief silence had a thinking quality, and then Doyle asked, "How can I make this easier?"

Lowering his hand, Larkin said, "I ignored Noah this morning and now he's weaponizing my mother to relay his message, knowing full well that my relationship with her makes it difficult to say no, and I'm—I'm so fucking frustrated that he doesn't get it." Larkin heard the break in his voice, but he didn't care. "No matter how many times I ask him to respect my boundaries, to understand I cannot simply drop what I'm doing to listen to him complain one more time about this divorce…. I feel like—like I'm misreading the situation. Like I don't quite understand the emotional expectations. Like I'm doing it all wrong."

"You're not misreading anything."

Larkin adjusted his suit coat and fixed the cuffs of his shirtsleeves. He looked back at the high glass walls of the café while pressing the back of his hand to his flushed face. "I just want it to be over."

"Would you like me to go inside with you?"

"My mother is unkind, Ira. I don't want it to be open season on you too."

Doyle smiled assuredly and said simply, "Don't worry about me."

Larkin opened his mouth to further deter Doyle's white knight sensibilities, but a fat drop of rain hit his nose, and that seemed to be all the confirmation Doyle needed before walking to the door of La Boîte and holding it open. Larkin reluctantly moved forward.

True to its name, La Boîte Dorée was fitted with gold. Lots of gold. From the wallpaper to the light fixtures to the flatware, the impression of luxury was loud and insistent, like the interiors of mansions from New York's past. There was also that small detail regarding menus… they were only available in French. And for a city that boasted a population of merely 80,000 who spoke French at home—according to the Census Bureau's 2015 American Community Survey—presenting a situation in which one was to order food in a language relatively uncommon to the general population was just another outdated ploy at maintaining certain levels of elitism and classism.

Larkin was unaffected by the intimidation tactic, however, responding in kind when the maître d' greeted them in French, and asking that they be directed to his mother's table.

"Wow," Doyle whispered, a step behind Larkin as they followed the young, clean-cut host toward a length of tables lining the glass wall. "Can you do that sexy R roll too?"

Larkin glanced back at Doyle. "It's called a voiced uvular fricative. And yes, I can."

Doyle winked.

And the way that Doyle could refocus Larkin's stressors with a passing tease, a smile, a twinkle from those pyrite eyes….

Larkin's shoulders relaxed a fraction. He continued toward the table the maître d' now stood beside.

Sitting before a lavish three-tier stand of elegant finger sandwiches and decadent desserts, a glass of champagne bubbling at her side, was Jacqueline Larkin. She was sixty-three years old but told everyone she was fifty-three, petite in both stature and height, and boasted the same ash-blond hair and gray eyes as her son. She wore a calf-length dress with short sleeves in an earthy off-white color, the cut a timeless and classy A-line silhouette, as well as stiletto heels with a pointed toe in a pinkish blush. Jacqueline looked intimidating, important, and rich.

Nodding to the maître d', Larkin said, "Hi, Mom."

"Everett, darling, I'm so glad you could make it." She bussed his cheek when he leaned down. "You look tired."

"I'm fine."

"I can give you the number of my medical spa on Seventy-Fifth."

"*Mom.*" Larkin straightened and motioned Doyle forward. "This is my partner, Ira Doyle. Ira, my mother, Jacqueline."

"It's a pleasure to meet you, ma'am," Doyle said, reaching a hand out.

Jacqueline smiled politely as she allowed her hand to be briefly held. "Nice to meet you. Can I get either of you a drink?"

"We're on the clock," Larkin said as he took the seat on Jacquline's left, his back to the glass walls. "What did you need to talk about that couldn't wait."

"Your manners have become so plebeian, Everett," Jacqueline chastised in a hushed whisper. To Doyle, she asked, "Tell me about yourself, Mr. Doyle. You're a police officer too?"

"Yes, ma'am. A forensic artist."

She feigned mild interest. "Do you go to school for that?"

Doyle's fingers tapped in an off-beat rhythm against his thigh—not from nerves, Larkin knew, but his natural tendency to fidget while sitting. "I did my undergrad at SVA."

"I'm not familiar with them."

"It's an art school. On East Twenty-Third."

"Oh. An art school." Jacqueline picked up her champagne flute and took a sip.

There was no way Doyle hadn't caught the subtle shift, the quality of distaste in her attitude, but he persevered as if he hadn't just been insulted. "And I did my master's at NYU."

"Isn't that lovely," Jacqueline said, concluding the conversation that simply as she turned her attention onto Larkin. "I spoke with Noah this morning, darling."

"About what."

She made a moue of disapproval. "I hadn't expected you to bring company. Private affairs are hardly a matter to be discussed in front of strangers."

"Ira isn't a stranger. He's my boyfriend."

"What?"

Slower, and stressing each word, Larkin repeated, "Ira is my boyfriend."

Jacqueline's eyelashes fluttered. "I raised you better than this."

That was a laugh, Larkin thought, considering this was the same woman who'd hired a private doula to advise her on the best time to conceive, so Larkin would have that coveted autumn birthdate and always be the most developed child in his grade. This was the same woman who'd hired a play-date tutor to provide feedback on his spontaneous play deficiencies when he'd been a four-year-old in order to shape him into the ideal candidate for elite pre-K academies on the Upper East Side. This was the *very same woman* who'd hired Larkin a sports coach at six years old when he'd asked his mother to teach him to ride his bike at the park.

Jacqueline hadn't raised a child—she'd gotten herself a participation trophy. And she'd kept it polished and shined, touting it about town whenever she needed a vehicle in which to preen and accept accolades, and all the while, Larkin had been denied an upbringing founded in the principle of love and had instead only known unattainable expectation.

Larkin met Jacqueline's cold stare and asked, "Better than what."

"To be flaunting your *homewrecker*."

"We're leaving," Larkin said, pushing his chair back and getting to his feet.

"Sit down," Jacqueline hissed. She glanced toward nearby tables before whispering, "You're being a brat."

The insult was like a slap, and Larkin's cheeks stung with humiliation as he sank back into his chair.

Jacqueline stared at him for a long, withering minute before turning her attention to the finger sandwiches, picking at them. "You know, Everett, there's a vulgar saying: Don't—you know what—where you eat."

"I'm not shitting where I eat," Larkin replied.

"*Language*," Jacqueline reprimanded. "Honestly, you sound like you grew up in the public school system."

"I was a public school kid," Doyle stated.

Jacqueline looked across the table, staring at Doyle as if he were an unwelcome guest who'd shouldered his way into a private conversation.

But Doyle continued, "Born and raised in Hell's Kitchen, in fact."

Nonchalantly, she replied, "It shows."

Doyle's nonverbal response was apparent before he was likely even aware of his own emotional reaction—brow furrowed, jaw tense, his shoulders widening as he subconsciously puffed his chest. In the one hundred and two days he and Doyle had breathed the same air, Larkin had come to understand that his partner's one serious and unresolved trigger was that of an avoidant-dismissive mother. And while their upbringings couldn't have been more polar opposite—Michelin stars versus bodega candy bars—Larkin knew that Jacqueline's belittling nature was acting as something like a mirror, reflecting past abuse Doyle had suffered in childhood back onto him as an adult.

"Mom, what the fuck," Larkin spat.

Jacqueline said in a rush, "Everett, your husband called me because he couldn't reach you. It would seem that your new—new—*man* has been caught loitering outside his apartment."

"*What?*" Doyle protested.

"Just last night," Jacqueline insisted.

"I didn't—I wouldn't do that," Doyle said.

"Noah's lying," Larkin said to Jacqueline.

"You'd have never married a liar, darling. Noah told me it was a blue Honda Civic."

—the engine, the high beams, the Honda tearing away from the precinct—

Jacqueline was pointing a finger at Doyle that was both accusatory and dismissive. "He said it was this man's car."

"Do you know how many people own Hondas in the city?" But Doyle didn't seem to be anticipating an answer from her, instead turning toward Larkin. "Evie—"

Larkin said over him to Jacqueline, "Whatever Noah thinks has happened, he's mistaken."

"You're awfully certain, darling, for someone who wasn't there," Jacqueline said dispassionately before delicately wiping her hands on a cloth napkin. "Your father and I have been discussing this whole ordeal at length, but after this incident, we're in agreement. Going forward, we'll be handling Noah's legal fees."

The *tink, tink, tink* of rain hitting the glass wall punctuated the uneasy seconds that followed.

Larkin asked, utterly flabbergasted, "You're taking my ex-husband's side in the divorce?"

Doyle put his hands up in a placating gesture and said, "Mrs. Larkin, whoever Noah saw last night, it wasn't me."

Without missing a beat, Jacqueline said to him, "Noah's been part of this family for seven years. You've been around for seven minutes."

Lightning illuminated the lounge in a sudden flash of white. Larkin's breath caught like he'd been seized by the throat, his hearing swelled to a high-pitched ring, and then the thunder's resounding crack tore across the sky—its shockwave so strong, it ripped the Earth apart. And then Larkin was falling, six feet down into the open casket of his own rank and festering memories. And when the rotten bottom gave way, Larkin plunged headfirst into a dark abyss, surrounded by the hallucinogenic whispers of New York City's lost and forgotten as he fell down, down, down the never-ending hole he'd been digging since that fateful night eighteen years ago.

Boom.

Squish.

Crack.

Larkin jumped to his feet, knocking the table and sending Jacqueline's champagne glass to smash against the polished floor.

"Everett," Jacqueline protested. "Good grief, look at this mess!"

"Evie?" Doyle was standing, already reaching for Larkin.

But Larkin couldn't speak, couldn't linger in that prison of glass as lightning illuminated his terrors and the thunder gave them a voice. He shoved his chair back, stumbled around Doyle, and rushed across the lounge toward a hall marked with a discreet sign for the restrooms. He shoved open the door to the men's room and felt like he'd dropped into another pit of blackness—the mood lighting dialed far too low for inebriated men to hit the mark while taking a piss at the urinals along the wall.

Another crash of thunder sounded from outside, reaching this inner sanctuary and echoing off the tile walls.

The room began to spin.

But then Doyle was there, standing close and speaking with an authority that reached into the fall, grabbed Larkin, and pulled him back to the here, the now.

"Start counting."

"I—I—"

"No, I need you to count," Doyle reiterated.

"O-one, t-two—"

"You have to take a breath."

Vision blurring, black spots spreading like mold, Larkin grabbed for purchase, for Doyle. And as Doyle responded by putting his arms around him, encasing Larkin in the jubilance up to heaven, he finally began to cry.

Larkin was aware, in a sort of out-of-body sense, of being walked to the back of the bathroom, a door closing and lock being flipped, but he didn't dare open his eyes to the blackness, didn't dare let go of his buoy, instead focused with all his might on the steady rise and fall of Doyle's chest against his own.

In and out.

In and out.

In and out.

Larkin's manic breathing eventually subsided into a shallow rhythm, and as he inhaled, he focused on each scent note he could discern from Doyle's skin, cologne, clothes. The practice had a grounding effect, and the numbness in Larkin's hands began to give way to painful pinpricks. Sensation returned in the form of heat radiating from Doyle's back, chest, and belly.

And that heat, that pulse….

If Larkin could feel it, it meant he was alive too.

He didn't move for what felt like a long time—shaking when the storm roared and shuddering when Doyle stroked the back of his head in response. But eventually, the world outside of summer rain and survivor's guilt began to make itself known. Larkin noted the subdued Muzak piped into the bathroom via a speaker system, the smell of urinal cakes and Febreze air freshener, and a low conversation in Spanish between two employees outside the door before one laughed and their steps retreated.

Larkin lifted his head from Doyle's shoulder. His face felt raw and his eyes were sore. He probably looked puffy. He probably looked awful.

But Doyle put a hand under Larkin's chin, gave it a little nudge up, and smiled when their gazes met. "Hey, sunshine."

"Hi." Larkin looked around—they were inside the wheel-chair-accessible stall, with Doyle backed up against the tile wall, legs extended in a kind of lazy wall sit that was definitely utilizing his core strength, so he could take some of Larkin's weight and allow him to lean comfortably.

Doyle tugged some toilet paper free from the nearby dispenser and offered it.

"Thank you." Larkin took it and wiped his nose. He was still pressed flush against Doyle's body and could feel his partner shift, reach into his pocket— "What're you doing."

Doyle glanced at Larkin before holding up his phone. "Checking the weather."

Larkin looked at the screen. A radar map featured an outline of Manhattan covered in a radioactive green blob, its dark red center having already passed and currently on an eastern trajectory.

"It's supposed to end in about ten minutes," Doyle confirmed. He pocketed his phone and smiled again.

Larkin didn't reply. He was lost in the study of Doyle's face—a priceless piece of art crafted from gold and bronze—before he grabbed Doyle's hips, pulled him off-balance, and crushed their mouths together. Doyle reactively draped his arms over Larkin's shoulders, pressed into his body, and opened so easily, so affectionately to tongue and teeth and shared breath. Larkin touched everywhere, reading the story of Doyle's life through bone and muscle and skin. He rubbed the heated cotton of Doyle's button-down shirt, slipped a hand between his legs.

Doyle gasped against Larkin's lips. He grabbed Larkin's wrist to stop him, even as he pushed into the caress and a throaty moan escaped him, like a man truly coming apart at the seams. Larkin took Doyle's hand and put it to his own chest, nonverbal confirmation he wanted, *needed* the same, and Doyle was quick to take what he wasn't always allowed—hands roaming Larkin's chest, reaching under his shoulder holster, moving down his belly—relishing in the pleasure of their shared caress.

But Larkin pushed Doyle's hands lower, whispering, "Touch me." He'd set a precedent that when making out, he didn't want hands below the belt. It'd always made Larkin feel like shit that he could have a man as handsome as Doyle and still not get an erection when fooling around, and Doyle had respected the request.

But it was different this time.

And by the way Doyle's pupils blew wide, the way his breath came out in sharp, offbeat pants, the way he cupped and caressed—he'd realized it too.

"You remind me I'm alive," Larkin said.

"Fuck, Evie, I need you so bad."

Larkin moved for another kiss just as the door to the bathroom swung open and a man stepped inside. He was whistling off-tune as he unzipped at the bank of urinals and groaned loudly while relieving himself. The corners of Doyle's eyes crinkled in response and he shook in silent laughter. He brought Larkin's hands to his lips and began kissing the knuckles. Larkin stood on his toes and kissed Doyle's Adam's apple.

The pisser eventually finished, flushed the urinal, skipped a good handwashing, and left.

Doyle exhaled a deep breath before combing his fingers through Larkin's hair, fixing his side part.

Larkin didn't want for this to be over already, for that to have been it, for the fire to die out after seven goddamn months of feeling cold to his core, but he wasn't a randy teenager vying for a hookup, and Doyle wasn't a stranger. Their first time together surely wouldn't be in a fucking bathroom stall of an overpriced Midtown café. It would be at Doyle's apartment—at home—where Larkin could properly worship and delight in every inch of his partner's body and soul.

"I'm sorry," Larkin said.

"For what?"

"For manhandling you in public."

"I wouldn't say we're in public, exactly. Besides, you know I like a good manhandling." Doyle had to adjust himself, murmuring an apology as he did.

Larkin took Doyle's face in one hand. "Thank you for following me."

"To the ends of the Earth."

"Earth is spherical."

"Yeah, it is."

Larkin lowered his hand and stared at Doyle, who only smiled, unlocked the stall, and held the door open.

They exited and Larkin took a moment to freshen up at the sink. He frowned at his reflection in the mirror, touched under his eyes, and said, "I look old."

"You look fine," Doyle corrected, checking his phone a second time. "The storm's over the East River."

"'Fine' generally denotes you need Botox."

"'Fine' means 'fine,'" Doyle said. "I love the character in your face. Your mother is the one who suggested her thirty-five-year-old child needs Botox over a restful night's sleep."

Larkin looked at Doyle in the mirror.

Doyle caught his stare and slid his hands into his pockets. "I'm sorry. It's not my place to say—"

"I'm well aware of the kind of person she is."

Frankly, Doyle said, "I don't like the way she speaks to you."

"Neither do I." Larkin grabbed a paper towel and dried his hands. "My mother lives in a bubble of privilege and vanity, where one well-timed rumor can destroy a reputation. But since she has no career, no pursuits of her own, her reputation is that of her husband's, her son's. My mother has never given a damn that I'm gay. She does care, however, that my failed marriage and contested divorce will ostracize her from her little gossip club.

"Despite having a degree in psychology and recognizing her patterns of emotional invalidation, I still find myself seeking her approval. I know it's an exercise in futility. I've done my best to limit our interactions over the past several years, to protect myself, but severing that cord in its entirety is difficult. I find that I just keep thinking, hoping, this time, she'll care about me."

Doyle opened his mouth.

Larkin added, "I'm so sorry for what she called you."

"You don't have to apologize."

"I do. She never will, and you didn't deserve that."

"Thank you."

Larkin tossed the paper towel in the trash and opened the door.

"What about Noah?"

Larkin turned.

"I swear, I didn't—"

"I know. I'll find out what's going on." Larkin ushered Doyle out of the bathroom.

They were halfway across the lounge when Doyle slowed and took out his phone, but this time he swiped to accept an incoming call. "Hey, Craig."

Larkin stopped and waited.

"We're heading that way, actually. All right, see you soon." Doyle lowered the cell. "The courier from Queens just dropped off the brooch."

"Good." Larkin led the way back to the table still occupied by Jacqueline. The spilled champagne and broken glass had been cleaned up in their absence.

Jacqueline glanced up from her phone and said in a loud whisper, as if someone might be eavesdropping, "Everett, you've been in the bathroom nearly twenty minutes." Her eyes flicked to Doyle and she added, "Have some self-control."

Larkin replied, the flat effect of his speech now like gasoline meeting a lit match, "There was a thunderstorm."

"Oh, darling, are you still doing that?" She sighed, and somehow such a small action read as monumental. "I wish you wouldn't do it in public."

"Evie, will you wait outside?" Doyle's voice was its usual smooth and smoky top-shelf quality, but the expression on his face—Larkin had seen that unmasked outrage only once before.

—Doyle grabbing Gary Reynold like he were a ragdoll, screaming in his face, "She's a child. A fucking child, you disgusting pig!"—

But then his partner's face relaxed, and Doyle offered Larkin a smile that reminded him of quiet Sunday afternoons, the *chink* of melting ice in a glass of water, pencil lead scratching fresh paper.

Larkin said to his mother, "We have to get back to work." He leaned down and bussed her cheek. "Please stop talking to Noah. I don't want you or Dad involved in my divorce proceedings." And despite Jacqueline's protest, he turned and headed for the exit. Ignoring the maître d' at the front, Larkin pushed open the door and was met with a wall of overly warm and damp post-storm air. He suppressed a grunt of discomfort and looked over his shoulder.

Doyle still stood at the table, speaking far too quietly to be overheard at that distance, but when he finished, he didn't linger—didn't allow Jacqueline an opportunity to say her piece—instead strode across the café at a laidback pace while slipping his sunglasses on. Reaching Larkin, Doyle made a very conscious broadcast of their relationship by moving into the threshold and putting a hand on the back of Larkin's head.

Larkin didn't stop him.

Doyle kissed his forehead before asking, "How about I drive?"

CHAPTER SEVEN

Larkin had, unsurprisingly, fallen asleep on the drive downtown—his nap forty-eight minutes long, if the clock on the Audi's dash was to be believed. Taking the FDR should have saved them time, despite its additional two miles, so Larkin couldn't explain the discrepancy. That was, until Doyle said that a notification on Local4Locals had warned of a southbound accident on the parkway causing significant delays, so he'd opted to take Second Avenue instead. Doyle had insisted, in that usual, easygoing breeziness, that it hadn't been a big deal. Any excuse to relax behind the wheel of the Audi, even if it meant an hour of brake-tapping through midday, stop-and-go traffic on surface streets.

It was 1:02 p.m. when they stepped through the front doors of One Police Plaza. The official headquarters of the NYPD since 1973, the thirteen-story, god-awful Brutalist structure looked more like a prison than it did a suitable place to squirrel away the three-man Forensic Artists Unit, never mind a more heavy-hitting team like Major Cases or the actual police commissioner, whose offices were located on the top floor.

"I swear," Doyle was saying, but there was barely suppressed laughter in his words.

"You should never lie to the police."

"It's the truth, officer."

"Then why don't I see that traffic notification on Local4Locals," Larkin asked, coming to a stop in the middle of reception and holding his cell phone up.

Doyle leaned in, squinted at the screen, and then said with feigned thoughtfulness, "So strange…."

"Did you intentionally take the long way."

"That wouldn't make any sense." But then Doyle grinned. "How was your nap?"

Larkin's heart beat a little too hard under the steady gaze of those pyrite eyes. "It was good."

Doyle pinched the black hair tie around Larkin's still-raised left wrist, gave it a light snap, then started for the bank of elevators busy with administrators and uniformed and plainclothed officers coming and going in all directions. He pressed the Up button on the nearest panel before looking over his shoulder and motioning Larkin to join him.

It'd have been easy, Larkin thought, to walk away from his domestic problems. To get in that elevator with Doyle and leave behind the lawyers, the arguments, the tears. He could drop the dispute over finances, give Noah half of his life, and become strangers again.

—'til death do us part.—

But their love, like all loves, had been a conscious decision of vulnerability, of unfettered access to the soul, of trusting one person above all others with the parts of ourselves that were the most difficult, the most scared, and the most ugly.

And yes, their love hadn't lasted, hadn't endured, hadn't separated them only in death, but whether fault could be blamed or fingers pointed, it didn't negate that Larkin and

Noah had once tried to nurture and cultivate something beautiful together, had laid bare their inner workings to each other, and had forged memories that no other person would share.

Paperwork was easy.

Tying off a bleeding heart was hard.

The elevator doors opened and people exited, parting to either side of Doyle. He was still looking at Larkin, brows now raised expectantly.

Larkin raised his phone in response.

Doyle looked a little resigned, maybe a little worried, but he nodded once and then got on the elevator.

The doors shut.

Larkin turned right, away from reception, and walked down a long hall until he could hear the cafeteria, that familiar cacophony from his childhood school days of competing voices bouncing off too-high ceilings, chairs dragged across high-traffic linoleum, stacking lunch trays, banging pots and pans, the *ding, ding, ding* of the register.

Coming to a stop at the wall opposite the cafeteria entrance, Larkin leaned back against it, tapped a few buttons on the phone, and put it to his ear.

Noah answered on the second ring. "I'm so glad you called—"

"Explain yourself," Larkin interrupted.

Noah sounded a bit taken aback as he said, "I—I've been trying to reach you all morning."

"I can't always drop what I'm doing to take your call. I've told you this I don't know how many times."

"But you *never* take my call. That's the whole *problem*." Noah swore, his voice becoming distant, like he'd lowered the phone, and then he returned and said in a strained but civil tone, "I don't want to fight."

"I'm not convinced of that."

"You're being an ass."

"I just sat through my mother calling my partner a home-wrecker and then accusing him of what very much sounds like stalking, Noah. I'm a little irritated with you."

"I'm sorry I resorted to calling your mom, but you weren't answering and—no, don't interrupt me, Everett. I'm *telling* you, he was outside our—my—apartment last night."

"No, he wasn't. Ira's been with me, at work, since 3:48 in the morning."

Noah countered, a little smug, "It was around one o'clock when I saw his car."

"1:00 a.m. is not 'last night.'"

"Last night—this morning—*who cares*. The point is, I woke up, got a drink of water, couldn't fall back asleep, and that's when I noticed his car was parked directly across the street."

Larkin was quiet, considering.

For the last eighteen years, he'd been held at gunpoint by his interpersonal relations, his back to a wall of societal expectations, wearing a mask not of Melpomene's tragedy or Thalia's joy, but a paper bag with a drawn-on smiley face placating, pacifying, pleasing—*I can't see*—don't disagree, don't disappoint, don't disgrace—*I can't breathe*—a neurotypical poison of *Just Keep Smiling* for a world that wasn't perfect nor beautiful nor noble, but instead, one that was entirely indifferent to the inevitability of his death.

The world would see the same sunrise tomorrow.

The world wouldn't care about the suffering Everett Larkin had endured at the hands of the firing squad, wouldn't care if Larkin would even be alive to see the first early rays over the horizon, because the world was unaffected by morals and murder, beliefs and brutality.

The world simply *was*.

But Larkin wondered if, perhaps, his interpretation of Nietzsche's existentialism was too… literal.

Because yes, this world, with its seven billion people, really wasn't perfect, nor beautiful, nor noble.

But Ira Doyle *was*.

And Ira Doyle was Larkin's world.

"You still there?"

Larkin squared his shoulders and said into the phone, "Do you know what shape the Earth is."

Noah's uncertainty was nearly deafening. "What?"

"It's spherical."

"What are you talking about?"

"A sphere has no ends," Larkin explained. "When someone says they'll follow you to the ends of the Earth, that means they have every intention of being at your side forever."

"Everett—"

"Ira hasn't been skulking outside your apartment."

"I know what I saw."

"A blue Honda Civic."

"Yes!"

"Honda Civics are among the ten most common cars driven in New York City."

"Don't start with your goddamn statistics."

"What reason could Ira have for watching you."

"Under normal circumstances, I'd say, *you tell me*, but you fucked first and asked questions never, didn't you?"

"Stop it."

"This isn't the first time I've seen his car," Noah protested, almost shouting now. "Everett, it's *scaring* me. What if he does something? What if he hurts you?"

—a patient in the care of a father trained in the doctoring of childhood scrapes and bruises, seven stitches bandaged with such tenderness, such gentleness, his touch like butterfly wings—

Larkin rubbed his forehead, the gash he'd gotten from when Earl Wagner had shot at him outside Precinct 9 now a healed, slightly pink scar that'd fade with time. "Did you see him."

"Not—no. I mean, he was in the car the entire time."

"Did you get a plate number."

"No."

"Ira is not a vindictive, insecure, or jealous man."

"You can't just—"

"I've seen this car too," Larkin said over Noah.

"Wh-what?"

"Last night, a little after one in the morning."

"Where?"

"Outside my precinct."

"And where was *Ira*?" Noah asked pointedly.

"At home."

"Maybe he wasn't."

"He was," Larkin confirmed with unwavering finality.

"Then you tell me—what the fuck's going on?"

"I need to know the dates and times and where you've seen this car."

"I'd have to think."

"I need you to be exact."

Noah blew out a breath, and its shakiness could be heard even as it distorted over the line. "Can I call you back?"

"About this, yes. Are you posting on social media at all."

"Just on Facebook."

"Stop immediately."

"Everett?" Noah sounded scared now.

"I won't let anything happen to you," Larkin concluded. He ended the call with a terse goodbye before swearing under his breath. Larkin pocketed the phone, rubbed his tired eyes, then headed for the elevators.

Doyle's office was on the fifth floor, on the most western end of the building, and to get there, Larkin had to proceed through an obstacle course of sensory overload: a breakroom that smelled like half a dozen different lunches all recently reheated in the microwave—the clear winner was someone's leftover salmon and broccoli—two maintenance men, one on an open ladder and the other holding the side rail for safety, who were replacing an overhead tube light that flickered like an impromptu rave, and then a dozen private offices, some doors closed, conversations muffled, others wide open, offering a peek into the lives of the elite squads that called 1PP home.

Larkin came to a stop outside the partially closed door with the nameplate: Ira Doyle, Forensic Artists Unit. He patted his suit coat, reached inside, and retrieved the travel-sized tube of Tylenol that had recently become a permanent fixture in his life—his very own Clancy's Candy Counter lemon drops. Larkin popped two pills, hoping to dissuade his headache from becoming a full-blown stress migraine, then pushed open the office door.

Doyle had this kind of touch, a presence, a *magic* when it came to making a space feel lived-in, Larkin decided. He couldn't pinpoint what it was exactly, because the room was a standard office with its drafting desk to the left, flanked by shelves cluttered with tools and supplies, the bulletin board with its drawings from child victims, and the large worktable to the right, but every time Larkin stepped in here, he could feel the tension ease in his neck, his shoulders.

It felt… safe.

Doyle's back was to the door as he stood at the worktable, snapping on a pair of latex gloves while staring at the contents of the evidence package open before him.

Larkin strode across the room, the *tap, tap, tap* of his derbies causing Doyle to turn. But before Doyle could speak, could ask how the call went, Larkin grabbed his tie, gave it a yank, and Doyle willingly moved forward with the action.

With the distance closed, Larkin wrapped his arms around Doyle's neck, hugging him hard.

Doyle returned the embrace tenfold.

"I love you," Larkin murmured, pulling back after a moment. "I didn't tell you that today."

Almost immediately, Doyle looked like he was about to cry.

It'd been like this since June 12. Nearly every time, because growing up, Doyle had been so fucking starved for affection that his emotional response to receiving unconditional love in adulthood was all off. He literally couldn't maintain an appropriate intensity—the scale tipping past joy, past wonder, somewhere beyond ecstasy—and that overwhelm usually resulted in tears.

Larkin stepped back and gave Doyle a minute.

Doyle hastily wiped his face in the crook of his arm. He cleared his throat and said, "I love you too."

Larkin's mouth twitched, but he said grimly, "I think we have a problem. Noah's not wrong about the Honda Civic."

"What do you mean?"

"I saw it too."

Doyle's brows drew together.

"Last night," Larkin clarified. "It was double-parked outside the precinct. Honestly, I only gave it a second thought because it looked like your car, and we'd just been speaking. But when I started walking toward it, the driver sped away."

"Someone followed you from Pier 34?"

"That's what I'm thinking."

"But who'd have known you were even there?"

"Unfortunately, a good number of people. O'Halloran said Port Authority called it in, and because of the message on the fridge, were already inquiring if someone by my name worked for the department. The press was also there, although I didn't note from which outlets."

"How does that align with… with what Noah told you?"

"He said he's seen this particular vehicle several times, the most recent being around one o'clock this morning."

Doyle was already shaking his head, saying insistently, "I locked the door like you asked and got back in bed. I didn't—"

"Ira, you don't have to convince me. Noah's going to call back with the times and locations he remembers seeing the car. Perhaps it'll be enough to piece together a timeline that'll allow for identification. You haven't noticed any similar activity lately, have you."

"No."

Larkin frowned but said, "I'd like to keep it that way. I can't afford whatever this distraction is—not right now."

Doyle reluctantly returned his attention to the evidence. He fiddled with the packaging for a long minute before retrieving the brooch from inside. He held it in his gloved hand and then went to the drafting desk, took a seat in the tall chair, turned on the magnifying lamp, and swung its head down. "Black enamel on a gold backing," he called. "Looks like there's been some oxidation."

"Is that relevant," Larkin asked, following and standing in front of the desk, looking at the brooch upside down.

"Only from a historical standpoint. There was this law in England that introduced fifteen, thirteen, and nine karats—the 1854 Hallmarking Act—which made gold more accessible to the emerging middle class."

"But alloy additives cause gold to tarnish," Larkin concluded.

"Tells you a little about who once owned this, don't you think?"

"Very interesting. So this wasn't American-made."

"It's got the trappings of English design, but that doesn't mean it couldn't have been sold to an American client. Looks like there're a few seed pearls missing…. Those prongs can loosen over time, especially if they've passed their centennial celebration." Doyle turned the brooch around. Without taking his eyes off the magnified backside, he flipped open the sketch pad on the desk, grabbed a pencil, then began writing what he could decipher of the inscription.

Larkin slowly moved around the desk to stand behind the chair. He watched over Doyle's shoulder, entranced by the juxtaposition of such masculine hands producing delicate penmanship.

"It's not an exact match," Doyle began. "But this script is pretty similar to English round hand. Spencerian was the dominant style in America during the latter half of the nineteenth century." He motioned to the spaces between letters on the paper—an incomplete name.

Cha ot aur Fu

"It's ironic…," Doyle said thoughtfully. "This person was loved so much that their name's been lost *because* of grief."

"The middle name is Laura."

Doyle turned in his seat, one eyebrow cocked.

Larkin said, "A-U-R is a very specific combination of letters in a name. And since this brooch is mid-nineteenth century in origin—" He paused for clarification.

"Based not only on the oxidation, but that mourning jewelry really took off after the Civil War, yeah."

"Laura was one of the top fifty most common female names throughout the latter decades of the nineteenth century," Larkin explained. "In comparison, the name Maura never even hit the top two hundred since the Social Security Administration began logging names in 1879. And since the A is lowercase, we can presume it's not Aurora—which is one, too many letters for the space available, but two, has only in the last decade seen a considerable uptick in popularity."

"This is what I love about you."

"My willingness to trawl the archives of government websites?" Larkin asked with a noted inflection.

Doyle smiled to himself while he filled in the missing letters. "Your dedication."

"Don't be mistaken. It's thinly veiled, unmitigated obsession." Larkin went back to the worktable where Doyle had deposited his suit coat on one of the stools. Over his shoulder, he said, "I can't outright claim there's a pattern when we've not yet had three examples in which to build upon, but given our established history with Adam Worth cases, I'm reluctantly willing to admit the brooch and earring are from the same set." Larkin retrieved the plastic evidence bag from the pocket of Doyle's suit. He returned to the drafting desk with the earring.

"The rest of the inscription is a death date," Doyle stated, tapping his pencil against the pad.

B Se 2 880 AE 13

Larkin stared at the jumble of letters and numbers Doyle had copied from the brooch. He said, "Even taking into account that portions of this inscription are missing, I don't see a date with the available information."

"Death dates on jewelry were written in a form of shorthand," Doyle replied. "There'd have been an O here—OB. That's short for obit, which is derived from the Latin obitus, or death. 'S e' was likely 'Sepr,' which was how they abbreviated September."

"Date of death, September 2, 1880," Larkin suggested.

"That'd be my guess," Doyle answered. "As for AE—"

"Aetat," Larkin interrupted. "Or aetatis, at age of. Yes, the shorthand makes perfect sense now, thank you."

"Next, recite all of the declensions of 'man.'"

"You just want me to say *homo*."

Doyle grinned.

"You're thirty-nine years old, Ira."

"It's still funny."

"Jesus Christ."

Doyle accepted the bag, opened it, and held the two pieces side-by-side under the magnifying lens. He turned them this way and that, studying details that'd have been lost on Larkin. "Same maker's mark," Doyle said suddenly. "I'm pretty confident these pieces belonged to the mother of this thirteen-year-old girl. But I guess this doesn't really tell us much without restoring her name."

Larkin stepped away from the desk again and crossed back and forth in front of it as he began to pace the width of the room. "Of the mementos found so far—death mask, post-mortem photography, mourning veil—one was not like the others."

Doyle said, "The mask was of Andrew Gorman's own likeness and the veil had personally belonged to Esther Haycox. But the photograph found on Niederman was more like… proof of his crimes."

"They were trophies. And Worth had plenty in which to blackmail Niederman simply due to their content," Larkin ruminated.

"Earlier you weren't so sure this jewelry was a trophy."

"No."

"But now you are?"

"The earring in Wagner's home is proof she had a set of mourning jewelry—C.L.F.'s, to be specific—in her possession until only a few weeks ago, the same time she tried to make a run for it. Now, one of these pieces has been presented on her body so blatantly, so boldly, as to be comparable to how the postmortem photograph was found on Niederman. It's a clue I can't ignore, even if it's not in alignment with her established pattern of taking a cut from the victim's clothing." Larkin stopped, looked at Doyle, and concluded, "It pains me to admit, but I *am* wrong on occasion."

"A wise man once told me that some serial killers experiment with their signature and ritual as they gain experience."

"I told you that."

Doyle leaned back in his chair with a teasing smile on his face. He threaded his fingers together to rest on the back of his head and absently swiveled left and right. "No matter how much planning goes into it—murder is messy. Even the most methodical killers sometimes have to adapt under pressure."

"I know."

"So maybe this mourning set *was* a trophy to Wagner. Maybe she took it as a one-off to see how she felt about it."

"She had just set you up to be murdered after offing her own husband, but spent precious seconds collecting the mourning jewelry from its hiding place before going on the lam. It meant too much to her to have been a mere experiment."

"She might've started with jewelry as her trophy-of-choice," Doyle suggested. "It could have held sentimental meaning."

Larkin considered this. "But not all women wear jewelry, so it wouldn't have been a dependable choice in the long term."

"Certainly not with sex workers," Doyle agreed. "Back then, the smart ones avoided wearing anything that could be torn out or used to choke them."

"One of Wagner's very early kills," Larkin concluded. "I suspect she murdered at least three patients at the New York Infirmary—when she was still learning how to kill with digoxin."

"Find the right victim and we'll find the owner of this jewelry, which'll potentially lead us to the cold case connection." Doyle puffed his cheeks as he let out a loud breath. "Piece of cake."

CHAPTER EIGHT

Larkin was no stranger to calling all sorts of different establishments in his never-ending quest for information as a Cold Case detective. He'd phoned golf clubs and strip clubs—which had an interesting amount of crossover he felt should be studied—repair shops and pawn shops, airlines, museums, every local and state government acronym to exist east of the Appalachian Mountains, and even a zoo, so Larkin considered an inquiry to a hospital to be rather mundane. But the folks at the New York Infirmary seemed to think the opposite, and after being punted to what felt like every single extension, voicemail, and unfriendly recipient on staff, Larkin was finally informed that the three individuals in question had each suffered a heart attack while in the care of the New York Infirmary and tragedies happen, detective, there was never anything suspicious about these deaths at the time of their occurrence.

Larkin lowered the cell from his ear, tapped End, and opened his mouth while turning toward the worktable. But as he took in Doyle—seated at one of the stools, hunched over an open laptop and digital tablet, stylus in hand and earbuds in— Larkin found that he'd completely blanked on what it was he'd wanted to say. Competence in the workplace would always be an attractive trait, but Doyle in his element took sexy to a whole other level. And while staring unabashedly, Larkin was struck with a sense of astonishment—that even fifty-one days into their romantic entanglement, the solace he found in Doyle wasn't abating, wasn't normalizing. It was still a wonder, like a tiny star going supernova in his chest.

Larkin's cell rang in his hand and he jumped a little in surprise.

Noah Rider.

He accepted the call. "Do you have the dates."

Noah made a sound of annoyance under his breath, and Larkin knew that if the circumstances had been different, his ex-husband would have commented on the lack of small talk, the lack of a polite greeting. "I wrote down what I could remember."

"Tell me."

"I saw the car three times before today. There might've been other instances… I'm sure there was… but I only started noticing about two weeks ago. The first was Monday, June 29, at seven in the morning. I was leaving to go to school. Summer programs were starting."

—*"Speaking of unnecessary overhead," Doyle was saying as he stood from the kitchen table. "Craig's been into these weekly morning meetings and I'm about to be late." He collected his suit coat, portfolio bag, and then leaned down to kiss Larkin goodbye—*

"And the next," Larkin prompted.

"I can't remember the specific day. Tuesday, Wednesday, Thursday kinda blur together, you know?"

"No, I don't."

Noah made a sound under his breath that almost indicated amusement. "I think it might have been Thursday the second. I do know it was 3:30 because I was actually leaving work on time for once."

—"Detective Doyle."

"Hi. It's me—Everett."

A smoky chuckle. "Hey."

"I'm sorry to bother you at the office with something so trivial, but I thought you might be familiar with a music venue called OK Astor. I'd ask Miyamoto, but she's not in the office."

"Oh wow, the OK A on Astor Place?"

"Yes. Your tone of recollection suggests familiarity. When did they go out of business."

"I want to say 1999, but I'll be honest, I was a freshman in college and there was a lot of drinking back then. Why?"

"I've adopted a case involving a young man who was murdered during the after-hours at the OK Astor. However, the city's documentation is a bit conflicting in regard to the actual year of their closure, and investigating a murder does, in fact, require a certain level of accuracy."—

"You still there?" Noah asked for a second time that afternoon.

Larkin blinked and shook his head. "Sorry. Thursday, July 2, 3:30 p.m. And the third."

"Last Sunday."

"July 5."

"Hm-hm. That one stuck out to me because it wasn't like, hey, maybe there're just a lot of blue Honda Civics around home or work. I went out for brunch with Lacy and Steph— from school, right?—and hand to God, Everett, that same car was parked outside the restaurant when we left."

"What's the name of the restaurant."

"It's a new place in Midtown—Sully's Bistro."

"What time."

"I had a lot of mimosas… maybe around two o'clock?"

—Walking in the park, the air warm, vegetation in full bloom, their skin heavy with the perfume of summer sunshine, and Larkin had stopped to say, "Ira, hang on."

"What?"

He'd raised his phone, turned the camera on, and said, "Smile."—

"Anything else," Larkin asked.

"I think that's it."

"There is a possibility that these incidents are related to a case I'm working," Larkin began.

"*Great*," Noah muttered.

"But if by some chance that's not what's happening, I need you to understand how difficult it is to prove stalking behavior in a legal context. The Bureau of Justice Statistics reported 3.4 million victims of stalking in 2019, and of the sixteen percent that sought help, seventy-four percent received it, but of that, only twenty-four percent was in the form of restraining or no-contact orders, or protection services. That's 96,000 people out of 3.4 million. In the meantime, I want you to document everything. And if you feel unsafe, don't waste time calling me—call 911."

"All right. Everett?"

"What."

"Thank you for taking this seriously."

Larkin said, "Change your routine. Leave earlier, walk a different route to the subway, don't go anywhere after dark. Understand."

Noah's voice was small as he said simply, "Yeah."

"I've got to go."

They had a late lunch delivered from a restaurant on nearby Mulberry Street: steamed rice rolls with shrimp, soup dumplings, and a complimentary salted egg yolk bun that Larkin was certain was due to Doyle's uncanny ability to befriend just about anyone, including whoever had taken his lunch order over the phone.

"Try a bite," Doyle said, holding the white bun out.

Larkin hesitated.

"It's good, I promise. When have I ever steered you wrong with food?"

Promptly, Larkin answered, "The quinoa meatloaf you made last week."

"I apologized for that, like, three times."

"I'm merely answering your question."

Doyle let out a long-suffering sort of sigh but was smiling as he waved the bun in a come-hither motion.

Larkin leaned over the corner of the worktable and took a cautious bite. The still-warm, creamy, and slightly grainy filling exploded in his mouth, mixing with the fluffy texture of the bun in a sweet and salty harmonization. He wiped yellow custard from his bottom lip and licked his thumb. "You win."

"Yeah?"

"It's very good."

Doyle was a little too smug as he took a bite.

Larkin returned his attention to his phone—the most recent email notification was his warrant for Marcom Refrigeration Systems, and so he forwarded it to the address that Good Ol' Ben had supplied during their morning chat.

"I've been thinking about Noah."

Larkin glanced up.

Doyle busied himself packing the empty take-out containers back into the paper bag they'd arrived in. "About him seeing the car last Sunday."

"You and I were in Washington Square Park at the time of—"

"No, I know," Doyle interrupted. He wiped his hands absently on a napkin before saying, "What I mean is, Noah doesn't drive, does he?"

"He takes the subway."

"So how did this person know what restaurant to show up at, to park outside of, if Noah commuted to Midtown underground?"

Larkin's brows rose a little. "I admit to overlooking that detail."

"It just seems like maybe there's more than one person involved."

"If this situation is the result of stalking behavior, then two individuals is highly unlikely. Stalking is an intimate, often one-on-one affair," Larkin said. "And multiple stalkers borders on the persecutory delusion of gang-stalking. It's more reasonable that this individual overheard him discussing weekend plans with his coworkers."

Doyle's lips were compressed. It was a subtle mannerism Larkin had seen time and again throughout his years as a detective—a subconscious attempt to physically restrain one's self from saying something, not because of deception, but because of distress or discomfort centered around a topic of conversation.

Larkin set his phone aside, threaded his fingers together atop the table, and stared expectantly. "You don't believe any of that."

Doyle shook his head.

"Why."

"Because you saw that car too."

Larkin slowly pulled his hands apart, pressing them palm down on the tabletop. He could feel sweat accumulating underneath them.

"And there's no way this isn't related to our case—or to Adam Worth." With that, Doyle turned his laptop at an angle so Larkin could see the screen. He'd opened two image files of the brooch and placed them side by side. The left had had its settings and colors wildly altered, bringing out subtle texture in the engraving that was all but invisible to the naked eye. The right was the same photo, but Doyle had traced the newly discovered details so that whole letters were visible.

"I know you said you were going to enhance the photographs," Larkin began as he scooted to the edge of his stool, "but this wasn't what I was expecting. I'm very impressed."

"I can do a whole lot more."

Larkin gave Doyle a sideways glance. "I have no doubt."

A hint of a smile flirted across Doyle's face, but then he said with all seriousness, "I'm confident that the first name is Charlotte. I thought maybe Charlotte Laura Fulton—it's definitely 'u' then 'l'—but I don't think I have the end of the last name right."

"Fuller," Larkin suggested.

"*Fuller*. That's a better fit. Was there a Fuller in any of the associated cases?"

Larkin closed his eyes and gave his mental Rolodex a hard spin. The faceless, the nameless, the lost and forgotten of New York City cascaded through his memory in a blur of colorless heartache at double, *triple* the industry standard of twenty-four frames per second; otherwise, it'd take a full six and a half minutes to recall each and every case, and Larkin might have been a psychopomp, but his heart was flesh and blood—as vulnerable as Achilles's heel—and he simply couldn't bleed out for that long.

"I haven't heard Andy's name in a long time."

"Marco will always be gone."

"That's my Mia."

"When Essie vanished—"

Larkin's eyes snapped open abruptly. "Barbara Fuller. Friday, June 12, when we interviewed Phyllis Clark—"

"She showed us Esther's belongings," Doyle hastily finished. "The IDs in the purse."

"Yes, exactly." Larkin stood. "This might be the circumstantial evidence that'll finally get me the warrant to collect Esther's belongings."

"Good to see you aren't holding a grudge about that."

"Phyllis Clark is an uncooperative and combative woman, but that judge is a bigger idiot than she is."

"You did include the phrase *mise en abyme* in the paperwork," Doyle reminded him.

"A lack of understanding of transmedial mirroring techniques is not sufficient reason to refuse a warrant to someone with my success rate."

Doyle was doing his best—and failing, Larkin noted—to not smirk. He asked, "Are we thinking this jewelry belonged to Esther in the same way the clothing did? A family heirloom?"

Larkin said, "Earlier, my suggestion was that we look at Matilde Wagner's early kills, but we needn't go all the way back to the New York Infirmary. Esther, whose legal name is looking more and more likely to have been Barbara Fuller, was the first of Wagner's *mission-oriented* kills—the one who gave her a taste for cleansing the city of its undesirables."

Doyle got to his feet as well. There was a glimmer in his eyes—like satisfaction at having finally solved a complex word problem. "Earl Wagner started working in the neighborhood in late '81, and Esther was murdered the night of October 2, 1982. Her veil was taken as a trophy, but maybe Matilde took more than that because she was still working out her ritual with the body."

"Something Phyllis said during our interview," Larkin began, before repeating a portion of their past conversation with the precision of a tape recorder, "Essie was still carrying a gym bag to work—she kept a few different costume changes inside.... Either way, that bag never resurfaced after whatever happened to her."

"That could explain why Esther would've had so much jewelry on hand at the time of her death," Doyle answered. "It was part of her costumes. She carried the set in her bag."

More thoughtfully, he added, "I wonder if that bag never reappeared because Matilde and Earl did away with it, or if it's simply lost in the office of the Property Clerk."

"We won't know without the original homicide casework," Larkin said. "Which I have to presume was filed under Jane Doe, seeing as her missing person report was never connected to a known murder."

"You've seen it?"

"Yes. Ulmer pulled it for me. It's about all he's done to help so far."

"Is it ridiculous of me to ask how many Does are in the system that would have to be sorted through to find Esther?"

Larkin rubbed his chin absently. It felt like sandpaper—a reminder he hadn't shaved that morning. He said, "A 2018 survey conducted by the Bureau of Justice Statistics found that from the 2,037 medical examiner and coroner offices within the United States who responded to their request for data collection, there were over 11,000 unidentified bodies on record with those agencies, of which, over 7,000 came from offices serving a population of more than 250,000 citizens."

"So a lot," Doyle concluded.

"Let's not be hasty," Larkin admonished. "The National Death Index breaks down their data into sets of five years—I need a calculator." Larkin picked up his phone from the tabletop and tapped in a series of numbers on the calculator app. "The crude death rate for New York state is roughly 150,000 a year… that makes 750,000 in five. However, if I'm not mistaken, during the period of 1980 to 1984—when Esther was murdered—the state reported a total of 10,151 *homicides*, which accounts for hardly more than one percent of the 750,000. However, roughly three-fourths of those homicides originated here in the city.

"Because I work Cold Cases, I'm privy to details the rest of the department outside of Homicide needn't concern them-selves with—namely, that one-third of those homicides from

'80 to '84 remain unsolved to this day—for a total of… 2,537 cold case murders. And according to the National Institute of Justice, with research conducted in part with NamUs, roughly ten percent of missing or unidentified bodies are the victim of a violent end—meaning that of those 2,537 city homicides, we're looking at about two hundred and fifty-three being cases of John and Jane Does."

"All right, well, that's not—"

Larkin held up a hand and said, "To bring us full circle, the Bureau of Justice Statistics further reports that, surprisingly, only twenty-four percent of all unidentified bodies are female. That gives us a working number of… sixty-one, rounded up." Larkin turned his phone around so Doyle could see the screen.

"We only have to sort through sixty-one Jane Does to find Esther Haycox?" Doyle asked with noted optimism.

"In theory. We will have to do so manually, of course."

"You're brilliant, Evie."

"Thank you, but it was only statistics and some simple math." Larkin looked at his phone again and tapped a few buttons. "If you don't mind, I need to call Marcom Refrigeration Systems about the warrant I forwarded." He put the cell to his ear, and for a second time that day, Larkin listened to the teeth-grinding free-form jazz music before a familiar voice eventually answered:

"—here's Ben. How can I help you?"

"Mr. Brooks, this is Detective Everett Larkin with the NYPD. I forwarded a warrant to obtain the 1997 home address we discussed this morning."

"Oh, right! The fridge that underwent home repair."

"That's correct."

"Lemme see…." Ben trailed off, and the *click-clack* of a mechanical keyboard could be heard. "How's your day going, Detective?"

Larkin figured the small talk was probably Southern hospitality and answered with the expected, "Fine, I suppose." At length, he asked, "And yourself."

"Each day's better than the last, sir."

"Does that not imply your own death would be the best day of your life."

"So long as I got no regrets, that sounds about right," Ben answered matter-of-factly. "Okay, got a message from my supervisor saying everything's on the up-and-up. Thank goodness I took an early lunch. I'da been real tore up if someone else got your call. You ready to take that address down?"

"Yes."

"239 Carroll Street. That's in Brooklyn—"

—red brick, two-story, a motorcycle parked in the tiny driveway, Doyle tapping the passenger window, saying, "That's it," and Phyllis Clark opening the front door—

Larkin abruptly lowered his phone, Ben's tinny voice still gabbing from the ear speaker, and he said to Doyle, "The fridge is from Phyllis Clark's home."

CHAPTER NINE

Larkin sped through the mouth of the Battery Tunnel. Formerly the Brooklyn-Battery Tunnel, its name was changed to the Hugh L. Carey in 2012, although no self-respecting New Yorker actually acknowledged the name changes being made to bridges and tunnels, since the honoring of self-congratulating politicians was, in Larkin's opinion, a waste of taxpayer money—not to mention getting rather out of hand—when the original location-oriented names made more sense to those who actually drove the city streets. The glow of artificial lights ricocheted off the white tile walls and ghosted over the Audi's windshield. Taking the tunnel tacked two additional miles onto their journey, but the bridges were already becoming congested with commuter traffic, and driving between boroughs on weekday evenings was all about finding a balance.

Larkin didn't mind. Because as they drove under the water of the East River, with nothing but that peculiar, bubble-like quality to sound, the glow of the dashboard, and the repetitive nature of the tungsten lights and road barriers to lead the way, it felt a bit like he was being recharged and reset before slamming headfirst into all new stimuli.

Doyle murmured something under his breath.

"What was that."

"I was trying to check property records," Doyle answered. "But I lost signal."

"I've already done that. 239 Carroll Street was purchased by Stephanie Sato in 1992. She is, presumably, Phyllis Clark's wife, but I wasn't able to confirm when Phyllis moved into the house, as further attempts to converse with her last month were met with a dial tone." Larkin abruptly smacked the wheel with his open palm. "I fucking knew something wasn't right with Phyllis."

"That's your gut speaking."

Larkin spared Doyle a brief, incredulous glance.

"After our interview," Doyle began, "you said you didn't trust her."

"I didn't. I don't."

Doyle was undeterred. "That's what us non-geniuses call a hunch."

"It's not a matter of intellect. It's a matter of having limited emotional intelligence. It's easier for me to deduce and detect if I look at only the facts."

Doyle tapped his fingers against his thigh. "Why'd you trust me? When we first met?"

Larkin was frowning. "What."

"What made you trust that I was a decent person?" Doyle reiterated.

"Your behavior told me," Larkin said simply. "In the same way Phyllis's told me she *wasn't* decent."

"But isn't that an emotional response?"

"Trust," Larkin explained, "is an ongoing exploration within human-to-human interdependent relationships. An interdependent relationship is critical when two or more parties work together to reach a mutually beneficial goal—such as justice for Esther Haycox. And the ability, benevolence, and integrity within that relationship are considered to be the most important factors in the development of trust.

"When we met, you showed professional competence in your readily available knowledge on nineteenth-century death masks and the culture surrounding them. You showed compassion in your declaration that cold case victims should be alive too. And you showed honesty in our every conversation, even when I pushed too far, even when I let my compulsive tendencies reveal what I wasn't given permission to inspect. Phyllis—on the other hand—while she might have delivered promptly on reporting Esther as a missing person, has been so dismissive of aid that, when combined with her hypocritical mindset and emotionally abusive tendencies, it completely negates all credibility, thereby destroying a healthy interdependent relationship with me. Trust is factual, not emotional."

They sped out of the mouth of the tunnel and into Brooklyn proper.

Doyle leaned to one side and tucked his phone into his pocket. "I think I read somewhere that Nietzsche once said, 'There are no facts, only interpretations.'"

"I see what you're trying to do, but Nietzsche must be read in context. You need to understand his position on Kant's argument of the noumenon and phenomenon, that morality is a misinterpretation of phenomena, and that knowing is based on perspective, *meaning*, to reduce philosophy to little more than good versus evil is tangential to philosophy itself."

"I think I've lost this argument."

"Philosophical debates aren't about winners or losers, Ira."

"I guess the point I was trying to make is, you aren't limited in your emotional intelligence and I don't like when you say that about yourself."

"But I am."

"It's easy for a majority to label someone they don't under-stand as lesser or lower or limited."

Larkin briefly took his eyes off I-478 and glanced sideways, his expression of curiosity reflected back in the dark lenses of Doyle's sunglasses.

"What you do, sunshine, is contextualize trust. Most of us can't do that."

—*"You're part of the human condition too."*—

Doyle's presence had been steadily filling the in-between moments in Larkin's life—where day and night shared the sky, where sleep and wake occupied the same mind—until it felt as if there'd never been a beginning to their relationship. That there'd be no end. That Doyle simply had been, and always would be, *here*.

It was a dangerous thought, but one Larkin couldn't suppress.

"Thank you," was all he said.

When Carroll came up on the right, Larkin turned. Towering ginkgoes and oaks lined the street, their overhead branches swaying lazily in the breeze. Debris had collected in the stag-nant water that filled gutters, suggesting this area of Brooklyn had been caught in the same noonday downpour. The approach-ing redbrick home with the tiny driveway, nestled among multimillion dollar brownstones, looked the same as it had on Friday, June 12. Larkin pulled up onto the curb, turned off the engine, and stared at the home out of the passenger window.

The engine *tick*, *tick*, *tick*ed.

"I don't trust Phyllis either," Doyle stated into the quiet. He pulled his sunglasses off and met Larkin's steady stare. "For the record."

"I'm glad we're in agreement on that." Larkin popped the driver's door and climbed out. He moved around the front bumper and onto the sidewalk. The driveway was empty and a curtain had been drawn taut across the living room windows.

"Want me to take point?" Doyle was asking as he joined Larkin's side. "Since you and Phyllis—what's wrong?"

"The living room has north-facing windows."

"So?"

"The north side of a home receives the least amount of light," Larkin answered. "On our first visit, I noted that Phyllis's wife had a number of succulents, a Boston fern, and a watermelon peperomia—all plants that thrive in bright, indirect sunlight. The living room windows were the only light source for the plants. It doesn't make sense to keep the curtains drawn."

"Maybe no one's home," Doyle noted. "And they close the drapes when they go out."

"But they've got sheer curtains too," Larkin replied. "Pull those shut and you've got both privacy and sunlight."

Doyle shrugged. "Maybe Phyllis is in the habit of walking around topless."

"Assuming she isn't exposing her breasts with the lewd intention of being seen from the street, under the amendment to Penal Law 245.01, women can go topless in New York wherever it's legal for a man."

"Let's just serve the warrant, Larkin."

They headed up the driveway. Larkin retrieved the paperwork—his second request for Esther Haycox's belongings having been approved upon the discovery of the refrigerator's origin—from the inside pocket of his suit coat before knocking on the door. "NYPD," he called loudly.

No movement sounded from within the home.

Doyle stood at an angle beside Larkin, able to watch both the street and front door with ease. "That's weird," he murmured.

"What is."

Doyle pointed over Larkin's shoulder.

Larkin turned to his left. A wall-mounted mailbox stood open and stuffed to absolute capacity. He distractedly passed Doyle the warrant and then tugged free a handful of mail. The envelopes and catalogues had the texture of paper that'd been left in the elements—soaked from rain, dried by sunshine, rinse and repeat. Larkin quickly sorted through the contents. The mail was a usual collection of preapproved credit cards, flyers from representatives running for local office, monthly account statements, even a few catalogues advertising upcoming exhibits at city museums and galleries. The oldest were postmarked from June 13 and, Larkin noted, every single one was in Stephanie Sato's name.

"Nothing here is addressed to Phyllis Clark," Larkin said.

Doyle said, "I *still* get mail addressed to previous tenants, and it's been six years."

Larkin returned the mail to the box. "I saw the Metropolitan Opera brochure on the kitchen table the other day."

"Dorothy Wallace," Doyle said by way of agreement. "I also get her quarterly catalogues from Ethan Allen."

"Ethan Allen isn't your style."

"Nor my tax bracket."

Larkin gave the front door another, louder knock. He put his hand on the knob and gave it a try.

The door opened, and stale, stagnant air carrying the unmistakable stink of death wafted out.

"*Jesus Christ,*" Larkin swore. He unholstered his SIG P226, checked Doyle, who already had his Glock 17 out, then pushed the door open with the toe of his shoe. "NYPD," he called again from the vestibule. "Ms. Clark, Ms. Sato, if you can, please make yourself known."

The silence was ear-piercingly loud.

Larkin warily stepped through the threshold. A set of stairs directly ahead went down to what he suspected was a basement studio, if Stephanie was indeed the artist Phyllis claimed her to be. But Larkin turned right and entered the bubblegum pink and mint-green living room, weapon raised in both hands. The house was a sauna, hot and humid, like there'd been no circulating air for weeks. Several houseplants were yellowed and limp. Larkin felt pricks of perspiration forming under his arms, at his hairline, beads of sweat already rolling down his lower back as he cleared the open layout and moved through the dimly lit home toward the bathroom. He glanced inside, but there was nothing more incriminating than a discarded bath towel on the floor.

Larkin reentered the hallway just as Doyle exited the bedroom.

"Bedroom's clear," Doyle said.

"The smell was stronger in the vestibule," Larkin replied. He motioned for Doyle, and with his pistol held at low ready, he returned to the front door before slowly descending the steps to the basement, following the smell of decay like a bloodhound. At the landing stood a door partially ajar, the interior within completely dark. Larkin nudged the door open farther with his shoulder. Behind him, Doyle sucked in a breath of air as the stench intensified. Larkin reached inside, felt along the wall, and switched on a light.

The space appeared to double as both a studio and storage. There was a wooden easel—a larger version of the exact one Doyle kept stored at home—and easily a dozen vertically stacked canvases along the left wall. There was a drop cloth on the floor, a table strewn with containers of well-loved brushes and palettes of paint, but also stacked boxes labeled as seasonal décor, a stationary bike, deflated yoga ball, industrial floor fan, an Igloo cooler that had the color trappings of the early '90s, and two cases of Pepsi Zero stacked beside a discarded pile of what looked to be salad dressing bottles and removeable refrigerator shelves. Right smack in the middle of the room was a decomposing body slumped in a foldable camping chair.

The remains were in the stage of active decay, with blackish liquid seeping from skin breaks caused by the bloating and putrefaction of internal organs. Skin sloughed from the hands hanging limp over the armrests, and long dark hair had slipped free from the scalp. The victim's head was tilted far back with their jaw hanging wide open. They wore a pair of stained and soiled overalls and were covered in so many wriggling maggots that the body gave off the illusion of movement.

"Sonofabitch…," Larkin whispered.

Doyle took a step closer, reaching over Larkin's shoulder to push the door back enough so that he could peer inside. "Holy—hang on, *Larkin*."

But Larkin stepped into the room so Doyle didn't have to. He cleared the corners, made certain there was no one lurking behind the New Year's resolutions and impulse buys, then approached the rotting corpse. Adult flies buzzed erratically around the body. Larkin put his free hand to his face, covering his mouth and nose while leaning in to inspect what remained of any defining characteristics. "It's not Phyllis," he announced around his cupped hand.

"How can you even tell?"

"The long hair," Larkin said, pointing his weapon at the goopy clumps of hair littering the floor.

"Could it be Stephanie Sato?" Doyle suggested, still hovering in the doorway.

"I don't know what she looks like." A writhing mass of maggots plopped to the floor like a splatter of paint, and Larkin took a few steps backward. "But it looks as if this woman was struck on the back of the head. There's an open gash on the scalp."

Doyle said, "If it *is* Stephanie, how has Phyllis not noticed her own wife is missing?"

"How has she not noticed the smell," Larkin corrected. He started toward the door when he heard a muffled *tap, tap, tap*. He stopped, looked up.

"What?"

Tap, tap, tap.

Larkin ducked out of the room and slipped around Doyle. Pistol still in hand and back pressed to the handrail, he slowly started up the stairs. He'd made it about halfway up when someone—a man—crept out of the living room and back into the vestibule. The stranger was dressed in khakis and a baby blue polo shirt, the sleeves bulging around his big biceps. He had an undercut and the kind of beard that belonged on either an Alaskan frontiersman or a barista from Williamsburg. The strap of a leather satchel was taut across his muscular chest, the bag resting on his backside, and he held an expensive-looking digital camera in one hand.

The stranger looked down, clicked a few buttons on the camera, then turned toward the basement steps, almost as if instinct had told him he wasn't alone. The man's gaze locked with Larkin's, and he immediately all but flung himself out the still-open front door.

Larkin charged up the stairs, shouting, "NYPD!"

The intruder was already across the driveway and onto the sidewalk by the time Larkin reached the threshold. Doyle was calling for Larkin, but he didn't stop. He raced out the door, back into the muggy aftermath of the storm, following the stranger along Carroll and west toward Clinton. Even in a suit and dress shoes, Larkin was fast. Gripping his SIG in his left hand, Larkin pumped his arms, pounded the sidewalk, and closed the distance.

At the corner, the stranger nearly plowed into two men carrying an ornamental sideboard from a funeral home toward a parked moving van, their angry voices filling the air like the drone of wasps. The man stumbled like a newborn foal into the crosswalk while keeping a desperate hold on his camera. A truck coming up Clinton laid on its horn. Larkin flew past the two still-shouting movers, into the road, and slammed into the suspect with all of his forward momentum—the two crashing to the pavement on the opposite side of the street and narrowly missing being flattened by an oversized pickup. The camera skittered and scraped loudly across the sidewalk, just out of reach.

"Get off of me!" the intruder shouted.

Larkin grabbed the man's right arm and yanked it back and up behind him, causing him to let out a high-pitched yelp. "Which letter in NY-goddamn-PD did you not understand?"

"This is police brutality!"

"The hell it is. *Stop moving!*"

Larkin's one-handed grip wasn't enough to hold the bigger man down, and he was able to yank free and awkwardly roll onto his back. Larkin clamped his thighs tight, straddling the intruder's hips, and by the way the stranger's face had taken on a sudden, almost waxy appearance, Larkin's look of rage was far outweighing any embarrassment regarding their physicality.

"Who are you," Larkin demanded.

"J-Joe Sinclair."

Larkin cocked his head as his Rolodex memory automatically spun. He knew this name. He knew this man—the reporter who'd endeavored for an interview during the Death Mask Murders. Unprompted, Larkin said, "*Out in NYC.*"

Joe's eyebrows rose. "Y-yeah. Wow, you remember—"

"What were you doing in that home."

"Following a story."

"You were following me," Larkin corrected.

"You're like no one I've ever met before," Joe said in a rush.

"Flattery will get you nowhere."

"I mean it," he protested. "It—it's not just that you're open in a conservative work environment, or that you're handsome and highly decorated—"

"Get to the fucking point," Larkin snapped.

"I've heard you're a genius—a literal genius. And that you're hunting your fourth serial killer in as many months."

"Were you at Pier 34 last night."

Joe swallowed and then nodded.

Larkin grabbed a fistful of Joe's polo and yanked him up. "Have you been following my ex-husband."

Joe was taken aback as he repeated, "*Ex*-husband?"

The sudden and profound relief that Doyle had been *wrong* nearly had Larkin as giddy as a schoolboy. It wasn't two or more stalkers, and the Honda Civic wasn't connected to Adam Worth. It was just a journalist—the same fucking journalist from earlier in the year—who'd clearly been lucky in his bit of online snooping to have discovered Noah, but not enough to have learned of the pending divorce. Joe had been hanging out around Larkin's former residence because the bastard thought Larkin still lived there.

Connor was going to have a stroke when he found out how close the media had inadvertently gotten to this case.

"Fourth degree stalking is a misdemeanor," Larkin said. "Do you want to spend the next three months on Rikers."

"Larkin!"

Larkin glanced to his right. Doyle was running toward them, coming up on the movers outside the funeral home across the street.

Joe's objections grew louder and more frantic. "It's not like that. Everyone wants you, Mr. Larkin, from the rags to the *Times*, but *I* can tell your real story without all the pandering Sherlockian bullshit. Consent to an interview—"

From the corner of his eye, Larkin saw a car slow at the intersection. He glanced sideways at… a blue Honda Civic. The passenger window rolled down, a sharp, cigarette scent wafted out; then there was a flash of a muzzle, a deafening boom—and Larkin's face and chest were splattered with blood as Joe slumped out of his hold and collapsed dead on the pavement.

Larkin looked down.

Joe's mouth was agape, his eyes wide as if surprised. A small entry wound glistened from the middle of his forehead. Taken out execution-style. The exit wound behind his right ear pumped a steady stream of wine-red blood into the gutter.

—rain and whiskey and blood like a hell-broth boil and bubble—

Larkin raised his head, and the pistol was leveled at him.

—"Since the day we met—I knew I was in love."—

CHAPTER TEN

—*sun-bleached planks rough against his skin, beads of water dripping like tears, dandelion heads a breadcrumb trail leading out farther, deeper, the lake a black hole of tannins and misery, and Patrick had jumped off the dock, swallowed whole by its gravitational pull.*

Larkin sank down after him and Patrick was there, asking, "Do you think we'll be together forever, Everett?" But Larkin couldn't breathe underwater, couldn't speak underwater, couldn't tell Patrick's memory that next month would be the eighteenth anniversary of his passing, the eighteenth year that Larkin was haunted by childish rhymes: he loves me, he loves me not, *the eighteenth year that Larkin had grown older without him, had become a man without him.*

A night of alcohol and kisses and murder for the hundredth, thousandth, millionth *time, only this memory, this confrontation with death, was met with being pulled up, toward the breath of now, the luminosity of today, life and love forevermore—*

"Evie?"

Larkin blinked. He sat on the curb, elbows on his knees, a half-empty water bottle in one hand that he didn't remember taking a drink from.

Doyle was crouched before him, and the way the evening sun hit his dark brown eyes—pyrite flecks shining like stardust—it was an all-access pass to his soul. Larkin saw a man who wanted to cry, to scream, to *rage*. He saw the ugly tragedies that had fashioned Doyle into the man he'd become, the knives in his back and Band-Aids holding his heart together. But despite the twisted shapes Doyle's hope and happiness had become, they cracked pavement like tree roots—stubborn and unrelenting—striving for the light.

It felt like the world had gone silent and still around them.

"Since the day we met—I knew I was in love."

Into that quiet, Larkin realized for the first time that he'd associated dying, not with guilt, but with love. And in doing so, he'd glimpsed an understanding of what it meant to exist: of life and death as a spectrum. Man's will yearned for purpose, and the purpose of senseless suffering was guilt. All that anger, uncertainty, could haves, should haves, would haves gave humanity something to cling to when cast out into the stormy sea of mourning. We didn't dare let go of what remained of those we so dearly loved, despite the certainty that this guilt was going to drown us, because this was *all that remained.*

To release ourselves of guilt would be to forget.

And remembrance was the greatest act of love there was.

But Nietzsche had said that man was a bridge, not a goal, so could such an interpretation of his philosophy of "perhaps" be that, like life, death was just another physical interim? A bridge along the spectrum?

Those we loved weren't gone. They were simply beyond the bridge, beyond the veil, somewhere that was difficult for us to see. And if they weren't gone—would never be gone—

what use was guilt? It wasn't a life preserver, but an anchor, pulling us away from the jubilance of heaven.

Man's will yearned for purpose, so what if, instead, that purpose was to love, and love again?

Over and over.

Forevermore.

Larkin shifted forward, dropped onto one knee, and pulled Doyle into a sudden embrace. He felt as if he'd returned from some faraway mountain peak, born again with a newly learned revelation ready to be shared with the world. But Larkin was conscious of how his complex relationship with dying, with death, was decidedly at odds with typical Western thinking, and that to exclaim *no one is truly dead*, especially to a bereaved father, wasn't so simple.

Speaking frankly of death had its time and place, and that wasn't now or here.

What *was* here was life and love and Ira Doyle.

Larkin placed a hand on the back of Doyle's head and whispered, "*I'm right here.*"

Doyle drew Larkin to his feet as he stood, bringing their bodies closer.

"We're okay," Larkin said.

Doyle nodded, his posture a bit stooped so as to press his face to the crook of Larkin's neck and shoulder.

"I love you more than you know."

Doyle tightened his hold but said nothing.

Because everything had already been said.

Like the sun coming up over the horizon to wake the world for another day, Larkin became aware of his senses, of his surroundings: the flashing lights of a parked ambulance, the voices of uniformed officers directing traffic and civilians around the cordoned-off crime scene, the stink of a corrupted body.

"'Scuse me, sir?"

Larkin let go of Doyle before turning to his right. An EMT stood several feet away, shifting his weight from one foot to the other. "What."

"Did you want to go to the hospital?"

"No." And with all honestly, he added, "I'm okay." Larkin watched as the EMT left, shut the back doors of the bus, then walked around to the driver's side door. His attention wandered next to the street corner, to the body of Joe Sinclair with a white sheet draped over him. Dried blood stained the pavement.

"Death doesn't seem to come for one of its own, does it?"

Both Larkin and Doyle looked in the opposite direction of the body and departing ambulance to see Neil Millett approaching. He wore partial PPE—booties over his shoes, gloves on his hands—with a digital camera hanging from his neck and his trusty evidence kit in one hand.

Larkin asked, "Why are you here."

Millett shrugged. "Ask my supervisor. I don't dole out the assignments." He set his kit down, scrutinized Larkin carefully, then said, "It first came over the radio as a 10-13. Someone had reported an officer down."

Larkin plucked at his bloody shirt. "Not yet."

Millett looked over Larkin's shoulder at the covered body, exchanged a knowing look with Doyle, then said with the usual toughness of a seasoned cop, "Glad to hear it." With that, he proceeded to take photos of Larkin's clothes, performed a GSR swab of his hands, confirmed the SIG hadn't been fired, and finished his evidence collection by saying, "I'm gonna need to take your clothes."

"That leaves me in an interesting predicament," Larkin answered, but he dutifully shrugged out of his suit coat and dropped it into the paper bag Millett held.

"You don't have a spare set for emergencies?"

Larkin unbuckled his shoulder holster and passed it to Doyle. "Field work is actually atypical to solving cold cases."

"What's your waist size?"

"Twenty-nine," Larkin answered.

"Wow, really?"

"Did you want my inseam too."

Doyle failed to entirely suppress a laugh, and Larkin was grateful for its authenticity.

Millett pushed the bag into Larkin's hands, said, "I'll be right back," then jogged toward Clinton Street where the CSU van was parked.

Doyle's introduction of some levity to the moment was a bit obvious when compared to smoother efforts of the past, but compartmentalizing was a vital tool in law enforcement, and now wasn't the time for either of them to ponder Larkin's near brush with death. In that gorgeous baritone, Doyle asked, "You think Millett's into you?"

Larkin set the bag at his feet and said, while handing Doyle the rest of his personal effects, "Millett's into the new ME."

That was a sufficient enough distraction, and Doyle's thick brows drew up as he clarified, "Dr. Baxter?"

"I'm uncertain if it's only mutual attraction or something more—"

"Are you serious?"

"Was it not obvious."

Doyle looked instinctively toward Clinton Street, then asked, "Anything else you want to share with the class?"

"It's not polite to gossip."

"Yeah, but I'm your work husband," Doyle reminded him. "You're morally and ethically obligated to keep me informed on matters of the heart."

"I wasn't aware the exchange of hot goss was part of my duties and responsibilities."

Doyle's smile was almost whimsical. "You're so cute."

Larkin's mouth twitched. He slid his tie free, unbuttoned his shirt, dropped the bloody mess into the bag, and had started on his trousers when Millett returned with a set of folded clothes in his hands.

"I've got—*okay*, you're not modest," Millett stated.

"No, I'm not," Larkin said as he maneuvered out of his trousers, standing on the side of the road in nothing but his mint-green derbies and a pair of low-rise black trunks.

Millett hastily offered the clothes. "Working CSU, you never know when you might find yourself in the garbage chute of a luxury high rise, helping to retrieve a decomposing body."

"Your nine-to-five is full of surprises," Doyle observed.

"You've no idea," Millett replied. As Larkin accepted the jeans, he added, "They might be a little big on you, but they're clean."

Larkin pulled on the jeans, which, yes, were both too big in the waist and too long in the leg, but after rolling the cuffs twice, they were at least manageable. He accepted a navy T-shirt that had CRIME SCENE UNIT printed in bold letters across the back.

"What's wrong?" Millett asked.

Doyle answered for Larkin, "He doesn't like wearing blue-on-blue."

Larkin pulled the T-shirt on. "A good wardrobe should have contrasting colors. Pink, orange—mustard pairs particularly well with dark blue jeans."

"I just don't see the NYPD adopting *mustard* as an official color anytime soon," Millett said.

"Thank you for the clothes."

"No problem." A van from the ME's office pulled onto the scene, and Millett murmured, "Looks like my long-lost medicolegal is finally here. I'll finish up with this DB and meet you guys at the house for the second one."

Larkin watched Millett greet the approaching medicolegal, the two of them pulling back the sheet from Joe Sinclair's body. He absently accepted his holster back from Doyle, strapping it on while saying, "He tried to interview me during the Regmore case. Joe Sinclair with *Out in NYC*."

Doyle looked incredulous. "They write about how to pair jockstraps with summer fashion trends."

"How's that for intellectual stimulation," Larkin said dryly. "Joe admitted to having been at Pier 34 last night. He admitted interacting, to some degree, with Noah."

"But the shooter was in a Honda Civic."

Larkin nodded stiffly. He'd been so happy, so *relieved*....

Doyle looked toward the street where the Honda's occupant had killed a man in cold blood, and wondered aloud, "Why would Adam Worth have a journalist from a gay entertainment press murdered?"

...since one intrusive little journalist wasn't a threat—he was just an unrelated annoyance.

Doyle set his hands on his hips. "It doesn't make any sense."

Larkin prided himself on being attracted to, and involved with, smart men, but he'd have given his left nut for Doyle to have been dead wrong about this.

Because Larkin had no idea where to go from here.

Doyle made a sound of being intrigued under his breath. He said, "I'll be right back," then headed toward Millett and the medicolegal, still hovering over the body.

Larkin pulled out his phone. He dialed a number, put it to his ear, and said when his call was answered, "Have you spoken to an individual by the name of Joe Sinclair."

"Who?" Noah asked.

"He wrote for *Out in NYC*."

"Is he the guy with the beard and biceps?"

"What did you say to him."

"Nothing."

"*Noah.*"

"Basically nothing," Noah course-corrected. "He called me, out of the blue, a few weeks ago. He introduced himself, said he was a reporter writing a piece on some cases you'd worked, and…."

"And what."

Defensively, Noah said, "No one's ever wanted to know about me. Four years we were married, and all I ever got asked were questions about you. From your coworkers, from *my* coworkers, our friends, family, even your psychiatrist."

"And you let a reporter butter you up."

"They weren't serious questions," Noah argued. "He asked where I grew up, what I did for a living, if I enjoyed it—and when's the last time someone gave a shit about a public school teacher? He asked if we were married and I said yes."

"Despite the contrary."

"We *are* still married, Everett."

"Goddamn it, this is not the time," Larkin said sternly. "What else did you tell him."

"That's all, I swear. After that, he started getting more interested in you, and I told him I wasn't going to answer on behalf of a cop."

"But you know what he looks like."

"I guess it wouldn't be too difficult for a reporter with basic research skills and an internet connection to have found our address, right? He came around and tried again, but I told him he needed to back off. That was the last time I heard from him."

"Why didn't you tell me."

"Because I handled it."

Larkin took in the active crime scene surrounding him—the investigators, the dead man, the bloody sheet. So much for handling it, he thought. "Did you see the Honda Civic before or after Joe Sinclair came to the apartment."

Noah's quiet had a thinking quality to it, and he said, "After. Maybe, like, only a day or two later." He hastened to ask, "What's going on?"

"It's an ongoing case," Larkin said by way of explanation. "Thank you, Noah." He ended the call as Doyle returned, now wearing a pair of latex gloves and studying the screen of Joe's camera. It seemed to be working, despite visible nicks and scratches on its body. Larkin said, "Joe tapped Noah for information. First on the phone, then again in person."

Doyle briefly looked up, and while Larkin hadn't ever met Doyle's grandmother, hadn't even seen a photograph of her, in fact, he could so easily imagine that same expression of skepticism time and again on the matriarch's face during Doyle's tumultuous boyhood years. Evenly, Doyle asked, "What'd Noah tell him?"

"He claims to have said nothing about me."

Doyle looked back down at the camera menu.

"He said the Honda showed up between twenty-four and forty-eight hours after Joe dropped by the apartment."

Still tapping buttons, Doyle murmured, "Given that it sounds a bit like the driver followed *Joe*, my first step would have been to ask Joe of any Honda Civic owners he might know."

Larkin grunted. "And if my job were so simple I'd have put in for early retirement already." He raised his phone a second time, pulling up Lieutenant Connor from his list of contacts.

"Look at this."

Larkin paused, thumb hovering over the Call button. He sidestepped closer and took a look at the digital screen as Doyle began to swipe through previously taken photographs, a timeline of their day, only played out in reverse: pictures of Phyllis Clark's bedroom, living room, like the photographer didn't know what the subject matter was. The next was of

Larkin and Doyle standing at the end of the driveway before they'd approached the front door, taken from behind and farther down the street. Another of Larkin entering Precinct 19 the night before, and at least a dozen more—these taken with a zoom lens—of him standing in a cone of orange light on the pier.

"How could I have not noticed."

Doyle lowered the camera but didn't say anything.

"*Fuck*." Larkin aggressively tapped Connor's number and put the phone to his ear.

His lieutenant had already been made aware of the immediate situation in Brooklyn, but after a succinct recap of Noah's claims involving the blue Honda, how it was noticed shortly after Joe attempted to obtain personal information on Larkin, and how both car and journalist had played a role in Larkin's life over the last twenty hours, Connor was well and truly pissed.

"What was I saying to you this morning about hack journalists?"

"I don't—*we* don't believe Joe's presence is unrelated," Larkin interjected. "There is a very real connection between his attempt to write some kind of tell-all and the fact that he was just silenced, execution-style, right in front of me. I don't know how he plays into our case, into a relationship with the sender, but he *does*."

Doyle was coming back from returning the camera to Millett so that it could be logged as evidence. He stopped beside Larkin and waited.

"Sounds a little conspiratorial to me," Connor was saying.

"If it wasn't all connected, I'd have an evidence marker next to my head too," Larkin countered, internally wincing when he caught the flash of distress roll across Doyle's face like a lightning strike. Hastily, Larkin continued, "But the sender doesn't want me dead. He wants a battle of intellect, and he doesn't want anyone in the way of his game. Right now, sir, he's winning."

Connor grunted. "Did you at least see the shooter?"

"He had to roll the window down," Larkin confirmed. "I saw his face in a three-quarter profile."

Doyle suddenly cut in with, "You did?"

Larkin looked at Doyle, nodded, but said to Connor, "I can look through some mugshots when I get back to the precinct. But first, I need to return to 239 Carroll Street. There's a DB in the basement who's not the owner, and the refrigerator Wagner's body was found in originated from this home."

"All right. I'll work on damage control from here. Grim?"

"Yes, sir."

"You're okay… *right*?" And the emphasis suggested Connor meant far more than being physically sound.

"I'm okay," Larkin confirmed. He ended the call and tucked the phone in his back pocket.

Doyle prompted, "You saw the shooter?"

"I saw his weapon first," Larkin answered as he started across the street in the direction of Phyllis's home. "An old-school revolver. But then I saw his face, yes."

Doyle caught up to Larkin with a few long-legged strides. "Would you remember his features?"

Larkin gave him a touch of exasperated side-eye.

"What I mean is, I think you should sit for a composite sketch."

—the antiseptic perfume of a hospital, languishing in bed, police asking, "What did he look like? What did he sound like?" but Larkin couldn't answer, couldn't speak, could do nothing but sob, and hope had died on the endnotes of a bad dream—

They had just walked past the wrought-iron fence of the funeral home when Larkin answered uncompromisingly, "I'm not a victim."

CHAPTER ELEVEN

"Larkin?"

"What."

"They have a fridge."

Larkin stopped walking as he reached the threshold of the bedroom he'd been inside of a month prior. He flicked on the overhead light. The walls were still that not-quite-orange-almost-pink color. The bedspread still lavender, the shag rug still white. Larkin turned around. Doyle stood behind him, tugging on a fresh pair of gloves. Sweat made the latex stick and pull over the backs of his hands. The house was still unbearably hot, and it showed in the kiss of pink across Doyle's cheekbones.

"Of course they have a fridge," Larkin agreed, cocking his head slightly.

"But the reason we came out here was because of the address on the repair order."

"The fridge was in the basement," Larkin clarified before stepping into the bedroom and around the corner to the left. This far into the home, away from the crackle of police radios and chatter of uniformed officers stationed at the open front door, it was notedly quiet.

"How do you know that?" Doyle asked.

The frame of the closet was swollen from the humidity and the bi-fold door squeaked obnoxiously as Larkin opened it. He leaned around the wall and explained, "There was an empty spot in the studio downstairs, roughly two feet wide by two feet deep. It was positioned directly in front of an electrical outlet, and there were discarded fridge shelves, cases of soda, and what appeared to be a prepper's worth of salad dressing—Wish-Bone by the branding, creamy French by the color."

Doyle stepped into the room. He loosened the knot of his tie while asking, "Is there a collective noun for maggots?"

Larkin arched one eyebrow. "Maggot isn't a technical term. But as far as I'm aware, the larval stage of a blowfly doesn't have a collective noun, no. Although, in common vernacular, I suppose 'mass of maggots' would be acceptable. Why."

"I was going to make a joke that compared the number of maggots downstairs to your 'prepper's worth of salad dressing' comment."

"I see. Did you still want to tell it."

"It won't be funny since I've had to explain it."

"I'll laugh," Larkin promised.

"Will it be a fake laugh?"

"Probably."

"I'll bide my time until the next one."

Larkin returned his attention to the contents of the closet, slid hangers across the rod, and studied what amounted to a thrifter's paradise of '90s wolf T-shirts, rayon blouses in cheetah and floral prints, grungy plaid, jeans with rhinestones, fur-lined satin robes, and countless other atrocities inflicted against the general population in the name of fashion. But the lack of any one style was, in fact, a style all its own, and the clothing vibes matched the mental image Larkin had constructed of Stephanie Sato, the artsy, sixty-something lesbian wife who'd painted the loud and brash, sexually explicit piece hanging in the living room, and who'd decorated the house in such a way that it resembled a painter's palette on an acid trip. And that was all well and fine, except where were the plain T-shirts, utilitarian cargo shorts, and tube socks of her more stereotypically butch wife Phyllis Clark?

Larkin took a step back and turned to face the room a second time. Jutting a thumb over his shoulder, he said absently, "The vacuum-sealed bag of Esther's belongings is gone."

"Oh, *come on*…," Doyle protested. He moved around Larkin, reached overhead, and began shuffling folded blankets and bedding around to confirm for himself.

Larkin got down on his hands and knees and checked under the bed. He mused, "Matilde Wagner, a confirmed killer—responsible for the death of Esther—was discovered dismembered inside a refrigerator that can be traced through financial records to *this* home, where the ex-girlfriend of Esther lives with her current wife.

"My initial interpretation of the facts was that of Phyllis having been responsible for Wagner's murder. A revenge killing. It wouldn't be difficult—especially after our interview with her—for Phyllis to have made the connection between Esther and Matilde Wagner. The media was all over that case like flies on shit. But even though that is a reasonable conclusion to come to, she would have had to have found Wagner before the police, which I find significantly less likely, given the manhunt that'd gone into tracking Wagner right up until last night's discovery." Larkin sat back up.

"Worth's involvement would never allow for such a simple and straightforward conclusion," Doyle added, turning to address Larkin.

"Certainly not," Larkin agreed. "There's a relationship between Wagner's body dump, this home, and Joe Sinclair's sudden and unexpected murder. I just can't… figure out how the pieces fit together."

Larkin blew out a breath, closed his eyes, and pinched the bridge of his nose. An adrenaline rush was the body's way of preparing for a fight-or-flight situation. Blood vessels contracted in order to keep blood pumping to major muscle groups necessary for attacking or defending. The heartrate increased to allow for more oxygen to the lungs. The liver burned off stored glucose for a quick source of much-needed energy.

Intellectually, Larkin knew all this. He'd had time to come down from the rush, to decompress, to grapple with a near-death experience. The waning high was why his muscles were a little shaky—he needed some sugar. It was why his headache had returned—he was still dehydrated. But Larkin knew, deep down and more than anything, what was catching up with him was the fact that he hadn't slept in weeks.

But he couldn't.

Not yet.

"Hey."

Larkin looked up, and Doyle was holding out two individually wrapped lemon candies. He felt his entire body unclench, release, relax, just a little. He pocketed one and popped the other in his mouth when a voice, loud and animated, emanated from the hallway.

"Okay, okay, okay, where's my Detective Larkin?"

Larkin looked over his shoulder from where he still sat on the floor as a third man appeared in the threshold, rubbing his hands together eagerly. He was in his early thirties, blond hair, blue eyes—a boyish Guy Pearce, Larkin thought—but with the energy of a young buck anxious to prove himself. He wore an off-white linen suit—a shade Larkin hazarded to guess was advertised as *antique* or perhaps *smoky white*—paired with a crisp white button-down and a polka-dotted burgundy tie.

The man took in CRIME SCENE UNIT stenciled across Larkin's T-shirt before seeming to write him off without further regard. Leaning around the corner, he made eye contact with Doyle, gave a subtle once-over, then stepped inside. "Val Hackett, Homicide," he said, shaking Doyle's hand. "It's a pleasure to be working this case alongside you. Anything you need from us in Brooklyn, just say the word. *Mi casa es su casa.* You know, I was supposed to meet you earlier this year, but a triple homicide landed in my lap the very afternoon you were hosting a lecture for Homicide and Major Cases—"

"On psychology of place," Larkin said as he got to his feet. "You talk an awful lot, Detective Hackett. So much so, you've not given my partner a chance to introduce himself."

Hackett glanced at Larkin, then back to Doyle, whose hand he was still shaking.

Doyle said, "Ira Doyle. I'm with Forensic Artists."

Hackett laughed self-consciously. "I'm sorry."

"That's all right."

Hackett turned and offered his hand to Larkin. "It's a real pleasure to finally meet you."

"I heard you the first time."

Hackett smiled wide, showed off his pearly whites, and laughed again. "Right."

"Why are you nervous," Larkin asked.

"I-I'm not."

"Do you know what dimorphous expressions are, Detective Hackett."

"I, uh—"

"When an individual has become overwhelmed with one particular emotion, to the point that it is no longer manageable, a phenomenon occurs wherein that person will exhibit the opposite expression. Examples include tears of joy or cute aggression. Researchers believe this is the brain's attempt to regulate emotions that, if left unchecked, would become detrimental to our health. So we cry at weddings, we squeeze babies, we smile when upset, as a means of cardiovascular recovery. A homicide scene certainly isn't funny, nor have I done or said anything particularly slapsticky, therefore, your laugh is not indicative of your environment but what's occurring mentally."

Hackett opened and closed his mouth like a landed fish, shook his head, then explained, "You're a bit of an institution, is all."

Larkin raised one fine eyebrow.

Hackett smiled once more, then sucked his cheeks in and rubbed his face with one hand, as if to scrub the expression away. "My dream is to work for Cold Cases someday. I've wanted to meet you since I made detective. And even though I couldn't make your lecture, I still read a transcript of it."

"I see." Larkin glanced at Doyle, who shrugged amusedly. To Hackett, Larkin said, "Tell me what you learned from my lecture."

"Let's see… one of the key concepts involved in geographical profiling is the psychological comfort zone of the offender."

"As it pertains to this scene," Larkin amended.

"Oh. Uh. Sure. Well… there's a dead woman downstairs, right? Patrol said there's no obvious signs of her having been killed elsewhere first, so it's likely she was murdered here—she's probably the homeowner. That could mean this house is within the offender's comfort zone. Of the four predatory patterns, the killer could be identified as a hunter—someone who searches within their comfort zone."

"No."

"No?"

Larkin said, "With that half-baked logic, this scene could have been the opportunity of a troller or the lure of a trapper."

Hackett hesitated.

"Murder, whether heat of passion or premeditated, is a series of chances—time, proximity, and location all factors taken into consideration before the opportunity is acted upon—but none of that matters if you don't first understand the victim. If the woman downstairs isn't the homeowner, would you still consider her killer to display a hunter personality."

"No, but, I mean, that opens up a whole new can of worms," Hackett protested. "Is the victim a stranger? Friend? Family member? Where's the homeowner? Because they'd now be a person of interest—"

"Your profile of place has changed completely, hasn't it," Larkin interrupted.

Hackett reluctantly nodded.

"You're never wrong to say you don't yet have enough information in which to build a profile. Is CSU in the house yet."

Sounding a touch disillusioned, Hackett said, "I think so, yeah."

Larkin sidestepped the Homicide detective and exited the bedroom. The footfalls of both Hackett and Doyle followed him through the home, and while the former's voice was too low to make out his words, Larkin picked up Doyle responding, "—already knows the answer. Admitting you don't know something will go a lot further toward impressing him than trying to bullshit him."

Larkin squeezed past two uniformed officers in the vestibule and started down the basement stairs. The stench of decomposition—a constant perfume that'd permeated the entire upstairs—grew in such intensity that by the time Larkin reached the landing, he could only theorize it'd been the adrenaline of entering the home with his pistol drawn that'd allowed him to investigate the basement at all. He already wore gloves and booties, but helped himself to an N95 mask from the boxes of PPE set to the side of the open studio door.

Larkin stepped inside while adjusting the nose piece.

Millett turned from staring down at the body in the camping chair and said, voice muffled by his own mask, "You could have warned me this was a full-body situation." He motioned to the white jumpsuit he was now wearing.

Larkin ignored the complaint and gave the body a wide berth as he walked toward the opposite end of the room. He crouched before the discarded shelving, Pepsi cases, and salad dressing to study grooves in the flooring—grooves made by dragging a hundred-and-seventy-pound fridge across a soft surface like linoleum.

"Did you know that over 140 million Americans prefer ranch on their salads?" Millett asked.

"According to who."

"NHCS."

"Interesting."

"I can't stand the smell." Millett continued, "Not since college. I woke up in the middle of the night to my roommate watching anime on his laptop and eating a bowl of canned peaches and ranch. A whole bowl. Like it was milk and cereal. I wonder what happened to that guy…."

"*Holy shit*. Lookit all those maggots!"

Larkin stood and turned around.

Hackett had bum-rushed the scene and was opposite Millett, taking in all the grisly details. His expression was hidden behind the mask, but his eyes were wide with surprise and disgust and utter fascination. Doyle, on the other hand, stood several steps behind Hackett, his posture stiff and arms crossed.

To Millett, Larkin said, "This is Detective Val Hackett with Brooklyn Homicide."

"Neil Millett, CSU."

"Yeah, hi, why're there so many?" Hackett asked, pointing.

"Ideal conditions," Millett answered. "It's warm, it's humid, and they've got a full-grown adult body to munch on."

"Why're they, like, clustered in groups?" Hackett asked next.

"A mass of maggots this big can generate heat at least forty degrees above the ambient temperature. Any higher than one twenty and they'll die. And since it's got to be at least ninety in this house already, they break away from the core—into these smaller groups here and here—to try and cool down."

"*Wow*."

Millett made a sound, something between a laugh and a snort. "How long have you been with Homicide?"

"Six months. But I haven't seen anything like this. It's mostly shootings out here."

Millett said, "The presence of pupa, both hatched casings and those still in development, tells me we're over halfway into our second lifecycle of blowflies. That's… oh, about three weeks, at least. I'd put time of death somewhere around June 8 to June 19."

Larkin answered as he approached the body, "That would correspond with the stack of uncollected mail and the watermelon peperomia upstairs."

"Peperomia?" Millett echoed.

"Yes. It's in no way as scientifically sound as the lifecycle of the blowfly, but a watermelon peperomia should be watered once it begins to exhibit signs of droopiness—every one to two weeks. The plant upstairs has completely collapsed and discolored."

"Larkin's a plant dad," Doyle interjected.

"Ah. Congratulations," Millett answered. "Boy or girl?"

"Watermelon peperomias are self-pollinating. Have you checked her pockets for an ID."

Millett turned his attention back to the body and carefully patted down the stained overalls. Maggots *plopp*ed and the body *squelch*ed. He reached into the right pocket, retrieved a leather wallet, and passed it to Larkin.

Larkin wiped dark viscous fluid with his gloved thumb, revealing a custom monogram in the corner that read *bitch*. He opened it. A New York driver's license, debit card, and health insurance card were all in the name of…. "Kathleen Gardner. Not the homeowner." Larkin checked the pocket for cash, but there were only soggy and discolored business cards all stuck together. He removed the mushy cardstock and could just make out three words. "Fur and Feather."

"My money's on either taxidermy or kink," Millett said off-handedly.

"It's an animal service," Hackett said suddenly.

Larkin looked up. "What kind of service."

"Dog walking and cat sitting, I think," Hackett replied. "I've seen her flyers in the neighborhood for years. The business name always stuck out to me, since I don't think she takes care of birds…. That and she prints them on neon orange paper." Hackett stared at Kathleen's body for a long minute before asking, "Do you think she was here to take care of the owner's cat?"

"What cat?" Doyle asked.

—orange tabby stretched out on the bedroom throw rug—

"Well, there's that cat stand in the living room," Hackett explained. "And I noticed one of those light-up balls under the dining table. Mine goes nuts for those. His name's Murphy—my cat."

"Doyle," Larkin hastily said. "It's an orange tabby."

Doyle was already moving to the doorway as he said over his shoulder, "I'll take a look."

Larkin redirected his stare to Hackett, who, after a moment, shifted under its intensity. "Did you know the victim."

"No way. But I live in Cobble Hill, and there're nice bars here in Carroll Gardens. I'm in the area a lot."

"I see." Larkin paused, then added, "Thank you."

Even with the mask on, Hackett beamed like a kinder-gartener who'd just gotten his first gold star sticker in class.

Larkin dropped the wallet into the evidence bag Millett held out before yanking his gloves off, turning them inside out as he did. He moved away from the body, closer to the easel, and studied the half-finished painting still propped and awaiting further work. Last month, Doyle had described Stephanie Sato as having a great sense of motion in her work, but all Larkin saw was art trying to *be* art. He didn't see technical skill or storytelling or those little flaws that were the foundation of an artist's signature style. He saw slapdash work devoid of meaning. He saw a pretentious concept with no soul. He saw an angry green woman fingering herself and was unable to understand who would desire to hang it over their dining table. Perhaps Stephanie's target market was not the collectors themselves, but those who chose their partner's art habits over their own sense of taste. Gift giving, in the language of love.

Perhaps a similar mindset would also explain the one-sided décor of the Clark-Sato home—something Larkin thought of as fauxhemian: the incorporation of bold colors and textures, layered elements, mismatching kitsch, but all curated in a very socially conventional manner. The interior design was loud, garish, and without personality, exactly like this painting.

Oh, there was personality, Larkin course-corrected—it just wasn't sincere. It wasn't a free-thinking nonconformist who lived and breathed their art, no matter how tacky Larkin thought it was. It was someone who wished to be *seen* as a free-thinking nonconformist who likely did art because it brought considerable satisfaction to their inflated self-worth.

The character seen in the upstairs didn't match who he knew Phyllis Clark to be: a no-nonsense woman of masculine tendencies who'd long-ago stripped those inclinations of their strict association to *maleness* by publicly wearing tube socks and cargo shorts, maintaining a short hairstyle, and riding a motorcycle for no other reason than she wanted to. Phyllis had also presented herself to be a rather pragmatic individual, quick to credit the home's aesthetic to Stephanie—almost like she didn't so much enjoy it as she did put up with it. So perhaps, then, Phyllis's gift to her wife was the compromise of shared space, the allowance of Stephanie's palette preferences and assertive style to dominate the home. Except the command of décor was so overwhelming that there was no discernable indicator of where Stephanie ended and Phyllis began.

On June 12, Larkin's sophisticated skepticism and refined understanding of the importance of place had been outfoxed by Phyllis's well-placed confidence, distracted by Doyle's personal shame, and now he had to contend with the consequences of that small but outrageous overlook.

He swore under his breath before asking, while still staring at the painting, "Do you live alone, Detective Hackett."

"Yeah."

"Have you ever lived with someone else—someone you were romantically involved with."

"A few years ago."

"What did your home look like."

"What do you mean?"

Larkin turned. "I live with someone. He was at that apartment for six years before I came along. Six years is a long time to accumulate belongings and refine one's sense of style. For example, he had a very nice linen throw—I despised it for no reason other than its texture—but six days after I'd moved in, he replaced it with a cotton blanket. I'm certain I made no overt signs of discomfort around that throw, but he's quite adept at picking up on my nonverbal cues, and when given the choice to keep an item he'd purchased based on his home's long-established aesthetic or see to my personal comfort, he chose me. It was the first of many compromises in sharing his space, and now, despite having lived together for only three and a half months, my presence cannot be overlooked.

"My key ring is by the door, my cuff links on the nightstand. My psychology textbooks have been shelved where only art and history and reference books lived before. My houseplants take up space where he used to keep his easel and painting supplies. I tell you this because no two people will have the exact same opinions on home décor, and living together forces compromise, no matter how small."

"Totally."

"Now that we know this DB is not the homeowner," Larkin continued, "would you like to give another go at establishing the psychology of place."

"Is this a trick? Am I supposed to say I don't know?"

"You may certainly say as much," Larkin answered. "But I've already given you a clue to hit the ground running."

Steps echoed on the basement stairs, and Larkin recognized the pace and footfall as Doyle's. When he appeared in the open doorway, Doyle said, "I didn't find the cat. And the dishes in the kitchen don't look to have been used by an animal for a while. But you know what I did find? A knife block with an incomplete set."

Larkin straightened his posture.

"There's a meat cleaver missing, for sure," Doyle concluded.

To Millett, Larkin asked, "After you're done here, will you inspect the bathroom for blood."

"The bathroom?"

"Please."

Millett looked between him and Doyle before shrugging. "Sure."

Larkin returned his attention to Hackett. "Twenty-eight days ago, we met the homeowner's alleged wife."

Hackett looked surprised. "I'd have never guessed two people lived here."

"Why."

"Well, it's like you said, when two people live together, compromises are made. But the home feels very, uh, uniform, I guess."

"And."

"And I didn't notice any wedding photos."

"Not everyone hangs those."

"Everyone I know who's married does," Hackett countered.

"I was married for four years," Larkin said. "My ex-husband and I never hung up our wedding photos. You may use generalities as guidelines and statistics to narrow down likelihoods, but you must not allow your own life experience to color a hypothesis."

Hackett was silent for one, two, three seconds. Then he asked, "So you… don't think the homeowner is married?"

Larkin answered, "Tell me why I think that."

"Wait a minute," Doyle interrupted. "Stephanie and Phyllis *aren't* married?"

Larkin held a hand up for silence.

Hackett said, slow and thoughtful, like he was feeling the concept out, "When my ex moved out, my place looked… not messy, but I suddenly had all these empty nooks and crannies. Places that he'd—" Hackett faltered, looked over his shoulder at Doyle, to Millett on his right, but continued when the use of that particular pronoun failed to garner a reaction. "—that he'd had his belongings. It kinda looked like I'd been robbed, but of only one personality."

"Interesting description. Continue."

Hackett pointed up, indicating the ground floor of the home. "The upstairs doesn't have that empty look, like someone recently walked out of a shared life only a month ago. Of course, the homeowner could have moved fast to erase all evidence of another person, but I don't think most people mourn the ending of a relationship like that, even more so a marriage. There's no evidence of a compromise once existing between two people." He shrugged before asking, "How'd I do?"

"You did quite well," Larkin said.

Hackett blinked a few times. He tugged his mask down. "Really?"

"Larkin—" Doyle tried.

"I did 'quite well!'" Hackett exclaimed. He looked around before saying to Millett, "Did you hear that?"

"Yeah, that's great, kid," Millett answered offhandedly. "You know, this is why I went into forensics. People are unpredictable."

"On the contrary," Larkin said. "Human behavior is almost too predictable. It can be a real bore."

"*Larkin*," Doyle said again, this time putting a stress on his name that couldn't be ignored.

"Yes," Larkin answered, obediently heading for the door. He slipped past Doyle, hiked up the stairs, stepped around the officers still stationed in the threshold, and entered the living room. Larkin tugged his mask off before raising the hem of his borrowed T-shirt and flashing a bit of skin as he wiped sweat from his brow.

"All right," Doyle said as he followed Larkin into the sweltering room. "Since when is Phyllis not the wife she claimed to be?"

"Detective Hackett did an acceptable—"

"Hackett is so desperate to impress you, I think he might've peed a little when you said *good job*." Doyle crossed his arms. "Why don't *you* think they're married?"

Larkin hesitated. He stared over Doyle's shoulder at the unoccupied dining table. His memory of June 12 played out like ghosts repeating their final moment in life. He could see

Doyle, see the look of surprise, of sorrow, of shame cross his features while Phyllis spoke of the Kitten Klub. It had been the exact moment Larkin understood the enormity of Doyle's childhood trauma, and he'd been so brokenhearted by its truth, so desperate to hide his insight into that baggage, to spare Doyle any further distress, that the clues all around him—so fucking obvious in retrospect—had become white noise.

But Larkin couldn't say any of that without effectively blaming Doyle for what was his own blunder. Instead, he said, "I-I sometimes become obsessed with the minute details, to the detriment of the bigger picture. I was guilty of this with Harry Regmore and—"

Doyle leaned forward, his arms still crossed. He said, quiet but firm, "Stop it."

"I'm trying to explain why I made a mistake."

"Did you make a mistake?" Doyle countered. "Or did your hypothesis change based on emerging data?"

"I need you to let me take blame for this."

"No."

"Doyle."

"You no longer believe Stephanie and Phyllis are married because…?"

With a touch of attitude, Larkin snapped, "Because confidence looks like strength, *goddammit*." He shook his head, slapped his mask against the palm of his open hand a few times, then tried again, calmer. "When someone is acting in a way that benefits us—Phyllis speaking about Esther's disappearance— we are more likely, more willing, to interpret their confidence as trust. Naturally, we desire a beneficial action or belief to be strong—might is right. Earlier in the car, I told you I questioned Phyllis's benevolence and integrity, but not her ability. I didn't because she was so sure of who Esther was and how she, herself, factored into Esther's life, that her confidence colored my perception of how Phyllis fit here, in this home.

"But there's nearly four weeks of uncollected mail, none of which is in her name. There's the lack of a second identity seen anywhere in the home's furnishings or possessions, and the one tangible object we could positively link Phyllis to, Esther's belongings—which included several forms of identification in the name of Barbara Fuller, quite possibly Esther's real name, which would mean the mourning jewelry *did* once belong to her—is now missing."

"Missing alongside Phyllis," Doyle clarified as an expression of disbelief slowly crossed his face.

Larkin said, "Insect activity puts the cat sitter's death between June 8 and 19, and the oldest postmark in the mailbox is June 13. The evidence, as it stands, suggests that Ms. Sato hired a cat sitter and went out of town sometime before June 12—because June 12 was when we interviewed Phyllis."

"You mean, while we were sitting there," Doyle turned and pointed to the dining table, "talking with her about Esther and the Broadway clubs, the cat sitter might have been downstairs? *Dead?*"

"It would explain why Phyllis had been comfortable and confident in her environment," Larkin answered. "She'd eliminated the only threat to the false narrative."

Doyle scrubbed his face with one hand. "This is a lot."

"Yes, I agree."

"But why would Phyllis be here? By your logic, does she even *know* the homeowner?"

Larkin motioned Doyle to follow him, and they stepped out of the home and into fresh air. The setting sun had left the sky a glazed-over gold with clouds like puffy pink cotton balls. A mild and much-welcomed breeze cooled the sweat under Larkin's arms. "Have you heard of the term erotomania."

"I don't think so."

"It's been called a number of rather inventive names over the centuries, including *maladie d'amour* and *psychose passionelle*—"

"You make it sound so romantic."

Larkin chuckled. "Erotomania has been classed as a subset of delusional disorder. It's primary, chronic, and seen more often in women—the delusion that another person is in love with the individual."

Doyle's brows rose.

"Often, the object of desire is someone of higher social status, someone who would have no idea who the individual even is, but that 'status' can also mean different things to different people. Sometimes there's no communication between the two parties."

"And other times?" Doyle warily asked.

"Other times it has led to the individual who is suffering from the delusion to break the law in order to establish contact with their object of desire."

"Like stalking?"

"Yes," Larkin said on the release of a breath. "Like stalking."

Doyle looked around, seemingly taking in the parked cruisers, the CSU van, the yellow crime scene tape, the comings and goings of uniformed personnel, everything a copy and paste of the corner of Carroll and Clinton. "Help me understand this. Did Phyllis just wake up one day and decide she was in love with the homeowner? Did she wait until Stephanie left and then break in to play house before going on the lam?"

"Erotomania can have a sudden onset, yes," Larkin agreed, "but I suspect Ms. Sato was not Phyllis's first delusion."

"It started with Esther?"

Larkin nodded. "Erotomania can lead to pathological jealousy, even violence, if the individual feels their advances are being rejected. This is only a working theory, of course, but Phyllis's behavior during our interview last month was… off. Her irrational disgust toward sex workers, when she *met* Esther as a patron of the burlesque scene, can certainly be viewed as jealousy."

Doyle said, "Phyllis claimed Esther left Frills because the industry was dying, and while that's historically true, what if Esther had further incentive to leave?"

"Like an obsessed patron," Larkin answered. "That was Phyllis's own description of herself. Esther might have snubbed Phyllis's interests, which could've made the delusion worse. Toward the end of their supposed relationship, Phyllis described Esther as coming home less often, staying with friends, carrying a gym bag to work with multiple changes of clothes…."

"When you say it like that, it sounds like a woman who was afraid to go home."

"Like she was being stalked," Larkin concluded.

"I guess the question is, how does Phyllis fit into all of these different events and timelines," Doyle said. "If she does have a history of stalking women, *did* her behavior escalate into something more dangerous? *Was* she involved with Wagner's murder? Could her presence have been total happenstance? And either way, where is she now?"

"She is most definitely a person of interest," Larkin said. "And one I'd like to speak with again, at considerable length." Hands on his hips, he turned to survey the row of multifamily homes.

Doyle was saying, "Three murders, two stalkers, one crime scene—"

"And a partridge in a pear tree," Larkin added sardonically before moving toward the set of cement stairs that led to the second-story neighbor.

A white woman sat on the landing outside her front door. She was middle-aged, dirty-blond hair piled into a bun atop her head, and she wore a pair of pajama shorts and matching tank top in baby blue, fluffy panda slippers, Dolce & Gabbana rose-tinted sunglasses, and was talking on her cell phone.

"Ma'am," Larkin started as he removed his badge and flashed the identification. "I'm Detective Everett Larkin—"

"Steph, hang on, some cop's finally decided to grace me with his presence." She lowered the phone and said, "It's about fuckin' time. I was told to wait here at least an hour ago. My shoulders are sunburned and I'd like to go inside and start dinner for my kid."

Larkin frowned. He wasn't about to waste what was left of his stamina being the unstoppable force to this woman's immovable object. He looked toward Doyle coming up the steps beside him.

Doyle was, as always, quick on the uptake. He said sympathetically, "We're very sorry to have kept you this long, ma'am."

"Becca. Friedman," she corrected.

"Ms. Friedman—"

"Look, I don't know anything. I didn't hear anything. I didn't see anything. Steph hasn't even been home and—"

"Are you speaking with the homeowner now," Larkin interrupted, pointing at the phone.

Becca looked at her cell too. "Yeah."

"Stephanie Sato," he reiterated.

"*Yes,*" she said, irritated.

"May I speak with her."

Becca returned the phone to her ear. "Steph? I'm gonna give the phone to this cop, he wants to talk to you. I've no idea. Okay, hang on." She held it out.

Larkin accepted the phone, tapped Speaker so that Doyle could hear the conversation, and said, "This is Detective Everett Larkin with the NYPD. Am I speaking with the owner of 239 Carroll Street."

"I'm Stephanie Sato, yes. Can you tell me what's going on?"

"I'm investigating a homicide, Ms. Sato."

"At *my* house?"

"Yes."

"But who—" Stephanie sucked in a harsh breath. "Did something happen to Kathy? Where's my cat?"

That kneejerk reaction to ask after the well-being of her *cat sitter*, not her supposed wife, was all the clarification Larkin needed to confirm his updated hypothesis was correct.

Larkin asked, "Who's Kathy."

"Kathleen Gardner, my cat sitter."

"I'm sorry to inform you that Ms. Gardner was found deceased in your basement this afternoon." Larkin thought to add, "We're unsure of where your cat is at the moment."

Stephanie gasped.

Becca choked.

"*Oh my God!*"

Between Stephanie's distorted speakerphone hyperventilating and Becca coughing up a lung, Larkin was barely able to get an additional word in edgewise. He raised his voice over the commotion. "Where are you, Ms. Sato."

"I-I'm upstate—at an artist-in-residence. I've been here almost four weeks. I'm not supposed to be home for another two."

"And the name of this location."

"The Adele Claremont Art Residency. It's outside Saratoga Springs."

"I'd like to speak with you in person," Larkin said. "When are you able to return to the city."

"She can't just *leave*," Becca protested.

"I can't just *leave*," Stephanie echoed at the same time. Her breathing steadied almost at once, and she said, "Do you know how coveted these positions are? If I leave, I forfeit my studio space."

"A dead woman was discovered in your home, Ms. Sato," Larkin reiterated.

Stephanie clapped back aggressively. "This is such typical chauvinistic male behavior. There's nothing a man hates more than a woman succeeding. My womanhood frightens you, doesn't it, Mr. Larkin?"

"I fail to understand what your gender has to do with my wanting to interview you."

"What my *gender* has to do with a *murder*, you mean? Over ten thousand women in this country are murdered every year, and you have the *audacity*—"

"That statistic is grossly incorrect," Larkin said over her. "A 2017 study put together by the United Nations Office on Drugs and Crime found that of the approximately 400,000 homicides committed globally, eighty percent of those victims were male. However, the 87,000 murdered women bore the greatest burden of intimate partner- or family-related homicide—fifty-eight percent of all deaths—leading to the continued and accurate usage of the term femicide. But the United States only saw roughly 3,600 of those 87,000 murders, not ten thousand. And it's Detective Larkin, ma'am."

Becca started coughing again.

Doyle gently pried the phone from Larkin's hand and said, "Ms. Sato? My name is Ira Doyle. I'm a detective with the NYPD's Forensic Artists Unit. I understand the prestige that comes with a residency at Adele Claremont, as well as your hesitancy to abandon such an opportunity sooner than anticipated."

Silence crackled loudly over the speakerphone before Stephanie asked woodenly, "You understand, huh? So have *you* resided at Claremont, Mr. Doyle?"

"Uh, no. They declined my portfolio."

"I guess we can't all be the three percent."

The problem with loving Ira Doyle, Larkin thought, was the unfettered access he had to his heart. It was in realizing how desperate, even as a grown man, Doyle was to be loved, to be accepted, to be validated. It was the gut punch in knowing Doyle's decades-old wounds had never scabbed over with cynicism, that his need for happiness kept those scrapes and cuts freshly bleeding, that he poured so much empathy into a career that treated him like the butt of a joke—*he draws pictures*. And in a world of performative cruelty, kindness stood little chance.

Yet, Doyle was *so determined* to never make another person suffer like he had—still did—that he would only ever swallow his anger and be gentle.

So gentle that then the world simply took advantage of him.

As expected, Doyle said, "Ms. Sato, if you can answer a few questions over the phone, my partner and I will be happy to wait until your residency concludes for an in-person conversation."

Larkin began to protest, but Doyle held a hand up.

"What're your questions?"

"When did you leave the city?"

"June 9—no, 10."

"Wednesday," Larkin murmured.

Doyle nodded in acknowledgment and asked next, "Was Kathy scheduled to visit the home every day?"

"Every morning starting the next day."

"And you weren't concerned when she didn't check in?"

"I don't have cell service," Stephanie explained. "We have a landline in the main cabin for emergencies—that's where I am now. Kathy knew to call that number if she needed to get in touch and someone would fetch me."

"No news is good news?"

"Exactly."

Doyle said next, "I'd like to give you a few names. Will you tell me if you recognize any of them?"

"Okay."

"Matilde Wagner."

"Hmm… no, I don't think so."

"Esther Haycox?"

"No."

"How about Barbara Fuller?"

"Nope."

"Phyllis Clark?"

"Sorry," Stephanie answered. "I've no idea who any of those women are."

CHAPTER TWELVE

It was 9:04 p.m. by the time Larkin and Doyle entered Precinct 19.

Larkin had been awake for nearly thirty-eight hours—since 6:30 a.m. the day before, when his alarm had gone off and Doyle, fresh from the shower and combing fingers through damp hair, stepped into the bedroom saying, "Good morning, sunshine." And after being in the car for the last thirty-four minutes, his body coming down fully from everything that had transpired in Brooklyn, gravity pushed at him. Larkin's derbies scuffed the stairs as he approached the nearly empty second-floor bullpen. He stopped before his desk, stared at the blinking light on his phone, the stack of ancient manila folders someone had dropped off in regard to any one of his dozens of open investigations, the pile of call receipts recorded by the officer at the front desk throughout the day, and it was a stark reminder that murder was a full-time job with no end in sight.

Adam Worth *wasn't* his only case.

Larkin tossed his ring of keys onto the desk, put one hand on his hip, and rubbed the grit from his eyes with the other.

The creak of Porter's chair preceded his "Grim?"

Larkin turned.

Porter was reclined as far back as the chair would allow, with his desk phone to one ear. The cord was a stretched and tangled mess. He put a hand over the mouthpiece and murmured, "Are you wearing someone else's pants?"

"Yes."

Porter took the answer at face value, shuffled his feet, and turned the chair toward the landing as Doyle reached the top step. Porter fist-bumped him while saying into the phone at the same time, "Cut me some slack, man. Rossi's been six feet under since '79."

Doyle continued across the bullpen. He stopped outside one of the two unused rooms beside Connor's office—light still on, door closed, deep voice resonating from within—then flipped on the bank of overheads. Larkin followed, passing Baker's desk before pausing and backtracking two steps.

He picked up a Lisa Frank pencil from amid the clutter. It'd gone missing from his pen cup a week ago. He spun it around, the holographic unicorn print highlighting fresh chew marks in the soft cedar. Larkin sighed and tossed it back onto Baker's desk. He entered the interview room and took in Doyle, already seated and digging a sketch pad out from the portfolio bag propped against the leg of the interview table.

Larkin quietly closed the door, leaned back against the wall to the left, and crossed his arms. Doyle had again brought up the necessity of a composite sketch on their drive back to the city, to which Larkin had said nothing, hoping his stoic silence was enough of a deterrent.

It had not been.

Doyle sharpened a few different pencils, testing the tips with the pad of his thumb. "Composite sketching can sometimes drum up strong emotion," he said. "Whatever you're feeling, just know that it's valid."

"I don't want to do this, Ira."

Doyle stopped.

Larkin felt a little like he were high—the exhaustion in his bones creating a sickening out-of-body sensation that was all too similar to one-too-many pills in his gut—and the return to that hazy no man's land, despite being sober, lowered his defenses, loosened his tongue. "I had to do this in the hospital, and I couldn't remember and I couldn't speak and I don't—" Larkin stopped. He pushed off the wall and moved to stand opposite Doyle at the table. More resolutely, he said, "I don't want to feel like a victim again."

Doyle met Larkin's eye, his stare unyielding but never unkind. "Composite sketching, for me, isn't about producing results. I know that sounds counterintuitive, but it's always ever been about giving an individual the chance to be heard. I want you to feel empowered, not demoralized."

Larkin let out a ragged breath. He straightened the chair before him, drummed his fingers against the tabletop in a quick succession of irritated movements, honestly considered playing his senior detective card and demanding they call it a night because he didn't—*couldn't*—be on this side of the law again. He couldn't bear reliving the questions, the interrogation, the despair, the injustice of still not knowing, eighteen years later, who had brutally murdered the love of his boyhood and who had stolen from him his entire sense of self.

"I think you can do this," Doyle began.

Man's will yearned for purpose.

"I would at least like to try."

And what if that purpose was to love?

"But I'll understand if you can't."

Larkin slowly pulled the chair out and took a seat. "I love you very much," he whispered.

Doyle whispered back, "I love you too, sunshine." He resumed sharpening pencils before opening the sketch pad to a blank page. "First we'll work on general proportions."

Doyle's patient demeanor never gave hint to the hundreds of times he'd given this same exact speech. "I'm going to provide you with a few six-packs—"

"I remember what he looks like."

Doyle let a few seconds settle between them before clarifying, "The six-packs are for me to reference." He dug through his bag a second time. "Race?"

"White."

"Age range?"

"Between sixty and seventy."

Doyle sifted through a handful of six-packs, put some away, and laid out the rest on the tabletop. He motioned to the strangers—all white males—and said, "I don't want you to pick who might look the most like the shooter, but instead pick similar individual aspects. Chin, mouth, ears, that sort of thing."

Larkin reluctantly leaned forward, but after studying the mugshots for several seconds, he pushed them away and said, "None of them."

"Evie—"

"None of them are similar, Ira."

"Don't raise your voice to me," Doyle warned.

Larkin sat back. He scrubbed his face with both hands and then ran them through his always so precisely parted conservative cut, causing his ash-blond hair to stick up like it did when he first rolled out of bed. Larkin reached into his pocket, retrieved the second lemon candy Doyle had given him in Brooklyn, and popped it into his mouth.

Doyle watched, waited, and eventually said, "I only need generalities."

"But I remember what he looked like," Larkin said again, the candy clicking against his teeth.

"If a composite sketch is *too* precise, its intended audience will be looking for that one individual instead of many *possible* individuals," Doyle explained. "And because I'm interpreting what you saw, it's not going to be a perfect match in the way a photograph would be. So what's better, an exact mismatch or an inexact possibility?"

"Neither."

Doyle made a sound under his breath, but he smiled nonetheless. "I know you're tired. I know you're stressed."

"No, I'm overcompensating to make up for past feelings of helplessness." Larkin took a breath. "He wore sunglasses and a ball cap."

"I can draw those," Doyle insisted.

"They were cheap aviators," Larkin continued. "Light brown lenses with a gradient."

"You were able to see his face behind them?"

Larkin nodded.

"Okay, good. What about the hat?"

"Yankees cap." Larkin leaned forward, unenthusiastically spread the six-packs out to study a second time, then tapped one of the mugshots. "I suppose this is a similar head shape. Rectangular, softened around the jawline but not jowls."

"I understand."

Larkin motioned to a second photograph. "And this nose. It was large. Very distinct."

"Anything else?" But Doyle corrected himself and asked, "Any other details that'll affect his face shape?"

"He had what I thought to be a rather prominent dimple on his right cheek, but—" Larkin closed his eyes. "—it's a vertical scar. About an inch in length."

"That's great." Doyle rolled his sleeves back, got as comfortable as he could in the unforgiving chair, then picked up a pencil. He began sketching the generic outline of a face, entirely unremarkable shapes meant to represent nose and hair and eyes, and Larkin would've never believed those rough strokes would amount to anything special if he hadn't experienced the magic unfold in real time on March 31, when Doyle had been able to tug free a twenty-two-year-old memory from Jessica Lopez's mind and then age-progress the drawing so exactly that they'd been able to interview Roger Hunt after he'd recognized himself in a post on Local4Locals.

Larkin checked his phone notifications while Doyle worked. Six new emails. Two voicemails. A flurry of texts sent from Hackett. It was all too much. He set his cell face down on the tabletop, leaned back in the chair, and stared at the ceiling.

Doyle asked, "Can I tell you something?"

"Of course."

"The Adele Claremont Art Residency."

"What about it."

"I resided there for four weeks—the summer before grad school."

Larkin leveled his gaze on Doyle. "Why did you lie."

He shrugged one shoulder. "People like Stephanie—people with a superiority complex—they thrive on validation that they're better than you. If you give them proof, they tend to be more agreeable and less combative. Claremont doesn't really mean much outside of the art world, so when her first comment was to challenge me… I kinda knew the type of person she was."

"Is it really a three percent acceptance rate."

"Yeah."

"And portfolio-based."

Doyle agreed a second time.

"As a student, your body of work would have been significantly smaller than Stephanie's is as an established full-time artist," Larkin said. "Whoever oversaw the selection process, they saw something special in you."

"It was a long time ago," Doyle concluded, but he had the sliver of a smile on his face. He looked at Larkin and asked, "Why don't you bring your chair around here?"

Larkin did as requested. He stifled a yawn with one hand as Doyle began to make nonleading inquiries regarding the blocked-out proportions on the paper: How is the shape and size of the sunglasses compared to the head mass? How is the width of the nose? Was it wider at the nostril flare, at the bridge, or overall? Doyle continued along that vein for a while, making changes where Larkin insisted it necessary, until the mess of rough lines began to look more and more like a distinct subject.

"Are the proportions on the paper within the realm of possibility?" Doyle asked.

"That really is such an oddly worded question," Larkin said, studying the sketch.

"We say that because most people can't recall like you can."

"It's acceptable at this current stage."

Doyle started on the characteristics next. He was quiet for, by Larkin's count, thirteen minutes, reworking previously established features to be anatomically correct. The slight adjustments took the composite from "drawing of man" to "interpretation of suspect" almost instantaneously.

Larkin leaned back in his chair again, far enough this time that his lower back no longer had support. He crossed his arms over his chest, crossed his legs at the ankle, and watched Doyle work from under a half-lidded gaze. "It's recognizable."

"Is it?" Doyle turned to him, his look of concentration momentarily broken as he gave Larkin an indulgent, sweet, *heart-melting* once-over. "Which aspects are similar to the shooter?"

"I got a better look at the lower portion of his face," Larkin said, his monotone notedly sleepy. "The chin and jawline. But the cheeks aren't right."

"Are you able to tell me why?"

"There's not enough age in them."

"I'll add lines and wrinkles—"

"And the scar."

"—And the scar, yes, I'll add those in the rendering stage. Is there anything else?"

Larkin shifted a little. "Anatomically, the eyes are correct."

"But?"

"Are you familiar with Stanley Kubrick."

"Sure."

"He's known for what some critics refer to as the Kubrick Stare. The shooter had that kind of soullessness in his eyes, despite smiling at me."

"I'll see what I can do."

Larkin listened to the scratch of pencil on paper—fought against the weight of his eyelids—listened to Doyle hum a distinct but unfamiliar melody under his breath—just a brief rest—listened to the HVAC system kick on—

"You said you'd been in love since we met. I think I was too."

—and then nothing.

—waves churning, twisting, crashing upward, throwing Larkin up and out of the lake onto the dock. His palms covered in splinters, like quills from a porcupine, blood drip, drip, dripping onto Joe Sinclair's forehead, drilling a hole through his skull, into his brain, his lips moving, repeating, "Everyone wants you, Mr. Larkin."—

Larkin jerked awake, instinctually grabbing either side of the chair to catch himself amid the sensation of the falling dream.

"Larkin?"

"You okay there, Grim?"

Larkin looked up. Doyle was still seated on his left and Lieutenant Connor stood opposite them, his hands planted on the tabletop, leaning over the composite sketch in front of him. "Sorry," Larkin whispered. He cleared his throat and straightened his posture. "Just a dream."

Connor grunted. He spun the sketch pad around and pushed it toward Larkin.

Larkin checked his watch—10:46 p.m.—then leaned forward. "Is this the finished composite."

Doyle asked, "What do you think?"

There were plenty on the force who thought the forensic artists having detective status was a joke, but what they failed to understand was just how good of an investigator Doyle had to be in order to pluck a monster from the mind of another person and prove, armed with nothing but a pencil, that the things bumping around in the night were *real*. Doyle had drawn a man in his midsixties, once-strong features softened by the natural lessening of skin elasticity, a large nose, a notable dimple in his cheek caused by an old scar, wearing a Yankees ball cap and ugly aviators. Most impressive—or disconcerting, Larkin considered—was how Doyle had absolutely *nailed* those deep-set eyes with the thousand-yard stare.

Larkin said, "That's the shooter."

"How's the scar placement?" Doyle inquired.

"Yes. I mean—it's correct."

"Ever seen this SOB, Grim?" Connor asked.

Larkin gave his mental Rolodex a hard spin, studied the blur of faces—of coworkers, of criminals, neighbors, strangers. "I don't think so."

"You don't *think*?" Connor repeated. He straightened his posture. "You must be dead on your feet to not be a hundred and ten percent certain."

Doyle said as he stood, "I'm going to scan and upload this sketch before packing it in."

Larkin watched Doyle exit, walk through a now-empty bullpen, and turn the corner to the copier room opposite the breakroom.

"I spoke with Detective Hackett out in Brooklyn."

Larkin returned his attention to Connor.

"What an excitable tyke he is."

"That's one way to describe him."

"Hackett's agreed to liaison with you in regard to whatever you need from the Sinclair and Gardner investigations. He'll be handling the warrants, so give him a ring when you're ready."

"I understand."

Connor looked like he had more he wanted to discuss—about Phyllis, about Esther, about the shooter, about this entire shitshow Larkin was caught up in—but he only tapped the tabletop and said, "Go home, Grim. Go to bed."

CHAPTER THIRTEEN

Larkin unlocked the door to 4A at 11:19 p.m.

The apartment was an uninviting black hole that demanded a routine he was too tired to see through, so Larkin simply ignored the sequence of events that'd been established for his own problematic short-term memory, and walked through the darkness, his path lit only by the orange halos put off by streetlights below, their murky glow bleeding in between the slats of the window blinds. He dropped his keys on the coffee table, phone, wallet—*I'll forget where I put these*—unbuckled his shoulder holster and dumped the weapon carelessly onto the couch.

At his back, the front door quietly shut and then the fairy lights clicked on. Their warm yellow twinkle washed away the dinginess of the city, fortified the walls, and welcomed them home. Doyle twisted the dead bolt on the door before letting out a long breath. Larkin heard him prop his portfolio bag against the bare brick wall before turning the window unit in the kitchen on.

The low, monotonous hum filled the shared space, marking their presence.

Larkin toed off his derbies and left them in the middle of the living room. He yanked the CSU T-shirt over his head, dropped it while walking to the bathroom, and shut the door behind himself. Inside, Larkin finished undressing, turned on the shower, and stepped under the spray.

It was a little too hot.

It made his head swim.

But he didn't care.

He needed to get the day out of his mind and off his body. He needed to feel squeaky clean and not like a lint roller that'd collected every little disgusting bit of humanity from the backseat of a taxi. He needed five minutes to himself, five minutes he didn't have to obsess about murders and stalking and the police asking him *why*, why can't you remember what your attacker looked like? Don't you want to help us find your buddy's killer?

Larkin needed more than his evening dose of Prozac.

He needed a hard factory reset.

He needed—

Larkin pressed his palms against the tile wall and tucked his chin to his chest, allowing the spray to pound the back of his skull. The rhythmic pulse kept good time, but Larkin didn't count the beats. He just stood still and let the shower strip away every negative emotion that burdened him, toyed with him, haunted him, like decades of landlord-white paint peeled away to reveal an original color that hadn't been seen in so long, even Larkin couldn't remember what it'd once been.

—yellow like a crown of dandelions—

—orange like campfire flames—

—red like blood—

The bathroom door clicked shut.

Larkin raised his head, wiped his face, pulled the curtain back.

His discarded clothes were gone from the floor. Placed on the counter beside the sink was his folded gray T-shirt and a pair of black trunks.

Gold.

Gold like Ira Oisín Doyle.

What he needed… was Doyle.

Larkin spit water from his mouth and snapped the curtain shut. He washed his hair and scrubbed his body, then turned off the shower and toweled down. Larkin dressed in the clean shirt and underwear before opening the bathroom door, steam wafting out like a cheap movie effect. The apartment had cooled down in his absence, and the circulating air raised gooseflesh on his bare legs.

His mint-green derbies weren't where he'd carelessly discarded them. Larkin glanced at the coffee table. His wallet and phone were gone, and the SIG wasn't on the couch. Larkin noticed his keys on the hook by the front door. His gaze moved right, following the brick wall, passing over the television, refrigerator, stove, and stopping on Doyle hovering over the kitchen sink. Forgoing the use of a plate, his partner was stuffing the last bite of what looked to be a sandwich in his mouth. Doyle looked over his shoulder, met Larkin's stare, and promptly coughed out a laugh around the food.

It'd been a long day of turbulent emotion and unfulfilled investigating and an actual fight for his life, but it had ended with Doyle still alive.

Still alive and silly and beautiful and noble and *perfect*.

And Larkin needed Doyle.

Around a mouthful, Doyle said, "'M sorry. Hungry." He pointed to the plate on the kitchen table. "I made you one too."

"Oh."

"I'm gonna wash up."

Larkin nodded. He watched until Doyle had closed the bathroom door behind himself, then went to the table. The sandwich was a grilled cheese, cut diagonally—the only acceptable cut for a sandwich, Doyle had claimed on more than one occasion—with a healthy slice of tomato added to it.

Doyle didn't like tomato in his grilled cheese.

But Larkin did.

Larkin wiped a rogue tear from his cheek with the heel of his hand, picked up the sandwich, and took several big bites. He finished the midnight meal and was standing before his shelf of plants in the far corner of the room by the time Doyle stepped out of the bathroom. Larkin's evening inspection of his carefully curated houseplant collection was a habit Doyle always left him to without interruption, so he wasn't surprised when his partner's bare feet didn't stop but padded all the way into the bedroom.

Larkin wasn't really checking his plants.

Not tonight, anyway.

He was awake again, with a physicality a hundred thousand times stronger than what he'd felt at La Boîte Dorée, and he was terrified any sudden movement would kill the desire he'd been robbed of for the last six months. Larkin glanced from the corner of his eye, watching Doyle through the glass french doors. His muscles flexed with each breath of oxygen, every pump of blood, his body a temple of vitality ready to sweat, gasp, be brought to his knees, pushed to his limits, no words but for more, more, more, God, *more*.

Larkin's skin prickled.

He felt flush.

He felt feverish.

He felt *alive*.

Larkin needed Ira Doyle.

And he'd have him.

Larkin strode across the apartment, opened the bedroom door, and as Doyle turned, wearing only a pair of boxer briefs,

Larkin pushed him. The back of Doyle's knees hit the bed and he fell onto the mattress with a sudden protest. Larkin moved after him while yanking his own T-shirt off, climbed on top of Doyle, and pressed their hungry mouths together.

And then Doyle's hands were in Larkin's hair, body thrusting up off the bed to meet him like they were opposite ends of two magnets. Larkin shoved back, rolled his hips, ignited a wildfire in his partner as he pinned Doyle's wrists overhead and bit his ear, his throat, his chest, marking Doyle as his and his alone. At one point, Larkin had to let go, had to sit up on his knees so that he could finish undressing them both, and Doyle followed suit. He pulled Larkin flush against his chest, groped his bare ass, and licked his stomach, down past the dark blond hair at his navel.

Larkin stopped Doyle from going lower, said breathlessly, "Let me make love to you," and kissed him.

Again.

And again and again.

His blood was pounding in his ears like a tidal wave, a tsunami, by the time Doyle slid out from underneath. Larkin watched as he wrenched open the nightstand, shoved aside its contents once, twice, before making a successful discovery of the lube in the very back of the drawer.

Doyle rejoined Larkin, this time straddling his lap. He leaned down and whispered, "Like this. So you can watch me."

Larkin put a hand on the back of Doyle's head and drew him into another tongue-heavy kiss. He swallowed Doyle's gasp, eliciting that now-familiar mewl of pleasure. Larkin kissed Doyle with the assurance of morning light burning away the nighttime mist, of spores making their home in rotten remains, of the first cry at the moment of birth, his fervor that of a learned man splitting the atom—their touch an explosive release of living, of dying, of matter from everything, *everywhere*—

Nietzsche had said that the concept of love was an expression of egoism, that the lover was ready to make every sacrifice, disturb every arrangement, put every other interest behind his own, that the lover wanted the unconditioned, sole possession of the person longed for, and Larkin agreed. He agreed because as Doyle, as *Ira*—who was every quality that gave pleasure to the senses and mind—gripped the headboard in both hands and rode him with total abandon, he couldn't imagine, couldn't *fathom*, not putting this man before every other person and thing in his life.

"More, more, mo—oh fuck, *oh fuck.*"

Call me selfish.

"Evie, don't—don't stop."

After all....

Larkin thrust up hard, and Doyle panted, begged, *screamed* Larkin's name as he came.

I'm only human.

Plunk, plunk, plunk.

The AC in 5A was dripping, each splash hitting the corner of Doyle's window unit with a metallic *ping* that broke the softness, the isolation, reminding Larkin that a world outside this room existed and he would be expected to be part of it when the sun rose in—well, in however many hours. Larkin couldn't read the face of the alarm clock from where he was sprawled among the tangled bedsheets and cast-aside pillows. He'd have to sit up, dislodge Doyle, who was lazily tracing the contours of Larkin's body, his collarbone, sternum, ribs—

"Sorry," Doyle whispered as Larkin's stomach involuntarily fluttered under the ministrations. He kissed the ticklish spot before setting a hand on Larkin's chest and resting his chin atop.

Larkin looked down and met Doyle's sated expression. He combed his fingers through thick brown hair and asked, "How do you feel."

"Reborn."

"Stop it."

Doyle laughed, easy and carefree. "I feel really good. And I feel even better knowing we're so sexually compatible."

Larkin snorted. "I've been told I don't give off top energy."

Doyle pushed up. He leaned over Larkin and murmured, "Anyone who's told you that is obviously not a bottom with only a small domination kink."

"Small domination kink," Larkin repeated, brows raised.

Doyle nodded, and he slowly drew one leg over Larkin in order to straddle his hips. "I'm not talking whips and chains. But I know what I like."

Larkin ran his hands up Doyle's haired thighs. "And what's that."

Doyle leaned down, their mouths a breath apart, and he whispered, "Being climbed like a tree."

"Jesus Christ, Ira."

Doyle laughed again, louder, and heat and smoke coiled in Larkin's belly like a live snake. "How'd you figure it out?"

"How did I know you... wanted to be climbed," Larkin slowly clarified. "When you flirt, you utilize a combination of physical and playful techniques, which are inherently more sexual in nature than what's seen in the sincere, traditional, or polite methods. But you don't go on the offense. You flirt to get a rise."

"You can't say it didn't work."

"Clearly." Larkin stroked Doyle's thighs again and said, "But I knew for certain after I mentioned the need to handcuff you when we were at the Property Clerk's warehouse."

Doyle's gaze momentarily rose upward, in a way that was typical of someone trying to recall a memory. He said suddenly, "Wait, that was you flirting back?"

"I wasn't flirting—I was being serious. You're very handsy."

"*Oh my God,*" Doyle moan-laughed. "I didn't anticipate you being such a tease." He took Larkin's face into both hands and kissed him. Doyle began rolling his hips, nice and slow, breaking the kiss to ask, "This all right?"

"Yeah."

He kept up the steady friction, the kissing, the touching that made Larkin feel intoxicated—all highs, no lows—before saying, "We really should get some sleep."

At the suggestion, Larkin opened his eyes, blinked against the glow of the touch lamp, and looked down. Doyle was ready. Him, not so much.

"We don't have to go again," Doyle insisted.

But Larkin pushed up and encouraged Doyle onto his back. Leaning over him, Larkin put his weight on his right hand and began stroking himself with the left. The sensory experience of their lovemaking was already stored in his long-term memory—the sharp scent of arousal, the taste of sweat, the glide of fingertips on heated skin, the desperate and delicious half-formed pleas Doyle made in the throes of passion, the way he looked like how having sex was a spiritual awakening—and those sensitive memories broke through Larkin's initial embarrassment and frustration and instead began to provoke a renewed physical interest.

"My recovery time isn't quite... what it was."

"It'll get better."

When Larkin was ready, he found the lube from within the folds of sheets, and Doyle—legs around Larkin's waist, their fingers entwined overhead—easily relented. Remembrance and touch explored, delighted in each other, while the room echoed with cries of "love" and gasps of "you," and Larkin wasn't sure—didn't care—who'd said what.

Only that it'd been said.

"I love you."

CHAPTER FOURTEEN

Larkin hadn't slept—really slept—for a very long time.

It was always in fits, lasting no more than a few hours, brought about by drug dependency or self-induced physical exhaustion, neither of which presented him with any sort of lasting restfulness. He woke tired, irritated, and since last month's threat against Doyle, afraid.

Afraid that in the handful of minutes he'd try to fit a full night's rest, some awful terror would befall his partner—something immediate, something that'd produce no sound, no cry to rouse Larkin to action—and so every morning, he woke with an uncontrollable sense of dread, certain he'd find Doyle dead beside him. It'd begun as an obsessive thought that had since manifested into a physical tic he couldn't quite contain, like a man forced to witness the same atrocity day in and day out, but each and every time he'd flinch, refusing to be conditioned.

So when Larkin sluggishly came to the next morning, belatedly registering the scratch of chest hair against his back and the weight of an arm draped over him, he lurched violently, turned so quickly that he ended up elbowing Doyle in the face.

"Ouch!"

"Ira?"

Doyle rubbed his nose while blinking sleep from his eyes. "I hope you weren't expecting someone else."

Larkin sat up. "Why're you in bed."

"Is that a rhetorical question?"

Larkin leaned over him and read the time on the clock: 9:22 a.m. He was supposed to be at the precinct an hour and twenty-two minutes ago.

"You're not late," Doyle warned.

Poised to launch from the bed, Larkin asked, "What."

"Connor was going to make you take a personal day, but I cautioned him against it."

Larkin's tension eased. He arched an eyebrow.

Doyle sat up, the sheet pooling around his waist. He seemed to fortify himself before saying, "The last Adam Worth case triggered some unhealthy tendencies in you that haven't… really abated. I think the right thing to do would be to remove an individual from the source of the compulsion, but what works for others, I know doesn't always work for you. And sometimes, not allowing you to confront the cause for an obsession ends up making it stronger." He clarified by tapping the side of his own head and adding, "Up here."

Larkin stared, silent and unblinking.

"I see what it's doing to you, and if you're going to solve *this* case, you need to make sure your basic needs are met or you're going to burn out. That's how mistakes are made and that's how people get hurt. But you've got me, and I won't let that happen. If getting you one step closer to catching the sender means making grilled cheeses at midnight or charming your lieutenant into a late call time, then that's what I'll do to support you."

After a moment of consideration, Larkin only said, "Connor never approves late call times. You either show up, or you don't."

Doyle leaned in. "I'm very convincing."

"What'd you do."

Smiling brightly, Doyle said, "Evie, we've been over this. I just smiled and asked."

Larkin grunted.

"How'd you sleep?"

"Is it in bad taste to say I slept like the dead."

Doyle kissed Larkin's shoulder before climbing out of bed. "I'm glad."

"You skipped your workout," Larkin noted.

Doyle went to the dresser and collected underwear from the top drawer. "Yeah. I was in a sex coma."

Larkin didn't typically hang on to ego strokes—compliments were unnecessary when he was already quite aware of his own capabilities—but that one he didn't mind. He planted his hands behind himself and leaned back, taking in the view of Doyle's naked body and its almost ethereal glow in the morning light.

Doyle turned. "Mind if I shower first?"

"No."

Larkin waited, waited until Doyle had left the bedroom, until the bathroom door had closed, until the shower had turned on, before he blew out a very cautious breath. He felt so—dare he say it—*good* that Larkin was scared one wrong move would send the euphoria into dormancy again. He could've kicked himself for lowering his guard so much that nearly eight hours of uninterrupted sleep had been obtained, but….

Larkin climbed out of bed, found his discarded T-shirt, pulled on a pair of low-rise trunks, and as he padded into the kitchen, drawing open the blinds to reveal a beautiful summer day, he considered the last time sleep had felt so simple and *pure*.

Certainly before he'd gotten addicted to benzos.

Larkin took his morning medication and flipped the switch on the coffeepot.

Before he'd become dependent on ZzzQuil.

He opened the fridge and collected a handful of ingredients.

Before he and Noah had tied the knot, even.

Larkin grabbed a cutting board and began dicing a few potatoes while the coffee brewed.

His promotion, he finally decided. It was the stress of working cold cases.

The stress of remembering the ever-fluctuating count—currently 9,024—of victims forgotten by the rest of the city. The stress of the race against time to bring solace to those left in mourning, before they, too, were nothing but a memory. The stress of simply being reminded daily what a fucking joke humanity was.

"You didn't have to make breakfast."

Larkin looked over his shoulder. Doyle stood in the threshold of the bedroom, wearing a pair of stark white boxer briefs, his damp hair already finger-combed, and even from this distance, Larkin could smell his freshly applied cologne of neroli and sandalwood and cardamom.

Perhaps not all of humanity.

Larkin added some salt and pepper to the cubed potatoes sizzling in the skillet. "Disliking something isn't the same as being incapable of doing something. It's only fair that I shoulder the responsibility now and then." He cracked eggs one-handed into a bowl. "Besides, recovery from two rounds of vigorous sex will require something hardier than greek yogurt and granola."

Doyle only chuckled in response, but that smooth and smoky voice settled over Larkin like a shield against all the world's trials and tribulations, and he realized he didn't just feel good.

He felt better.

He felt *amazing.*

Doyle returned a few moments later, dropped his suit coat and shoulder holster over the back of a kitchen chair, and joined Larkin. He reached overhead, collected two mugs from the cupboard, then fetched cream from the fridge. Doyle wore dark brown trousers and brown oxfords, a white button-down shirt, and a gold tie.

"Is that my tie."

Doyle closed the fridge before instinctively smoothing the tie against his chest. "Do you mind if I borrow it?"

"No, I don't. It looks very nice on you."

Doyle poured them each coffee. He leaned back against the counter, saying teasingly, "Thank you, Mr. Menswear Aficionado."

"I'm merely a product of my upbringing," Larkin corrected. "You've met my mother."

He poured the bowl of beaten eggs and finely chopped herbs into a pan bubbling with butter before hastily moving it back and forth over the burner while softly scrambling the contents with a fork. Larkin glanced sideways. Doyle had declined to comment on Jacqueline and was silently sipping his coffee.

Larkin folded the omelet a few times before banging his open palm against the handle of the pan, causing the other side of the omelet to bounce up and fold over, creating a seam. He grabbed one of the plates, tilted the pan, and let the omelet roll out, seam down. French omelets were deceptively difficult to master, and Larkin was satisfied he hadn't lost his touch in the intervening eleven months since he'd last made one. Noah had always preferred American-style, so Larkin rarely bothered more than once or twice a year to make one for himself. He shoveled some home fries onto the plate and then handed it to Doyle.

"Wow. What'd I do to deserve this?"

"It'd be easier to ask what you haven't done."

Doyle leaned down and kissed Larkin. "Thank you, sunshine."

Larkin nodded and returned to cracking more eggs for his own omelet. He melted butter, poured the mixture, worked the pan, and asked as he smacked the handle a second time, "What did you say to my mother yesterday—before we left." He plated the omelet and potatoes before collecting his coffee and taking a seat.

Doyle looked up from his breakfast but didn't answer.

Larkin said, "I assure you, she very well needed to hear whatever you said."

"I don't know about that." Doyle set his fork down. "I let anger get the best of me."

"Anger is a universal emotion."

Doyle leaned back in his chair. "I told her a child has a right to unconditional love and acceptance, but being a parent isn't the same. It's a privilege. And that… my grandmother would've prayed to St. Dymphna for intercession because, surely, any woman who treated their child as she did must be ill."

"You called my mother—"

"No, no. I only told her what an old Irish grandmother would've made of the situation."

Larkin smiled wryly and took a sip of coffee.

Doyle stretched his legs out under the table and recited rote, "'Lord, our God, you graciously chose St. Dymphna as patroness of those afflicted with mental and nervous disorders. Please grant, Lord, through the prayers of this pure youthful martyr, relief and consolation to all suffering such trials, and especially those for whom we pray.' Heard that one a lot growing up."

"About you," Larkin asked.

Doyle shook his head. "My mom. A lot of prayers to St. Monica too." He straightened in his seat, picked up his fork, and added, "But did you know there *is* a patron saint of juvenile delinquents?"

"I still struggle to picture you being a little hellraiser."

Doyle grinned like the Cheshire Cat.

"Oh, no, never mind," Larkin corrected.

They both laughed, and Doyle asked, "You're not mad, are you?"

"No. In fact, I wish I were also capable of telling my mother her behavior is bad enough to require the intervention of Catholicism."

"Sometimes there's no bettering people," Doyle said simply. "No matter how many saints you throw at them."

Larkin broached the next question with caution. "When was the last time you saw your mother."

Doyle's thick brows rose a little, but after a moment of reflection, he said, "My grandmother was awarded custody when I was nine. That was the last time."

It was 11:13 a.m. when Larkin and Doyle hiked the front steps of Precinct 19. They would have arrived at eleven o'clock exactly, had Larkin not been so indecisive about what to wear. He'd gone back and forth for quite some time between the gray glen plaid and navy windowpane before ultimately settling on the latter suit with a white button-down. The pattern popped when paired with a solid purple taupe tie, a polka dotted pocket square of black and gold, and, of course, his gold wingtips.

"You look like a million bucks," Doyle murmured.

"Is it obvious I dressed to match you."

Doyle paused midstep and leaned back to take in Larkin's full attire. "Nah. That'll be our little secret."

"It's about time you showed up," a third voice interjected.

Larkin and Doyle both turned to the front doors as Neil Millett exited the precinct, grimacing as he left the air-conditioned interior behind. He looked fantastic, though, wearing an olive-green suit—linen, not a cotton blend—with a striped, baby blue button-down and a plaid tie of forest green, red, white, and a bit of navy.

Larkin stated, "I like this suit. Olive is a good color on you."

Millett looked down at himself. "Thanks. I, uh, I like this power couple thing you've got going on." He motioned between Larkin's shoes and Doyle's tie.

Larkin shot Doyle a look, which Doyle pointedly didn't meet as he fought to control a self-satisfied grin. To the point, he asked, "Why're you hanging around my precinct."

"Remember how you asked me to check the bathroom at the Carroll Street house? It lit up like the Fourth of July under luminol. Tub, sink, walls—everywhere. Whoever it was, they tried to clean up the bloodbath with bleach, but they missed enough for me to get samples."

"Have it tested against Wagner's remains," Larkin said, and at the incredulous expression Millett shot him, he continued, "Dismemberments are most often performed in tubs. Texas, 2005, Ohio, 2012, Montana, 2018—"

"Larkin," Doyle murmured.

Larkin shook his head and redirected himself. "While the missing knives can only be considered circumstantial evidence, the fridge Wagner was found in unquestionably originated from the home. Whether or not she was murdered and then dismembered in that tub will go a long way in establishing who all was involved."

"All right," Millett answered without further facial criticism. "I also wanted to talk to you about yesterday's DB."

"Which one," Larkin asked.

"The gunshot vic—Sinclair, was it?"

"Joe Sinclair, yes. What about him."

Millett slid his hands into his pockets. "I thought you should be made aware that he's been harassing—well, maybe that's too strong of a word—*irritating* a number of cops over the last few months. Specifically, out cops."

"Yes, my first interaction with him was on April 1," Larkin said. "Wherein he exhibited undue interest in my sexuality."

"Then you heard about last month?" Millett asked. "What happened with the Homicide detective?"

"I do my very best to ignore those apes," Larkin answered.

Millett laughed—actually laughed—at that. "You and me both. And yet, they still call me. What I mean is, that Joe guy got into some deep shit last month after sticking his nose into a murder investigation. I think he might've even been a suspect at one point?"

"Why would he do something so…."

"Stupid?" Doyle suggested.

"I was going to say contradictory to his personal well-being," Larkin corrected.

"I think the guy was gaga for authority, if you know what I mean," Millett said, reaching into his back pocket and retrieving his wallet. He poked through the contents and continued, "My best friend's married to the Homicide detective who was on that case. That's how I learned about Joe's 'undue interests.'" Millett found the business card he'd been looking for and offered it to Larkin. "I don't know if this bears any relevancy to your case, but I couldn't stop thinking about it last night—about how the guy's been schooling around gay cops. That's Detective Winter's number, if you want to give him a ring. Can't hurt, right? Always trust your gut."

"That might very well be indigestion."

Doyle accepted the card on Larkin's behalf, saying, "We'll give him a call."

"Thank you, Millett," Larkin added.

"Sure thing." Millett turned to start down the opposite set of stairs but stopped, looked back, and said, "Oh, by the way, ballistics came back on Wagner's third eye. Bullet was a .38 special."

"A lot of handguns use .38 caliber bullets, do they not," Larkin asked.

"A lot of revolvers," Millett corrected. "But when you consider how unlikely it'd be to see revolvers on US streets originating from Spain or France or the Philippines, it was most likely shot by a Colt, Ruger, or Smith & Wesson."

—summer sun glinting off the blued barrel as it leveled on him and the black abyss of the muzzle swallowed him whole—

"It's strange to see a revolver on the street at all," Doyle said thoughtfully.

"Bad guys aren't singly loading cartridges into their cowboy six-shooters these days," Millett agreed dryly.

Larkin interrupted. "Can you have the bullet from Joe's autopsy compared to Wagner's."

Millett looked puzzled.

"Yesterday's shooter used a revolver."

"I'll give the doc a call."

"Thank you." Larkin watched as Millett started for the street, already putting his phone to his ear. To Doyle, he asked, "What do you know about revolvers."

"Not that much."

"That's unfortunate."

"What about you?"

Larkin shook his head with dissatisfaction. "I know my way around semiautomatics." He walked up the remaining stairs, pulled open the door, and gestured for Doyle to follow.

In the quiet of last night, Larkin had been able to disregard the overload of stimulation his workspace had presented, but in the bright light of a new day, the stark reminders of the brutality of man couldn't be brushed aside so easily. It was all right there for him to think about, obsess about, until it'd been properly catalogued, stored, and responded to. Larkin preferred a desk be kept like military barracks—succulent and Lisa Frank aside—and this was more akin to a tweens' sugar-fueled slumber party.

The light for the phone's voice mailbox was still blinking. The stack of delivered manila folders hadn't been moved from where it leaned precariously to one side, threatening to spill across the keyboard and onto the floor in a dramatic interpretation of a publishing house's slush pile. Loose call receipts looked to have been scattered by the circulating air and the comings and goings of detectives all morning. One lay beside the wheel of his chair.

Doyle had already shed his suit coat and was rolling back the sleeves of his shirt when he asked, "What is it?"

"We have to begin the arduous process of manually digging through Jane Does to find Esther's homicide report, but I won't be able to focus on that knowing this"—Larkin indicated by making a circle with his index finger in the direction of the mess—"is sitting here, getting worse by the hour."

"How about I tidy up for you?" Doyle suggested.

Larkin was good at keeping his dislike to himself when it meant protecting the emotional well-being of a romantic partner—a necessary white lie, they were sometimes called— but Doyle still knew, *somehow*, that Larkin utterly despised even the thought of him touching the desk. Larkin quickly said, "It's not that I think you can't put things away. It's just— I'm very particular."

"I know," Doyle answered, his tone indulgent and not the least bit hurt. "How about I check on the status of the composite sketch?" He raised the business card. "And then I'll touch base with Homicide. You can work on organizing while I do that."

"I suppose that's acceptable."

Doyle walked around to the left side of Larkin's desk, leaned over Baker's, pulled the phone forward, and punched in a few numbers.

"What is my tell," Larkin asked.

Doyle turned, receiver to his ear, looking expectant.

"I didn't say anything."

"Exactly." Doyle winked before his call was answered and he said, "Debra, it's Ira. Have they got you working Saturdays now?"

While Doyle did his usual flirting with Debra Baan of Public Relations, Larkin sifted through the stack of newly acquired cold case files—some decades old—scanning cracked typeset and regulating details to his infallible long-term memory before putting them away. And while each name and date and cause of death activated the recall of Larkin's initial request *for* the paperwork, they also triggered associations with other cases already in his rotation.

New case, Antonio Williams, found stabbed to death on Bleecker Street, January 3, 1974, had the same date of death as Destiny Marshall. New case, Gracie Feinberg, a transgender sex worker whose nude body had been discovered in the early hours of September 29, 1988, in the Meatpacking District, had the same circumstances of death as Kristal Black, one year prior. New case, Billy Donovan, pushed from a sixth-story window on September 13, 2003, had the same name but different spelling as *Billie* Donovan, a Hell's Kitchen local who'd been shot execution-style on April 6, 1984, and whose body had been found dismembered and distributed between two black trash bags in the East River.

Larkin snapped shut the folder in his hands.

So often, his associations were too personal, too conceptual, too tortured to be anything but a disruption and a burden on every second of every day of his life. But every once in a while, those associations were like pins in a tumbler lock finally lining up.

Click.

Larkin leaned over the open second drawer of his desk—hanging files all precisely aligned and organized—and snatched Hell's Kitchen Billie Donovan out of it. He'd been unable to dedicate much time to Billie's murder since adopting the case early in his career, had even considered recommending Porter to take it on instead, as the circumstances screamed gang violence and the senior detective was far more versed in organized crime than Larkin was, but despite the most noble of intentions to see Billie's case solved, here Billie sat.

Still waiting for justice all these years later.

Larkin next collected Wagner's crisp new file and, while holding them both up, said, "Porter."

Porter turned in his chair.

"Was it common for a mob hit to be made to disappear."

"Depends on the mob, but sure," Porter said, looking between the two manila folders with mild interest. "The Italian mafia's buried more than a few bodies along the border of Brooklyn and Queens. That was one of my first investigations when I came to Cold Cases back in 2004, you know. Just me, the FBI, and Bonanno crime family vics found at the Hole."

Larkin gave Billie's case a shake. "Gunshot, execution-style. Body dismembered, placed into trash bags, and dumped into the East River."

"When?"

"1984."

Porter snorted. "Sounds an awful lot like some of the Irish wackos from back in the day."

"What do you mean."

"Used to be, the last Irish mobsters in the city would hack up bodies in a tub, put the pieces in trash bags, and drive 'em to the river for dumping."

"Are you talking about the Westies?"

Both Larkin and Porter directed their attention to Doyle, who was hanging up the phone.

"You know them?" Porter asked.

"I grew up in Hell's Kitchen," Doyle answered, moving around the front of Larkin's desk to join them in conversation. "Grandma would sit on the stoop in the evenings with other ladies from the tenement and talk about the good old days— about McGrath and Spillane, the old-school gangsters who used to run the neighborhood. Her generation wasn't very fond of the Westies."

Larkin lowered the folders in his hands. "Your grandmother approved of mob behavior."

"It's not that she approved," Doyle answered. "That's just... kind of how it was back then."

"Hell's Kitchen was under gang influence for well over a hundred years," Porter explained to Larkin. "But the violence got real bad after Mickey Spillane was murdered in '77 and the Westies opened the neighborhood up to working with the Italian mafia. RICO charges didn't take the Westies out until the late '80s, though, which is why that body dump sounds like their MO."

Larkin considered for a moment. "Why, when the neighborhood is only a block or two from the Hudson, would they traverse crosstown to dump the body."

Porter said, "The Irish mob used to control the dockworkers union. The longshoremen were all from Hell's Kitchen. It wouldn't look good to toss vics into the same body of water your neighbor works."

Larkin raised Wagner's file next. "Gunshot, execution-style. Body dismembered, placed into a refrigerator, and dumped in the Hudson River."

Porter's eyebrows crept toward his nonexistent hairline. "Interesting parallels."

"Larkin?" Doyle asked with noted uncertainty.

To Doyle, Larkin said, "We've been focused on the details *within* Wagner's death, but not the death itself. The fridge, the brooch—important, yes—but what about the MO of the murderer. *How* someone kills can also tell a story. Is there a complex psychological urge to do harm, such as the ritualistic serial murders associated with Harry Regmore, Alfred Niederman, and Matilde Wagner, or is it perhaps more indicative of the killer's associations or past influences. Do they kill not out of known psychopathic lifestyle behaviors, such as stimulation-seeking, impulsivity, or parasitic orientation, but because it's their job."

"You think we're dealing with a street thug and not an organized killer this time?" Doyle asked.

"On the contrary, this individual is fairly organized. And patient. It takes a considerable amount of time to butcher an adult human and then dispose of the remains. But the sender has done business with all manner of monsters, from mission-oriented serial killers to necrophiliacs. Why wouldn't he also do business with, say, a former mobster."

"Wagner wasn't necessarily a 'mob hit,' Doyle started. "But is instead reflective of how this individual might have been trained to kill."

"And the deviation of trash bags to fridge is because it wasn't ever about making Wagner disappear," Larkin added. "Silenced, yes, but her body needed to keep the game going ad nauseam. We know from past cases that the sender is framing her killer, and that Wagner's murder will also eventually point us toward a seemingly unrelated cold case—"

"Barbara Fuller!" Doyle interjected. Animatedly, he said, "That's the cold case connection. Think about it: Last month, we had to identify Esther from old VHS footage in order to find her killer. But in doing so, we learned her name might've actually been Barbara Fuller. Now her killer is dead and the mourning imagery—jewelry, in this case—is bringing us right back around to the name, Fuller. There must be something about her, specifically, that the sender wants us to learn. Something more than her legal name."

"Why she ran away," Larkin suggested. "What life did Barbara leave, and why was making ends meet as Esther— existing on the fringes of society—the better option."

"It might've been the only option," Doyle corrected with noted somberness.

"I've no idea what the fuck you two are on about," Porter finally put in, "but I hope I helped."

Larkin returned his attention to Porter. "Yes, you were of great assistance. Thank you."

Porter grunted.

Larkin spun on his heel, returned to his desk, and began to hastily store the last of the cases sitting out. "Actually, Porter, I have one last question."

"I don't like feeling used."

Larkin finished storing the folders, closed the desk drawer, and straightened his stooped posture. Porter had turned in his chair and was staring at him. "You may have my cake batter donut."

"The stale cake batter donut that's been sitting on the counter since yesterday morning?"

"Yes."

Porter mulled over the offer. "What's the question?"

"The Hudson River was once a significant location to Hell's Kitchen. It employed much of the neighborhood, which then employed the Westies."

"That's right."

"Do toothpicks hold any sort of significance to the Hudson. Something symbolic, or historic, perhaps."

Porter's mouth fixed into a shrug before he said, "There's a story—can't say how true it might be—that back in the day, prospecting dockworkers would line up at the pier each morning, and if they tucked a toothpick behind one ear, it signaled to the foreman that they were game."

Doyle asked, "Game for what?"

"That they'd kickback some of their wages in return for the job," Porter clarified as he got up from his chair. "It perpetuated the system of racketeering and loan-sharking—kept the Irish mob alive a few decades longer than they shoulda been."

"Thank you," Larkin said.

"Thanks, Jim."

Porter gave them a lazy salute before heading toward the breakroom.

Larkin shrugged out of his suit coat and draped it over the back of his chair. "The history of the Hudson is relevant in this case the same way that the subway and Broadway locations were in the past."

"It's sounding more and more like Hell's Kitchen mob activity," Doyle agreed with a nod. "Last month, Phyllis said that Esther—uh, should we start referring to her as Barbara?"

"I do believe we should consider this an opportunity to give Barbara her identity back."

"Sure. Phyllis said that Barbara had the quintessential New York accent, making her a local. On top of that, she's a beautiful young woman possibly from Hell's Kitchen. What if the reason she turned to a life on Broadway was to get away from someone in the neighborhood?"

"It's not an unreasonable theory, especially given the extra work she put into changing her identity. She didn't buy a fake ID and call it done—she went to considerable lengths to obtain those legal documents we had a brief look at." Larkin motioned Doyle to follow him as he started across the bullpen. "But we need to speak with someone who knew her—knew her as Barbara."

Doyle switched gears. "Debra's a little backed up in Public Relations, but she said your composite sketch should be up on Local4Locals sometime today."

"Good."

"And Detective Winter in Homicide confirmed what Millett said: Joe was horny for a story. He ran a background check last month—no arrests, no priors. But Winter echoed Millett's concern: The guy tried speaking with queer officers in Vice, Transit, and Homicide before circling back to you." They reached the threshold that led to the breakroom on the right and copy room on the left, and Doyle followed Larkin left. "Winter's investigation ended up going in another direction and he lost the opportunity to delve further into Joe, but from all accounts, Joe was pretty pushy with the other officers too."

Larkin came to a stop outside of a closed door at the end of the hall. "Based on what Joe said yesterday, that all of the media outlets want to interview me—which is correct—but only he could tell my story without pandering—which I found extremely doubtful—I would have believed his fixation was on me. But this only proves my original read of Joe was correct: So long as the subject of his narrative fucks other men, the individual themself is interchangeable, which, to be quite frank, I find more than a little offensive, considering the call is coming from inside the room."

Doyle winced and said, "If it was only about landing an interview with a gay cop, you'd be the *last one* I'd harass a second time."

Larkin raised a quizzical eyebrow.

"Respectfully."

Larkin retrieved the keys from his pocket. "So it is about me."

"I think, whatever Joe was *actually* trying to accomplish, it did become about you, yeah. It was about more than an interview. He wouldn't have been shot, otherwise."

—dead eyes reflecting back his final living seconds like a still image caught on film, that of a man with a puckered scar—

Larkin shuddered. He quickly unlocked the door before them, pushed it open, and took Doyle's hand, leading him inside. He flipped a switch on the wall, and an overhead light flickered once, twice, and with an audible hum, illuminated a windowless space roughly the size of the breakroom. Cream-colored metal filing cabinets from the '90s lined the wall directly ahead and to the right. A worktable with a faux-wood laminate top was pushed to the left, and beside it was metal shelving that reached to the ceiling. It'd been packed tighter than tinned sardines with bankers boxes. Plastic totes were stacked two and three high along the floor and shoved as far out of the way as possible, suggesting no one had anticipated humanity being such a disappointment that detectives would run out of space in which to shelve unsolved murders. The room had a musty, old paper smell, and Doyle promptly sneezed.

"Welcome to the Morgue," Larkin replied. He turned to face Doyle. "These are our unassigned cold cases."

"There're hundreds."

"Thousands," Larkin corrected. "9,024 is our current total of unsolved cases. If we estimate each detective has about two dozen assigned and open investigations, there are nearly 8,800 cases left in this room. Of course, these numbers don't take into account any cold cases Homicide detectives might still be sitting on."

Doyle swore quietly.

"You can ignore the filing cabinets," Larkin explained. "That's everything from the turn of the century to the 1960s. Ignore the tubs as well. Those are all from the '90s and later." Larkin put a hand on one of the boxes shoved onto the metal shelving. "These are the '70s and '80s. John and Jane Does will be marked with a red tag."

"I'm having Property Clerk flashbacks."

"I assure you, there will be no maggots in these boxes."

Doyle smiled at that, but as he walked over to the shelving, he said, "I have to ask… because I haven't been able to stop thinking about it. Did you ever doubt me?"

"What are you talking about."

Doyle stared at the faded case numbers on the side of the nearest eye-level box. "The stalker-turned-shooter," he clarified. "Driving the same make, model, color even, as my car? It's Worth trying to get in your head again, I know it." Doyle tapped the box absently before sparing Larkin a sideways glance. "You made a really stupid decision last month that almost cost you your life. He knows he can't brute-force us apart, so if he doesn't want me helping you, wants to keep the game between the two of you, best to lean back into the emotional manipulation tactics. And if you thought, for even a moment, that there was a chance I could've been harassing Noah—"

"Ira," Larkin interrupted, and his voice sounded harsh, even to his own ears. "I haven't been able to sleep for weeks. It's not because of the Prozac. It's because I'm waiting for that sonofabitch to walk through our front door so I can put a bullet in his brain. I would *kill* for you."

Doyle didn't move, like a deer caught in the headlights.

"Adam Worth will never make me doubt the love of my life."

It was seven very, very long seconds before Doyle finally exhaled, and the tension in his posture, the stiffness in his shoulders, the flexed muscles in his forearms—they all relaxed like a noose around his neck had been loosened. "I didn't mean to upset you."

Larkin shook his head in a manner that seemed to say, *You didn't*, and joined Doyle at the wall of boxes.

"We're gonna talk about the no-sleeping thing. You know that, right?"

"One crisis at a time."

The smart move would have been for the Cold Case Squad to store boxes, and the files therein, chronologically from the get-go.

They hadn't been, of course.

Larkin and Doyle split the search—Larkin crouched to pull red-tagged cases on the bottom shelves, while Doyle stood and reached the ones from overhead. Despite the work hardly being more than a monotonous chore, Larkin had to exert considerable effort in maintaining both mental and emotional distance from the reality of the task at hand. Each file was someone born, someone named, someone who had dreamed and hoped and loved, and despite his recent revelation about the spectrum of existence, these were still people who had been robbed of having a good death, and the injustice of it could and *would* send Larkin into a spiral if he let it.

Porter appeared in the threshold of the Morgue at 12:07 p.m., nursing a fresh cup of coffee and holding the final bite of a chocolate-frosted donut. "Whaddya fishin' for?"

Larkin reached and set another red-tagged folder on the table before pivoting on one foot to address Porter in his crouch. "A Jane Doe from 1982."

"Good luck."

"Did you not want the cake batter donut," Larkin asked, furrowing his brow a little.

Porter looked at the frosting melting between his thumb and index finger before shrugging. "Moto got it for you."

Larkin opened his mouth to say… well, he didn't quite know, but a phone call cut short his consideration. He looked over his shoulder as Doyle retrieved the cell from his pocket and answered, "Hey, Craig."

"Who's Craig?" Porter asked before eating the last piece of donut.

"Doyle's supervisor," Larkin answered distractedly.

"Right now?" Doyle asked into the phone.

Larkin frowned. "Bailey already approved my request for your assistance on this case. Is he negating—"

Doyle held a hand up to stop Larkin's protestations.

"Uh-oh," Porter said. "Trouble in paradise."

"Thank you, Porter," Larkin said, clipped.

"Maybe you and Craig should arm wrestle over Doyle," Porter suggested amusedly.

Larkin pivoted on his heel a second time. "I'm deceptively strong."

"Uh-huh."

Larkin arched a brow at the tone of disbelief. "But that is irrelevant, as the man has about as much muscle mass as a ham sandwich."

Porter tried to suppress a sudden laugh, but the snort jostled his coffee cup and he spilled the contents. "*Shit*…." He quickly switched the mug to his other hand, shaking the wet one while leaving the doorway of the Morgue and calling, "I got coffee on my damn shoes, Grim!"

A smile tugged the corner of Larkin's mouth as he got to his feet.

"All right," Doyle concluded. "I'll be there shortly."

Larkin said, as Doyle lowered the phone, "This is not what was promised to me."

"I know. But it sounds like SVU's just tapped Forensic Artists for a minor emergency—"

"And both Loving and Bailey are either unavailable or underqualified for the particulars of said emergency," Larkin concluded. He rested his hands on his hips before adding, "I can't even be irritated without sounding like a jerk, because survivors always come before cold cases, and SVU has requested the most competent artist for the job."

"You're just saying that."

"Not without empirical evidence."

Doyle's gaze flicked over Larkin's shoulder toward the open door before he offered a placating smile. "Hopefully it won't take too much time."

"It'll take as long as it takes," Larkin corrected. "Don't rush good work for my sake."

"I'll call you."

Larkin nodded. He pulled Doyle down by his tie and kissed his mouth. "I love you."

"I love you too."

Larkin watched Doyle disappear around the corner. His smoky voice bid farewell to the few other detectives working that Saturday, and then he was gone. Alone, Larkin blew out a breath, looked around, then dragged a molded plastic chair out from under a stack of boxes. He pushed it up against the metal shelving, stood on the seat, and resumed searching where Doyle had left off.

Some of the boxes were easy examinations, holding no more than two or three bulging folders several inches thick, while others were packed tight with dozens of files containing nothing more than the bare bones of an investigation that'd gone nowhere. Larkin made sure to go through the latter with particular care, as he was all but certain the original Jane Doe homicide would hardly contain enough to fill a greeting card, otherwise Barbara would have, at the very least, been linked to the missing person report filed under Esther's name only a few days later in October of 1982.

It was a dusty and monotonous process, and the quiet was interrupted by the *beep, beep, beep* of the copier across the hall as someone struggled in vain to make a two-sided copy, desk phones in the bullpen ringing until voicemail picked up, and eventually, Ulmer's snide "You ready to include me on this case for real, or what?"

Hand poised to pluck a red-tagged folder, Larkin turned to see Ulmer leaning in the open doorway. Mildly, he said, "Hello, Ulmer. No, I'm not."

"I don't get you."

"That's fine."

"Three times you've asked me to dig up missing persons reports, and three times I've delivered. You don't have to like me—I can't fucking stand you—but it's time to put me on this case in an official capacity."

Larkin ignored the demand. He removed the file in question before fitting the lid on the box and shoving it back against the wall.

"I wrote that complaint, you know," Ulmer continued. "I guess it's up to you whether I file it or not."

Larkin tapped his fingers against the box—one, two, three times—before he got off the chair. He moved toward the doorway, taking a stand before Ulmer. "Do you know the term, ressentiment."

Ulmer's brows narrowed. He didn't answer either way, and instead crossed his arms defensively.

"Ressentiment, as Nietzsche used it, is a philosophical concept in which one assigns their own inferiority, their own grudge, their own hostility, onto an external scapegoat. The ego seeks to create an enemy—a cause that can be blamed—for one's station as a plebian. Slave morality is reactive of the master morality. It's an inversion of values—bad is now good, good is now evil.

"We all have slave morality within us. Nietzsche's exploration of the genealogy of morals within Western society demonstrates this. But our labor of today should not be in returning to the high-minded aristocratic morality of the past, but in reaching beyond the binary, beyond good and evil, to transcend into tomorrow. My achievements, for the sake of this argument, may be viewed as values of strength—a value which is arguably *good*. But because you are unwilling to seek self-actualization, to accept reality as it actually exists, you twist my strength into something prideful, sinful, *evil*.

"And you, Ulmer, with that cunning projection of false humility, are utilizing your *resentment* by filing a complaint and claiming I keep you from elevating your station when this can be easily accomplished by putting in the necessary time and work. You poison us all with base and slavish thinking. You can't stand me because I represent everything you want but cannot have—not because I'm holding you back, but because it's more comfortable to be perceived as a victim."

Ulmer's complexion darkened. His nostrils flared like a bull seeing red.

Larkin waited, but when Ulmer continued to say nothing, he concluded, "You go ahead and file that report."

"You're an arrogant, conceited, entitled, pompous little prick—"

"Man despairs for reason, Ulmer. And whether you will against the most central conditions of life, or choose to instead embrace that which makes us most human—pain and happiness and beauty and death—that is entirely up to you. But before the slave morality's life-denying rationale slides you further down that dangerous ascetic precipice, of which only nihilism awaits, I suggest visiting the breakroom. There're donuts."

Through gritted teeth, Ulmer said, "You're too fucking much."

Larkin closed the distance between them. "Then go find less."

Ulmer smacked the folder in Larkin's hand, causing the contents to spill across the floor. "Clean up your shit." He turned and stormed down the hall.

"Asshole," Larkin muttered with a small shake of his head. He crouched, collected the documents with their faded and cracked typeset, and brought them to the worktable. He'd only reordered a few pages before his eyes caught: *October 2, 1982.*

Larkin looked at the stack of folders he and Doyle had pulled, had intended to spend the better part of the day reading through, then reactively turned toward the vacant doorway. His heart fluttered uncomfortably, like it'd missed a beat, and his fingertips tingled as his body reacted to the oncoming spike of adrenaline.

Larkin was not a religious man.

He wasn't even particularly spiritual.

But he did believe the dead were never truly gone. He believed that what lay beyond the veil was not the business of the living to understand—it was merely the next step in the spectrum of existence for those whose physical bodies had returned to stardust—and he believed that until then, his purpose was to *live.*

To love and love again.

But still, Larkin could envision her standing there, with that shag-cut brown hair, the prominent nose, those big doe eyes. She wasn't looking for retribution or justice. Such concerns mattered to the living. She was only looking to free herself of the guilt and anger that accompanied a bad death.

She was looking to be remembered.

To be shown the way.

Larkin's throat was tight as he said to the empty room, "Don't worry, Barbara. I've found you."

CHAPTER FIFTEEN

On the fateful night of October 2, 1982, Jane Doe had been seen entering the once grand, then fleabag, now razed Hotel Cavalier on Forty-Third Street between Sixth and Broadway. The man she'd been with had rented a room by the hour under the name of D-Day. (Responding Homicide detective Ralph Noonan had scribbled beside the alias: *Animal House*.) The front desk clerk of the Cavalier claimed D-Day and *a* woman (he did not specifically claim her to be the same Jane Doe who'd entered, and Noonan failed to ask for clarification) had returned the key "about an hour later."

At approximately three o'clock in the morning on October 3, a different "newlywed couple" found Jane Doe dead atop an unmade bed with a harvest gold comforter, arms stretched wide as if she'd been crucified, nude from the waist up. The description was a perfect match to the VHS tape Larkin and Doyle had watched of who they knew at the time to be Esther Haycox—Matilde Wagner's first mission-oriented kill.

D-Day had been Earl Wagner, her husband.

And the woman who'd returned the room key had actually been Matilde herself, on their way out after the two committed that first murder together.

When it came to the available forensics, police had snapped a dozen grainy photographs and made a notation that they'd taken a gym bag into evidence, which corresponded with Phyllis's dubious claim that Barbara had been going to her job at the Kitten Klub with a bag of costumes, but there was nothing to indicate CSU had collected fibers, DNA, not even fingerprints.

NHI—no human involved.

"This is Detective Everett Larkin with the—"

"I know who you are, detective," Roz from the office of the Property Clerk interrupted. Her unperturbed, slow, and gravelly voice was arguably even worse over the phone. "What do you want?"

"To schedule a property pick up," Larkin answered, barely managing to not tack on an, *Obviously.*

"What's the case number?"

Larkin read aloud the string of numbers from the Jane Doe file before Roz put him on hold. With the receiver still pressed to his ear, Larkin leaned back in his desk chair, crossed his legs, and continued reading the homicide report.

If he'd been underwhelmed by the evidence retrieved from the scene, the ME's report had been enough to bring Larkin's blood to a boiling point. The medical examiner had noted that Barbara came in with bruising around her neck— enough to suggest a homicide—as well as the needle tracks of a "habitual user." There'd been no accompanying documentation of an autopsy having been performed, however, despite Barbara's condition clearly falling within the OCME's responsibility to investigate deaths of an unusual or suspicious manner. And if that goddamn doctor had done his job in 1982, he'd have realized Barbara wasn't a user at all, but had instead been administered a lethal dose of digoxin, perhaps while she'd been held down—while Earl was crushing her windpipe. Had such a finding been properly documented, perhaps it'd have provided Detective Noonan with more clues and more administrative support to get further in his investigation than he ever did.

Matilde and Earl Wagner might never have had an opportunity to kill a second time.

Mia Ramos could have grown up.

And Alfred Niederman never would have gotten a taste for dead children.

Could have.

Would have.

Should have.

"Stupid sonofabitch," Larkin murmured.

"I'm still here, detective," Roz croaked, and Larkin startled at the unexpected response.

"I thought I was on hold."

Roz harrumphed.

Larkin added, "I wasn't referring to you."

"Your request is in-progress."

"Thank—"

"You can pick up after three and before five."

"What. No, that won't work. I need it now."

Roz drawled, "Do you think you've been my only call today?"

"Of course not," Larkin answered. "But as a first grade with triple the average closure rate, I do feel my request shouldn't languish in the first come, first served queue."

"How very humble of you, detective."

"I can be there in twenty minutes."

"I don't care if you're here in five and call me pretty," Roz said, and somehow, a voice that sounded as if she gargled sharp rocks every morning came off as utterly flippant. "You can pick up after—"

As far as Hail Marys went, this was worse than when Larkin told Dr. Baxter he had eyes like the moon and Doyle had overheard that face-planting attempt at flirtation, not least of all because Larkin was openly gay and Roz—in fact, he didn't even know her real name—was a woman of nearly sixty who he'd compared to a slug monster from a Pixar movie, but desperation made a dedicated man do funny things, and he blurted out, "You're very pretty."

There was a prolonged pause, then Roz sighed, said, "Your evidence will be available after three," and hung up.

Larkin set the receiver down. Under his breath, he said, "I will never understand how Ira does it."

He added a reminder to his phone before returning to the content of Barbara's homicide. Detective Noonan claimed to have tried questioning women who'd been working Forty-Third Street the night of the murder. He'd been armed with a Polaroid snapshot of Esther on her deathbed, asking if anyone could identify the victim, but all he'd gotten from walking the beat were cold shoulders and zipped lips. The lack of cooperation from sex workers wasn't at all surprising to Larkin. To demonstrate an association with Barbara—a woman who'd been soliciting sex—would have meant they'd face possible arrest for prostitution as well. Women on the street were exceptionally vulnerable and profoundly mistreated, be it by their pimp, johns, or the system, and staying quiet meant staying alive.

Larkin didn't blame them one bit.

He did blame Noonan, though.

Because while the man had patrolled the street Hotel Cavalier once stood on, at the end of the block was the Kitten Klub, where Barbara had worked, where Earl would have watched her perform, and Noonan never thought to pop his head in and ask questions.

He'd been *right there*.

This murder could have been solved before the sun had risen the morning of October 3.

But instead, Barbara had been restless for thirty-eight agonizing years.

Noonan had, at least, thought to jot down basic descriptions of the sex workers he'd spoken with. Most didn't come with names, since they didn't offer and he didn't seem to know any of the women, but there were two he must have been *acquainted* with through past arrests, because he'd not only recorded their names, but he'd attached their current, as of 1982, rap sheets to the report as well.

Sharon King, twenty-nine at the time of Noonan's report, had been deceased since 1991 of a drug overdose, according to Larkin's research. Bridget Cohen, however, then twenty-three, was still alive and living uptown in Washington Heights.

His desk phone rang.

Larkin glanced at it before leaning forward to check the ID—he wouldn't answer if it was Roz. He accepted the call when he saw it was the downstairs front desk. "Detective Larkin."

Officer Cruz, one of the star players of the department's softball team, said, "I have a Detective Val Hackett from Brooklyn here to see you."

Larkin turned in his chair before standing and looking over the banister to the ground floor. Sure enough, Hackett stood near the entrance, soaking up Precinct 19 as if he were a sponge, like his own station house wasn't the same organized chaos of both uniformed and plain-clothed officers moving every which way, overlaid with the competing stinks of industrial cleaner, toner, and coffee, and sounds of half a dozen conversations being interrupted by ringing telephones. That's when Hackett looked up, spotted Larkin, and waved enthusiastically.

Into the phone, Larkin said, "I see that."

"Do you want me to send him up?"

"God, no."

Cruz snorted.

"I'll be right down." Larkin hung up, put away Barbara's file, and grabbed his suit coat. He drew his arms through the sleeves on his way downstairs.

Hackett met him halfway across the floor with an eager, "Good afternoon, Larkin."

"Why're you here."

"Straight to the point—got it." Hackett retrieved a folded warrant from his inner pocket and held it up like a treasure map. "Your lieutenant called last night and said to keep you involved with the Brooklyn murders, since they relate to a case you're working? So, anyway, I got warrants for Joe Sinclair's place of employment and his home. He was a reporter for *Out in NYC*. Do you read it?"

"It's not in my usual rotation, no," Larkin said dryly.

"Well, I stopped by their office this morning. His boss confirmed that Joe mostly worked from home, so he didn't keep anything at work." Hackett tucked the warrant back into his pocket. "I thought you might want to join me at his apartment, though. Psychology of place and all that."

"I don't know how he plays into our case, into a relationship with the sender, but he does.*"*

"I would, actually."

"I'm on my way there now. The manager from the landlord's office is supposed to meet me."

Larkin checked his watch: 1:12 p.m.

"Is this not a good time?" Hackett asked, his voice tinged with disappointment.

Larkin sighed a little. "No, it's fine. I have one hour and forty-eight minutes before an evidence pick up is ready downtown."

Hackett was beaming—all sunshine and roses—as they stepped out of the precinct. "Joe's place is on East Sixty-Second. It's only a few blocks, if you fancy a stroll."

"I just had my suit dry-cleaned," Larkin answered, discreetly noting none of the surrounding vehicles were a blue Honda Civic, and he wasn't sure if that gave him more anxiety than not.

Hackett was motioning to a black-and-white parked two spaces away on their left. "I borrowed a cruiser to come into the city. I will warn you, though… it smells a little like Friday night upchuck."

March 10, 2011, Larkin had turned his overheads on, sounded the siren, and deftly wove through late-night traffic in the Grand Central area to catch up with an erratic driver. He followed the Toyota Prius as it had swerved left onto East Forty-Second and cruised down the uptown bus lane before narrowly missing a lamppost, jumping the sidewalk, and then crashing into one of the massive sidewalk pots that, in the summer, would be full of flowers. Larkin and his then-partner had gotten out of their vehicle, approached the Prius driver as he stumbled out from behind the wheel of his totaled car, and who then promptly projectile vomited all over the front of Larkin's uniform.

The only difference was that it had been a Thursday night.

Nose wrinkled, Larkin said, "I'll drive." He led the way across the street to the parallel-parked Audi. Larkin tapped the key fob, the locks releasing with a beep, and opened the door. He slid behind the wheel as Hackett hurried around the back bumper and opened the passenger side.

"Wow. *This* is class," he said as he took a seat. Hackett laughed in that little self-conscious way Larkin had made note of the day before as he drew his seat up a few clicks. "Did you have a giant riding shotgun?"

"Detective Doyle."

"Oh. Ha. Yeah, he's pretty tall, I guess."

Larkin started the car, adjusted the AC, checked his mirrors, and pulled onto the street. "Which avenue."

"Between Second and Third."

At the end of the block, Larkin turned south onto Lexington. Afternoon sun bounced off apartment windows overlooking the avenue, washed-out storefront displays and signs, and refracted off the looming glass high-rises farther downtown. Larkin pulled the sun visor down.

"Can I ask you a personal question?"

Larkin cast a critical look at Hackett.

Seeming to take silence as an indicator of yes, Hackett asked, "Are you autistic?"

Rolling to a stop at the next red light, Larkin looked at Hackett a second time. "No."

"I just got that spicy vibe from you."

"Spicy," Larkin repeated, unblinking.

"Neurospicy."

"You mean neurodivergent."

Another laugh. "Yeah."

Larkin had heard enough watercooler gossip over the years to know how he was perceived by fellow officers. To some, he was weird; to others, socially stunted. He was arrogant, he was unsettling, he was brilliant but strange, he was so many negative facets, and never once had he overheard someone suggest: maybe he's neurodivergent. Not that such diversity didn't come with its own stigmas, its own biases, its own challenges, but if just *one person* in the last ten years on the force had thought to challenge their own preconceived notion of what was "normal" and understand that Larkin was a human being… how different would his career be?

His reputation?

His social circle?

Hackett asked next, "Would you have guessed I have ADHD?"

Larkin looked at the light, pressed down on the gas when it changed, and said mildly, "Yes."

"I think it makes me a pretty good cop, actually," Hackett continued, unperturbed. "When I was still a patrolman, anyway. Juggling different situations at the drop of a hat was great. And I love being a detective, but I guess it's tougher now. Time management is the bane of my existence, especially when it comes to all the paperwork."

"What is your current time-management technique."

"Uh, I don't really have one. I suppose I just raw dog it."

Larkin said, "Try the Pomodoro."

"What's that?"

"The Pomodoro Technique is a low-tech method that's been shown to aid adults with ADHD by allowing for a fixed period of hyperfocus, followed by relaxation as a form of reward."

"How'd you learn about it?"

"I have a psychology degree and don't read *Out in NYC*."

Hackett laughed again.

Larkin turned onto East Sixty-Second and parked the Audi behind a mud-splattered Jeep Wrangler with Jersey plates. He turned off the engine and unbuckled his seat belt.

"I know I shouldn't have asked something so personal to someone with seniority," Hackett spoke up before Larkin could open his door. He looked so young and so uncertain just then. "It's only, I practically idolize you—"

"*Don't*," Larkin warned. "Hero worship locks us in a perpetual cycle of belief that excellence is obtainable in only a select few, and at the cost of our own character, self-worth, and skill set." Larkin studied Hackett as he sunk into the seat. "You said you want to work Cold Cases."

That perked him up again. "More than anything."

"To do so, you must be critical," Larkin said. "But never unkind. You only need to work on the first one."

Hackett smiled from ear-to-ear. He might've been blushing a little too.

Larkin popped the door and climbed out.

The street was busy with the usual foot traffic seen on weekends: Two young guys in their twenties schlepping a love seat down the block like they were trying to save a few bucks on the cost of a moving company, a mom in designer leggings and a matching top—a color Larkin could only describe as Millennial Beige—was pushing a stroller while talking animatedly on the phone, a middle-aged mail carrier sat on a nearby stoop, scrolling on her phone and holding a rechargeable fan that blew dyed black hair crunchy with hairspray away from her face, and a well-dressed, middle-aged man was busy shouting, "Fuck you, fuck you, and fuck you too," to every individual he passed on the sidewalk.

Larkin looked away from the mail carrier and watched the man for a moment, making certain the vitriol wouldn't escalate into some form of physical violence, before he followed Hackett. They came to a stop outside of a six-story, prewar walk-up of white terra cotta and opulent ornamentation in need of a good scrubbing. A man of roughly forty, of medium complexion, with thick black hair, and who probably had a five o'clock shadow at 9:00 a.m., stood on the stoop with a phone to his ear, talking loud and fast.

"—apartment won't be here tomorrow. Hm-hm … Yeah … Yeah, for sure, but listen, I got a guy ready to drop *cash money* right now. Yeah, but look, I told him you were first in line and I gotta honor—" He moved the phone away from his mouth and asked Larkin and Hackett, "Are you the couple here to see 4F?"

Hackett looked all parts delighted with having been mistaken as Larkin's romantic partner. But still, he removed his wallet, flashed his badge, and said with perfect professionalism, "Detective Val Hackett, Brooklyn Homicide. Would you be Marcus Holland?"

Marcus said into the phone, "Think about those high ceilings and the fireplace mantel, and I'll give you a call back in twenty, okay?" He hung up and shook Hackett's hand. "That's me."

Hackett introduced Larkin next and then handed Marcus the search warrant.

"Everything looks to be in order," Marcus concluded after scanning the paperwork. "Come with me." He tapped a code on the panel beside the front door and the locks disengaged with a loud buzz.

Hackett motioned Larkin to go ahead while he took up the rear. They followed Marcus through the vestibule and up the stairs, their steps echoing off the bare walls as they criss-crossed the halls from one staircase to the next, and Larkin noted that even in an upscale neighborhood like Lenox Hill, if you weren't living in a recently built luxury condo, complete with a doorman and concierge, a private Pilates studio, rooftop bar, and whatever the fuck a resident's lounge was, there were going to be missing tiles in floor mosaics and the grout was going to be a little grungy and there wasn't going to be an elevator in this grandfathered building and their dead journalist was going to live on the top floor because the rent was cheaper.

Larkin's thighs were on fire by the time he reached the sixth-floor landing, but the physical exertions that were to blame for his discomfort—

—knees clasped against his flanks, arms wound around his back, those chest-heaving cries for more *as he fucked Doyle into the mattress and relished in the shared delight all night long—*

—that was a haptic memory that could cause some inappropriate scenarios if Larkin wasn't careful with the association relay.

Marcus was winded as he said, "Here it is," approaching the door to 6B.

"Thank God," Hackett murmured at Larkin's back.

Marcus retrieved a ring of keys from his pocket, checking sticker labels on each of them before finding the one he needed. He unlocked the front door, gave it an extra nudge when it resisted in the swollen frame, and then ushered the detectives inside.

Larkin retrieved a pair of latex gloves from his pocket, studying the extremely small and oddly shaped studio as he tugged them on. To his right was the kitchen, recently refurbished, as the chrome appliances and solid white cupboards didn't match the personality of the bathroom just beyond, if the yellow-tiled walls and mint-green pedestal sink were any indicator. To his left was a long and narrow space that curved at the end, lit by one window that looked out over the back of the property. Joe seemed to have been using that area as a living room. A flat-screen television was mounted to the wall and a single armchair, upholstered in a cream color, sat opposite with hardly more than seven feet between. There was a single framed photo on the wall, a black and white of a woman eating spaghetti with a headline reading: Hot Girls Don't Need No Man. It looked like something that'd been bought at an arts and craft store.

In terms of visible belongings… that was it.

Hackett moved around Larkin and looked toward the living room. "It continues around the corner?" he asked, looking to Marcus.

The manager gave him a quizzical look and said, "No. This is it. Real shame to hear about Joe. He was a nice guy."

"How was he as a tenant," Larkin asked, turning to Marcus.

"He was fine," Marcus said with a shrug. "Paid first of the month, every month."

"Have there been any complaints filed against him."

"Nah. Ideal neighbor from what I can tell. So, was he shot or…?"

"We're not at liberty to say," Hackett answered.

"Hope it wasn't a hate crime," Marcus said, but when neither detective went for the dangling bait, he clarified, "Joe was gay, you know."

"We understand," Hackett answered. "How much was he paying for this apartment?"

"Thirty-five a month."

"For *this*?" Hackett squawked, all pretense of professionalism cast aside. "There's not even room for a bed!"

Marcus frowned and pointed to a set of double doors beside the chair. "That's a Murphy bed."

"And this," Larkin asked, more coolly, motioning to the single door beside the hidden bed.

"That's a closet," Marcus answered. The cell in his hand began to ring. He glanced at the caller ID before asking, "Either of you mind if I go downstairs? I've got a showing and—"

Larkin signaled for him to go.

"I'll be on the fourth floor if you need anything." Marcus left the open doorway, answering the call with a loud, "You're outside? I'll be right there."

Hackett moved farther into the living room and said, while motioning like he was pulling the bed down, "Imagine bringing a guy over here—'One sec while I get my bed out.'"

Larkin cracked a smile before turning, walking across the kitchen, and flipping on the bathroom light. He took a look in the medicine cabinet, finding only a tube of toothpaste and brush, floss, deodorant, cologne, an all-in-one lotion—which was mildly horrifying—a razor, nail clippers, and a half-empty box of condoms. No sample or travel-size products that people so often accumulated over time, no medications—prescription or otherwise—or any sort of skincare. Larkin pulled back the curtain on the bathtub, but all that was inside was another all-in-one bottle—this of shampoo, conditioner, and body wash—and a loofah.

He turned the light off, returned to the kitchen, and opened the nearest cupboard. One dinner plate, one bread-and-butter plate, one bowl, one cup. He tried the next cupboard and found a single coffee mug, a pour-over, and a nutribullet with a smoothie cup. Larkin pulled open the drawer beside the empty sink. One knife, spoon, and fork. One wooden spoon, a paring knife, and a set of measuring spoons. In the bottom cabinet, he found more of the same: one pan, one pot, a bag of rice, a box of crackers, a can of beans, and a jug of protein powder. The refrigerator held only a gallon of almond milk, one container of strawberries, another of blueberries, and a prechopped bag of kale. He found two gluten-free burritos in the freezer.

"Must have been laundry day," Hackett said suddenly.

Larkin closed the door on the freezer. "Why do you say that."

"Guy's got nothing to wear," Hackett replied. He was standing in front of the open closet. "A pair of jeans, and… two, three… five polo shirts. Oh, and one white T-shirt."

Larkin moved to join Hackett. He studied the bare bones collection before saying suddenly, "He's a minimalist. A rather extreme one, in fact. They use what are referred to as a capsule wardrobe. The idea is to own as little as possible while still maintaining a high degree of attire variability. He died wearing khakis and a blue polo, so that's two pairs of pants and seven shirts total, which is fourteen different outfits. If you add one sweater and one accessory, then you've got even more options. For some, the idea is to reduce decision paralysis, but the choice of becoming an extreme minimalist can range from trauma to financial to laziness to simply not *wanting* beyond the most basic of necessities."

"Yeah, well, if I paid thirty-five hundred a month for a shoebox six stories up, it'd be a financial choice for me too."

Hackett moved toward the armchair and picked up a slim silver MacBook from its cushion.

Larkin tugged his trousers at the knees before crouching down. He pushed aside the empty bin for dirty laundry and found a padded diploma cover propped against the wall. Inside was a bachelor's degree in journalism from the University of Missouri and two photographs. One was of a young Joe Sinclair in his graduation cap and gown, flanked on either side by an older couple—mother and father perhaps, although they could have been his grandparents—and the other was a candid, interior shot of a hoarder's house. Chaos was stacked nearly to the ceiling, copious piles of trash among the belongings, no discernable path—Larkin could practically smell the room in that picture and he shuddered.

"His laptop is password-protected," Hackett stated.

Larkin stood.

"We can have the lab guys crack it open and see if he's got anything on it to suggest an enemy or—hey, why do you think Joe, specifically, chose the life of self-flagellation?"

"Control," Larkin answered.

"How do you mean?"

Larkin didn't prescribe to the concept of minimalism from an anticonsumerism point of view, but he did understand it from a trauma perspective—the inherent relief in keeping one's personal space visually quiet. He didn't like unnecessary possessions because it was always *one more thing* for his brain to memorize, catalogue, pack into his exhausted long-term memory, and on days where he was so fucking sick and tired of thinking, he'd find himself in a screaming match with his ex-husband over a pine cone that been left on the kitchen counter—the last bit of visual information that'd sent him completely over the edge—only to find out one of Noah's students had given it to him as a gift, and Larkin didn't know that, hadn't intentionally tossed something of sentimental value, but Jesus fucking Christ, it's a pine cone, Noah, and I can't—*I can't*—

Larkin winced, jerked his head, and took a breath. He turned to Hackett, who was watching him curiously, and said in his careful monotone, "I think minimalism this severe might be a trauma response, most likely originating from a time when Joe felt he had little or no control in his life. Typically, cleaning, decluttering, or organizing one's living conditions provides a sense of accomplishment, but for some, their surroundings are almost a physical manifestation of the anxiety or fear they have inside, so removing possessions is, quite literally, akin to tossing out unwanted emotions." Larkin offered the hoarder photograph.

Hackett took it, his face twisting into one of horror. "Holy shit."

"Mental illness in the children of hoarders can manifest in many ways, but one of note is the tendency to purge belongings at an excessive rate. Even a reasonable quantity of possessions can trigger the same stress, anxiety, embarrassment, and fear they grew up with while surrounded by their parent's hoard. Without proper therapy, these individuals can and do become minimalists, not for its aesthetics, but for control of their environment. Having things *just so* gives them that sense of order they didn't have as a child. Unfortunately, it's a Band-Aid for a bigger problem, which is how reasonable minimalism reaches this sort of an extreme."

Hackett's brows were knitted together. "Why would he keep this picture, though?"

"It's a fear tactic. Something he used as a reminder to keep himself in check."

"Where was it?"

"Tucked inside his unframed diploma." Larkin considered his own words for a moment.

"What?" Hackett asked into the sudden silence.

"How do we use psychology of place on one such as this."

Hackett snorted and shrugged.

"I told you where I found that photo."

"Inside his diploma."

"His *unframed* diploma," Larkin corrected. "That, in and of itself, is not strange. But in an apartment with no personal touches, no mementos, where he's one duffel bag away from being able to up and leave, the only intimate belonging was found on the floor, behind the laundry bin, which was used to store a photograph that brings him stress and shame. There's a second photo in the diploma, Joe at his graduation with who I suspect are his later-in-life parents." Larkin rested his hands on his hips and finished, "His education was clearly something he was proud of. He's so far resisted divesting himself of that diploma and picture of himself all smiles in his cap and gown, but at the same time, he's treating it as a source of humiliation."

Hackett was staring at Larkin with that same awestruck expression as yesterday before seemingly catching himself and shaking it off. He said, "You can be happy with your education and still be disillusioned with where it leads you. Like, uh… oh, say you go to school to study acting. You do great, learn a lot, graduate, but end up slinging lattes in SoHo and getting bit parts in TV shows when you imagined being an A-list star."

Larkin raised a brow. "That's rather insightful."

"Yeah?"

"Did my lieutenant tell you about Joe Sinclair's final movements."

"He told me that Joe's been trying to get a tell-all interview with you," Hackett answered. "That he wasn't taking no for an answer."

"Does that sound like the sort of story a man who works for *Out in NYC* would spend his time covering." Larkin could practically see the light behind Hackett's eyes turn on.

"Now that you mention it—not really. I think the most thought-provoking article I've seen them publish was in support of a bi celeb who was getting dragged for their het-presenting relationship. Usually it's porn-star gossip and reviews of new underwear lines."

"I believe Joe had aspirations of those beyond that of *Out in NYC*," Larkin said. "I suspect he would have used an interview with me as a way of advancing into a more… heavy-hitting career in journalism." At that, Larkin went to the double doors that hid the Murphy bed, grabbed the handles, pulled them wide open, and before he could censor himself, said, "*Jesus Christ.*"

Pinned across the inside of both doors were the makings of a Hollywood murder wall, complete with dozens of news clippings, crisscrossing red strings, and prominently displayed throughout, photographs of Everett Larkin.

CHAPTER SIXTEEN

Larkin stepped off the elevator at the fifth floor of One Police Plaza with a box in both hands and a case file balanced atop. He strode down the long hall toward the most western end, sidestepping two detectives who'd decided the middle of the corridor was an ideal place for a conversation. Their voices went from full volume to a sudden hush, one whispering, "That's the Grim Reaper," and the other answering, "I heard he's playing patty-cake with the doodle squad." Larkin stopped, turned, and stared.

Abbott and Costello scurried into their respective offices.

Larkin rolled his eyes and continued down the hall, only to be stopped a second time when he was less than six feet from Doyle's closed door.

"Hey! Larkin!"

Larkin backtracked a few steps and peered through the partially open door of Senior Artist Bailey's office. "Good afternoon."

Bailey motioned him inside with a friendly wave.

Larkin glanced a final time in the direction of Doyle's office.

"Don't worry, he's not going anywhere," Bailey said.

Larkin used the box to push open the door the rest of the way before parking himself in the threshold, not so subtly suggesting he had other places to be and couldn't stay. "It wasn't my intention to interrupt Doyle during an interview—"

"Oh, he's not working on a composite sketch," Bailey answered. He sat behind his desk, hands on the back of his head, and a smile somewhere under that bushy Selleck mustache. He wore a wide polyester tie of muddy greens, sickly yellows, and rusty reds that'd been the height of men's fashion sometime in the '80s. "Do you know what vein pattern recognition is?"

"I understand it as a concept," Larkin answered.

"It's the practice of matching veins in an extremity to their corresponding individual," Bailey answered. "They're as unique as a fingerprint, did you know that? When it comes to child exploitation, sometimes it's all we've got to work with."

"A… *vein*?" Larkin asked, now confused.

Bailey lowered his hands. He drummed his messy desktop idly. "Like in a forearm or the back of the hand—something that might be in a video or photograph. Scumbags like that, they're not big on showing their faces. We don't have a federal budget or access to more state-of-the-art methods, but we've got Doyle. He's been tinkering with image-enhancement techniques for the last year."

"How does it work," Larkin asked.

Bailey pursed his lips, and his mustache wriggled like it was alive. "I know you put an RGB image into grayscale and finagle the contrast levels to such a degree that veins usually invisible to the camera will *become* visible. It's not foolproof, and it's pretty technical, but Doyle understands all those doodads a lot more than me or Loving does."

"That's fascinating," Larkin answered, realizing now the method Doyle had used for making "Charlotte Laura Fuller" once again visible on their brooch had been repurposed from his trial and error at combating a far more insidious crime.

Bailey smiled, a combination of both pride and indulgence. "Yeah, and you know him… always taking the cases with kids. I don't know how he stomachs it, to be honest. But they trust him and SVU likes him. I don't get in the way of that relationship."

"Yes. Well…." Larkin allowed his gaze to briefly wander as he considered his choice of words. He'd been inside Bailey's office only once before—on March 30, when he'd been dropping off Andrew Gorman's skull casting for a facial reconstruction—and the room hadn't changed much. It was smaller than Doyle's, with no supply closet, and instead of a flat work surface like where Doyle did his sculpting, Bailey had a large office desk laden with paperwork.

He did have a drafting desk, though, and that entire section of the room looked a bit like a bomb had gone off in an art supply store. Sketchpads lay open, loose papers with half-finished composites and warm-up exercises were scattered about, heaps of expensive pencils and messy charcoal bits appeared to have no permanent home, and by the looks of paintbrushes sticking out from among piles of tracing paper and micron pens mixed in with plastic bags of clay, had never once been organized.

A diploma was hung crookedly on the wall behind Bailey's desk—Parsons School of Design—with a massive corkboard taking up the rest of the available real estate. Unlike Doyle's, which displayed drawings given by the child victims he worked with, Bailey's board was burdened with newspaper clippings going back a decade, if not more, praising the successful arrests based on the work of the Forensic Artists Unit.

Looking at Bailey again, Larkin concluded simply, "Doyle is a very good man."

"He sure sets the standard, doesn't he?" Bailey pointed at the box in Larkin's arms. "That your refrigerated lady case?"

"No." But then Larkin added more tactfully, "It's related."

"Did you want to leave it here?"

"I'd rather drop it off with Doyle. I won't stay."

Bailey waved a hand. "He's been at it nearly… what… three hours? I'm sure he's close to finishing. But hey, thanks for sending him back downtown for this. I know it's not ideal—"

"Crime never is."

Bailey chuckled. He shifted forward in his chair and rested his elbows on the desk, papers crinkling under the weight. He said, voice low, "Try not to get him killed, hmm? I still plan to be living *la vida loca* when I hit sixty, and Doyle's going to be promoted to Senior Artist when I tap out."

Larkin raised both brows. "Does he know."

"Not yet. Let's keep it that way for a while longer, okay?"

"I understand."

Bailey winked and gave Larkin a finger-gun salute.

Larkin took a step backward, more than ready to make himself scarce before Bailey could meander on to another topic, but his eye caught the corkboard a second time, and he stared at a muddy photograph of a young skinny cop with a familiar mustache, who smiled awkwardly for the camera while holding up a piece of paper—its details lost in the poor quality of the newsprint. Larkin inclined his head and asked, "Is that you."

Bailey spun in his chair. He pointed and said, "Oh, that? What gave it away?" He grinned at Larkin while stroking his mustache. "Yeah, that was about a thousand years ago. Look at me. I was still in uniform."

"What're you displaying."

"My very first composite sketch. Back then, the detectives, they'd just ask around, 'Hey! Can any of you guys draw?'

Well, I was fresh outta art school, dead broke—go figure—and joined the ranks for the steady paycheck. One night, they came around saying, 'We need a composite!' and drawing a suspect was a hell of a lot more up my alley than responding to domestics at 2:00 a.m., so I said, 'Yeah, I'll do it.' Next thing you know, my fate's been sealed."

"Are you wearing a hip holster."

Bailey laughed. "Sure am. My trusty six-shooter."

Larkin's gaze darted to Bailey with renewed interest. "You used a revolver."

"Standard issue back then. When did we transition to 9mm… '93? '94? Something like that. All us old-timers had to go to the range and get recertified." Bailey waved a hand and concluded, "I don't miss it. I mean, I've got a service weapon, but I prefer not having to wear it, thank you very much."

"Doyle too," Larkin commented, almost automatically.

"Smart man."

Larkin looked down at his box, offered Bailey a curt goodbye, and left the threshold. He went to Doyle's office, the last door on the left, and opened it. He stepped partially inside and looked toward the worktable.

Doyle sat perched on a stool with his back to the door, his left hand raised up and balled into a fist, temple leaning against it. His laptop was open, tablet out, and stylus working in his right hand. Loud and angry music bled from his cheap earbuds.

Larkin slipped inside, crossed the room, and approached Doyle from the left side. He noted several discarded candy wrappers on the tabletop and a Post-it stuck to a section of the computer screen, which didn't make sense for about three seconds, and then Larkin realized what Doyle was doing— understood that he was offering a modicum of respect for the underage victim by covering their young body while he worked on identifying the adult who had violated them in this image they shared.

Doyle must have sensed he was no longer alone. He raised his head, glanced to his left, then quickly tugged his earbuds free. "Evie?"

"Sorry." Larkin watched Doyle instinctively close the laptop, the viewing of such abuse an atonement he'd been conditioned to believe—like so many victims were—was his alone to make. Larkin slid the box onto the table. "I didn't intend to drop in unannounced, but I was just downstairs."

Doyle nudged the box to one side, revealing an ancient case number. He asked, "Were you harassing the property clerk?"

"I called in advance," Larkin clarified.

Doyle's infectious smile didn't quite reach his eyes just then.

Larkin wanted to ask why—why do you insist on working the cases *no one* can, the cases that break hearts and blacken souls and destroy careers, why, Ira, won't you believe me when I say it wasn't your fault, but you use those very words to comfort the children who come through this office like a revolving door's been installed, why do you freely give so much of yourself that you leave nothing for *you*?

But he couldn't ask any of that.

Because he already knew the answer.

And acknowledging Doyle's shame, calling it out, dragging it into the light before he was ready, would only put a distance between them that Larkin wasn't sure they'd be able to recover from.

So he said, "Bailey told me you're working on vein pattern recognition techniques."

Doyle instinctively looked at the laptop.

"He explained the process—tried to, anyway—but I understand how you got the idea for restoring the engraving in the brooch, now."

Doyle got to his feet. "Lucky shot, is all." He stretched his arms overhead and cracked something in his back. "What's the box? Did you find Barbara's homicide case?"

Larkin picked up the old file. "Found it," he confirmed.

"Really?"

"I've had a very productive afternoon. I also checked out Joe's apartment with Hackett."

"How'd that go?"

Larkin removed his cell, opened the images stored on the Cloud, and then offered it to Doyle. "I'll spare you the nitty-gritty psychoanalysis: Joe despised his job as an entertainment reporter and was actively working on a story that would land him a position in big boy journalism—"

"What in the *CSI: Miami* is this?" Doyle interrupted. He swiped with his thumb, scrolling through photos taken of the murder wall found in the closet with the Murphy bed. "Am I supposed to think Joe is a serial killer?"

"No. But what if he was getting help from an aphid."

Doyle's thumb hovered over the screen. He glanced up, his tangled brown hair partially obscuring his eyes. "Joe was in touch with Worth?"

"I think so."

Doyle set the phone on the tabletop. "Give it to me straight, Butch."

"The best I can do is gay and marginally effeminate." Larkin smiled when Doyle abruptly laughed. He watched the last of the tension ease from Doyle, and he took on that more relaxed, big cat posture. "This morning, we were in agreement that Worth doesn't limit who he works with."

"Right."

"What if it were more than just the most vile of society."

"Please, Mr. Worth, help me land a story that'll put me on the staff of the *Times*, the *Journal*, the *Tribune*?"

"Why not," Larkin asked. "So long as Worth gets his dues."

Doyle turned, leaned his backside against the table, and absently stroked the stubble along his jaw as he considered Larkin's suggestion.

Larkin continued. "Joe's been relentlessly working the queer officer angle for months. His obsession with this specific theme goes beyond having a kink for law enforcement. But for as persistent as he was, Joe was also terribly unfocused—almost like he didn't know *who* the subject was."

Doyle twisted, picked up Larkin's phone again, and studied the photos of the murder wall. There had been countless newspaper clippings and printed online articles about major crimes happening throughout the city over the last half a decade, which were connected by red strings to different photographed individuals, their likenesses sourced from either the internet or candid snapshots taken without their knowing. In Larkin's case, there were photos of him from years ago, still in uniform and featured in an article about diversity hiring, as well as more up-to-date images clipped from coverage of his recent cases. It'd become clear where Joe's energy had been redirected.

"These other people on the wall," Doyle started. "Might they be the other officers Joe tried interviewing?"

"Based on the content of the pinned articles surrounding them, yes. Hackett is still with CSU at the apartment, and he'll make sure they cross-check identities." Larkin moved around to Doyle's side, leaned close, and swiped through a few of the pictures before stopping on a cluster of Post-its scribbled in what was probably Joe's hand. "He was tracking my case history."

Larkin swiped to the next picture—that of a sheet of unlined white paper, creased vertically and horizontally, unremarkable penmanship reading: *There's a legacy in queers-in-blue.* He explained, "During the subway incident, Noel Hernandez received an anonymous tip with just enough information for him to make a choice regarding the man who'd murdered his childhood best friend. I think this is the same thing—a suggested starting point for a down-and-out reporter looking to make a lasting name for himself." Larkin met Doyle's gaze and added, "It just took Joe a while to figure out *which* queer in blue he was supposed to write about."

Doyle gave Larkin the phone, saying, "Joe called you before we arrested Regmore."

"Correct."

"That suggests Worth knew about our investigation even earlier than suspected."

Larkin nodded while pocketing his cell. He returned to the left side of the table, shrugging out of his suit coat and resting it beside the evidence box.

"*Shit*...." Doyle turned around and braced his hands on the table. "Do you think Worth is responsible for Joe's murder?"

"I find it unlikely that Joe's usefulness had already run its course. After all, he hadn't yet written a story about me. I don't expect to find much on his laptop beyond notes, either. What I think is more likely is his sleuthing went noticed by someone else who perhaps deemed him in the way or a danger to their operation."

"Mr. Honda Civic," Doyle concluded.

Larkin picked up the case file a second time and said, "May I update you on the original 1982 homicide."

"Should I sit down?"

"You should remain standing. I like looking at you."

That won Larkin a mile-wide smile.

"Detective Ralph Noonan of Homicide, whether through a general disregard for human life, gross incompetence, struggling against an underfunded department still reeling from the fiscal crisis of the 1970s, or all of the above, did a piss-poor job in the investigation of Barbara's murder," Larkin began. "He asked no clarifying details of the Hotel Cavalier staff. When overseeing the crime scene, he didn't demand the collection of trace evidence. He didn't second-guess the ME's decision to not perform an autopsy. The Kitten Klub, where Barbara worked, was on the very same block as the hotel, but from his notes, there's no indication he bothered checking the place out. He makes note of having questioned women working West Forty-Third that night—"

"They wouldn't have said anything," Doyle interjected.

"You're correct. He did record the identity of two sex workers he spoke to: Sharon King, deceased since 1991, and Bridget Cohen—"

"Who?"

Larkin paused. "What."

Doyle had such an… *odd* expression just then. An amalgamation of so many juxtaposing emotions that Larkin couldn't interpret his facial grammar.

Doyle repeated, "Who? Who did you say?"

A misplaced sensation of self-doubt made Larkin open the file and double-check what he already knew. "Bridget Cohen. She lives in—"

Doyle moved forward and snatched the folder from Larkin's hands with uncharacteristic aggression. He quickly went through the yellowed reports and DD5s, coming to a brief stop at the first rap sheet, then lifted the page so vigorously to view the next that it tore.

Larkin had known Ira Oisín Doyle for one hundred and three days, had been steadily peeling away the layers of misinterpretation and self-preservation to see beyond the veil to who the man *really* was, only to conclude Doyle truly was everything he presented himself to be.

He was gentleness.

He was love.

He was hope.

He was *jubilant up to the heavens*.

He was *depression unto death*.

He was fragile.

He was wounded.

And he was so, *so* angry inside.

For one hundred and three days, Larkin had been finding tiny shards of Doyle's soul everywhere he went, had been collecting them, putting together those fragments to reveal unprecedented guilt and betrayal and shame, lacquering their edges together with gold because Larkin just wanted Doyle to see, to *understand*, that he was still beautiful, that he deserved to be whole, that he had done nothing to warrant being shattered into these millions of little pieces.

Larkin wanted his partner to know only love.

Yet he had somehow, inadvertently, just broken Doyle's heart.

"Ira?"

Doyle looked up from the folder. He was the epitome of picturesque despair. "I think I have to recuse myself from this case."

"What?"

And like a man drowning, Doyle said, "Bridget Cohen is my mother."

CHAPTER SEVENTEEN

Doyle wiped his cheek with the heel of his hand. He turned his back to Larkin and took a few steps before his shoulders shuddered, hunched, the same hand came up to his mouth, and he dropped into a squat.

Doyle began to cry.

First a crack, a tear, then a fissure opened, and everything ugly poured out of him in one great big heartbreaking sob.

Larkin's immediate panic kept him frozen on the spot. Doyle's love language was touch. He craved physical affection. Hugs, kisses, fingertips following a path pebbled with gooseflesh. He wanted it when he was awake, when he was falling asleep, after a long day, a hard day, a good day, and he freely offered that affection in return—even when he must have known Larkin would turn it down—because Doyle's love language was touch, and his hug meant: *I'm here.*

But Larkin didn't move.

Because this wasn't a long day or a hard day. This was a wound Doyle had been inflicted with at too young an age, a wound that had been poisoning him for decades, and now it'd ruptured, and Larkin didn't know what to do. Doyle had seen him at some of his worst and weakest moments. He'd seen

Larkin's suicide ideation, the near overdose, the out-of-control addiction. He'd seen Larkin's tics when compulsions flared into overdrive, and he'd seen violent reactions to memories relived. But what had Larkin seen of Doyle?

A man who weaponized his own empathy.

Who atoned for the sins of others.

Who was ashamed of his inner child.

Larkin had only ever seen a man who knew how to heal everyone but himself.

Who betrayed your trust and broke your heart. Who made such a gentle man so angry inside.

Your mother.

Spurred into motion, Larkin first went to the door, shutting and then locking it, before cautiously approaching his partner. Doyle was still in a low crouch, the manila folder crushed between his chest and arms. Larkin got down on one knee. He tried to reach for the file, to simply get it out of the way, but Doyle tightened his hold, needing something, anything, to protect him as his world crumbled.

Larkin went back to the table and returned with his coat. Carefully, he draped it over Doyle's shoulders, waited, and then breathed a sigh of considerable relief as Doyle's gut-wrenching sobs began to wane. Doyle slowly dropped to the floor, crossed his legs, and pulled the coat around to his chest, discarding the file in the process, which Larkin quickly moved out of sight. Taking a seat on the floor beside him, Larkin watched Doyle bury his face into the coat.

His shoulders shook. He was still crying.

"I lie awake and try to pinpoint the exact moment that our trajectories intertwined," Larkin began. "Surely it's something less than fate but more than chance. But I end up somewhere around the Big Bang and realize the thought is too enormous. It's an existential crisis." He was thoughtful for a moment before continuing. "You are everything quiet and beautiful in this world. You're a field of sunflowers and the iridescence on a soap bubble. You're sunlight refracting on water and fog settled deep in a valley.

"I love you more than you'll ever really understand. And I've come to accept that my difficulty in articulating these emotions might not be the fault of my TBI, but is instead because this love is ineffable. For me, you transcend words— you exist in a place of nature and emotion."

Doyle lowered the suit coat. It was spotted with tear stains. His mouth trembled, but the crying had come to a slow and uneasy rest.

Larkin said, "For the first time in eighteen years, I've been able to associate death not with guilt, but with love. Because of you. And if an old dog like me can still learn new tricks, then someday you'll see yourself the way I see you. You'll see you've become the adult you needed as a child. And the day you believe it is the day you begin healing."

Doyle didn't move, didn't speak.

Larkin hesitantly asked, "Do you want a hug."

Doyle nodded without looking up.

Larkin moved onto one knee and loosely wrapped his arms around Doyle's shoulders, but then Doyle pulled him closer—gripped him so tight around the waist that Larkin didn't think a pry bar could separate them—so he pressed Doyle's head to his chest and stroked the mess of dark hair.

"She worked at the Kitten Klub," Doyle murmured.

Larkin wanted to say, *I know*.

"I don't—" Doyle cleared his throat. "I don't know who my father is."

Larkin wanted to shout, *I know*.

"Bridget had a lot of issues, and she attracted the wrong kind of men. When Grandma found out about the last guy and what he—" Doyle pushed out of Larkin's hold while shaking his head. He was trying so hard to keep his anger tucked away, out of sight, but it'd finally been shown the light after decades of darkness, and it couldn't escape fast enough. "I was *nine*."

Larkin wanted to scream, *I know*.

Doyle wiped a few more tears from his face—a product not of sadness, but of liberated rage—and said, "It's been thirty years and she's never reached out, never once asked how I was doing. She knows my name—she gave it to me. It's *Ira Doyle*." He finally looked at Larkin, and the brightness in Doyle's eyes was like the spark on a long, long fuse having finally reached a bundle of dynamite. "Despite everything, I have two degrees. I have a home, a career. I was a dad." Doyle flinched at his own words before amending with a quiet intensity, "I was a *good* dad. I did everything no one in my family could, and I—I just want someone to be proud of me."

Larkin didn't hate most people. He fervently disliked them and rarely kept that truth to himself, but to loathe, abhor, utterly detest another human being? He saved such sentiments for the truly evil among us. But to see Doyle, who was so kind and so tender, who rivaled the holiness of those saints of yore, reduced to such crippling heartache—there was no other way for Larkin to describe how he felt toward Bridget Cohen.

He hated her.

Doyle shook his head and expelled a painful sigh. "All my life, I've felt like a falling tree."

Larkin narrowed his eyes and said, "Berkeley's philosophy is garbage. He argues that only the mind exists. If what we perceive is only an idea—and we perceive with our physical senses—then aren't our senses only an idea. And if our physical self is an idea, then that would imply our ideas are only ideas. It's *reductio ad absurdum*. *I* hear you."

Doyle met Larkin's steady stare.

Larkin got to his feet. He held out both hands and pulled Doyle to stand in one smooth motion. "*I* see you," he continued, seeking out the familiar callus on Doyle's ring finger—years of holding not a pistol, but a pencil—and rubbed the pad of his thumb over the spot. "And *I* am so proud of you, Ira."

Doyle's chin quivered. He didn't say anything.

Larkin kissed the back of Doyle's hand before letting go. He stepped away just long enough to collect a box of ULINE tissues from the shelf behind the drafting desk. Doyle was setting the now-wrinkled coat aside and leaning back against the table, arms tightly crossed. Larkin offered the box.

Doyle took a few tissues—they tore, of course, but that was to be expected from the money-saving brand the department opted for. He wadded the one-ply mess into a ball and wiped his eyes and nose. He drew in a breath—the steadiest so far—and crossed his arms again, not quite hugging himself, but almost. "Are you going to speak with Bridget?"

"Yes," Larkin answered, intently watching Doyle for a reaction.

But all that hurt and all that sadness and all that anger—it'd whipped through Doyle like a tornado without a warning, and he looked absolutely spent. "Cohen isn't her real name" was all he said before shrugging a little. "I mean, it is, but she didn't marry."

"Ghosting was a form of identity theft, back in the day."

Larkin did his best to soften his tone, to speak not as a cop, but as a partner. "Why did she change it."

"I don't know. If she wanted to distance herself from the neighborhood, or from Grandma, maybe, that could've been why." He spared Larkin a sideways glance before adding, "They didn't have a great relationship."

"What about Detective Noonan."

"What about him?"

"Noonan knew her—named her in his report."

Doyle did a sort of shoulder-shrug-headshake.

"Bridget's arrests prior to October of '82 were made by Vice. Noonan worked Homicide."

"Maybe he transferred departments," Doyle suggested. "Like Charlie Stolle did."

Larkin had his doubts, but he said nothing as he crossed in front of Doyle, scooped up the discarded folder from the floor, and made his way around the far side of the table—providing a sort of buffer between Doyle and the explosive contents therein.

"They could've known each other," Doyle said. He turned and set his hands on the tabletop before leaning forward a little. "They would've known each other," he corrected. "Bridget and Barbara."

"That's what I hope," Larkin agreed. He set the folder beside the unopened evidence box. "If we factor in location— the Hudson—and historical context—the toothpick representative of Hell's Kitchen longshoremen—then Wagner's homicide very much has the trappings of a mob killing. We might be looking for a former Westie, or perhaps an old associate. And the mourning jewelry has led us all the way back to Barbara again, who worked at the same club as your mother—who was also from Hell's Kitchen, yes."

Doyle nodded.

"Who Barbara really was," Larkin said, "that's where the final clue lies. And the only person alive, the only person who might have that answer, is Bridget Cohen," he finished, tapping the folder.

Doyle was quiet again.

"Tell me what you're thinking."

"I'm thinking… how terrible it is that you hold me in such high regard," Doyle answered. He ran his hand over his closed laptop—back and forth, back and forth—not looking up. "Because I don't care who took out a serial killer—I really don't. And because I don't give a fuck what my mother might contribute to the investigation. I don't want to see her or hear her or—" Doyle's hand stilled. "I want you to choose me over this case, but I know you won't and I hate that I'm pitting you against your job." Doyle finally looked up. "I'm not a good person—"

"You're *my* person," Larkin interrupted, like the brutal honesty of Doyle's words hadn't just hit him so hard in the chest that they could've formed a crater. "And that makes you perfect." He flipped the file open and sifted through the yellowed, curled pages. He found the document associated with Bridget Cohen. "I want to solve this case," he confirmed. "But I believe my first and most important job is loving you."

"What're you—"

Larkin raised the paperwork and promptly tore it in two.

"*Evie!*" Doyle dashed around the table.

Larkin held the report out of reach and said, "I told you that I would kill for you, Ira. That wasn't an exaggeration. I will *always* choose you."

"You can't destroy evidence," Doyle protested, grabbing for it a second time. "Come on—no, no, I've changed my mind. I've changed my mind, Evie!"

Larkin narrowed his eyes, cocking his head in uncertainty.

Doyle quickly snatched the report on the third try.

He looked at the torn pieces.

He looked back at Larkin.

And maybe Doyle understood then just how much power he had in their relationship, because he wrapped his arms around Larkin's shoulders and didn't let go for a very long time.

Bridget Cohen's rap sheet lay to one side on the worktable, mended together with three strips of Scotch tape.

Doyle lifted the lid on the evidence box before saying without his usual humor, "Smells like Reaganomics and rock 'n' roll."

Larkin snapped his latex gloves on. He removed a paper bag, read the tag, and said, "Gym bag."

Doyle took out the next and read, "Clothes." He reached inside it and removed a skimpy top that appeared to have been cut from the same crape material they'd seen of the costumes Phyllis had kept in a vacuum-sealed bag. "Fabric is nineteenth century," Doyle murmured, studying the handiwork closely. "I'd say it's a visual match to the other upcycled pieces." He tucked it back into the evidence bag.

Larkin retrieved a handful of crime scene photos next. He sifted through them in quick succession, but even a flipbook of the past couldn't reanimate the sad, half-naked body on the mattress. He dropped them to the tabletop and reached for the last bag—this a pair of blue satin pumps in size six. Larkin made a *tsk* sound.

"Looking for something in particular?" Doyle asked. He reached across the table and pulled free an empty, red nylon duffel from one of the paper bags.

"Something concrete." Larkin gestured at the evidence before them. "The circumstantial evidence is good: We've one hundred percent linked the mourning clothes from Barbara Fuller's homicide case to Esther Haycox's missing person report, proving they are, in fact, the same person."

Doyle leaned to one side, picked up his cell from the tabletop, turned on the flashlight app, and used it to illuminate the inside of the duffel.

Larkin continued. "But the jewelry has only been linked to her via the surname, and there are thousands of people in the United States with the name Fuller. I don't like such a critical clue standing on unsure ground in a courtroom setting. I want tangible proof that the brooch found on Wagner once belonged—what is that."

Doyle was pinching something tiny between his thumb and index finger. He set his phone aside and dropped the item into his gloved palm, rolling it this way and that. "It's a seed pearl."

Larkin moved to the edge of the table to stand beside Doyle. "That was inside the gym bag."

"Stuck in the lining," Doyle confirmed.

"Where's the brooch."

"On the shelf—behind my desk," Doyle said, pointing with his free hand.

Larkin spun on his heel, strode across the room, and collected the plastic evidence bag. He returned to the table, removed the brooch, and handed it over.

Doyle accepted it and, while squinting, tried fitting the pearl back into place. One setting was too big, the second too small, but the third— "Bingo."

"This jewelry belonged to Barbara."

"Yeah."

"She's the cold case link that'll solve Wagner's murder."

"Yeah."

"We have to interview Bridget."

And Doyle said, very quietly, "Yeah."

CHAPTER EIGHTEEN

The corner bodega on 172nd and Broadway had sun-faded posters in the windows, complete with clipart images of household staples, proclaiming: EMBUTIDOS Y MAS! FRUTAS Y VEGETALES! JUGOS, AGUA Y MAS! ACEPTAMOS EBT Y CREDIT CARD! The front door was propped open with a brick, and a Spanish radio station—baseball commentary, Larkin was fairly certain—played loud enough for passersby to get the latest updates. Overhead were four stories of apartments, units whirring away in some of the windows, while others were open, curtains limp, tenants hoping for the same breeze the bodega owner seemed to be waiting on to cool the baking neighborhood a few degrees. Halfway down the block, a dozen people waited at a bus stop, shading their eyes or fanning themselves, and right underneath FRUTAS Y VEGETALES! a middle-aged man with a potbelly had set up a folding card table and appeared to be selling area rugs—ten dollars each or two for fifteen.

Larkin checked his watch.

5:41 p.m.

"Evie."

Larkin turned around.

Doyle was a few feet away, leaning against the passenger side of the Audi and hugging himself. "I feel like I'm going to be sick."

Larkin quickly returned to the car. He took Doyle's forearm and pulled him away, enough to open the door, then said, "Sit down." He put a hand on Doyle's head, gently guiding him into the seat, and once his partner had one leg in the footwell and the other on the curb, Larkin reached over him, opened the center console, and collected a water bottle from within. He cracked the top off and handed it to Doyle, and even though it wasn't cold—in fact, was probably a little too warm—he downed half of it in one long swallow.

Larkin tugged his trousers at the knees before crouching. He took Doyle's free hand, gave him a reassuring squeeze, and even though it was too hot for skin-on-skin—Doyle's hand was uncomfortably clammy—Larkin didn't let go.

"I can't do this." Doyle tucked the bottle between his legs before pulling his sunglasses back to rest on his head. His eyes were dry, but he brushed his cheeks anyway. "I'm sorry."

Larkin moved into a stoop so that he could press his forehead to Doyle's. He asked, voice low, "Do you remember what you said, when you were the one standing here, in the rain, pacifying a heartbroken drug addict who just wanted to feel alive again. You said, 'I don't want you to be sorry. I want you to be okay.'" Larkin crouched again so he could look at Doyle properly. "You're so good with the living. You're able to read their hearts when I have to read their faces. I have to empathize in a way that leaves me vulnerable to negative associations—something I think you know, because you've been shielding me from outrageous fortune since we began working together. But a partnership means we both carry those burdens."

Doyle tightened his hold on Larkin's hand.

"I promised you, when you were ready, that I would listen. And now I hear you telling me you're at your limit, so I want you to stay in the car—"

"What?" Doyle interjected.

Larkin arched one eyebrow.

"I can't let you do the interview alone," Doyle said, but there wasn't any fight in his voice.

"Why."

"She's *my* mother."

"I hesitate to credit her with anything beyond birthing you, Ira." Larkin fished his keys from his pocket and pushed them into Doyle's hand. "Your selflessness is beautiful, dear, but I need you to put yourself first. Just this once."

Doyle tightened his hold on the set of keys.

"Please."

He finally nodded once and whispered, "All right."

Larkin leaned in, kissed Doyle, then straightened and moved onto the sidewalk. He headed toward the apartment entrance on the street side and only looked back once to confirm Doyle was still in the car. Larkin stepped through the unlocked front door and into the vestibule. He considered the intercom beside the wall of mailboxes. He had Bridget's apartment number, thanks to DMV records, but experience had taught him that when dealing with a witness who had a long (and legitimate) history of distrust when it came to law enforcement, it was ideal to introduce yourself face-to-face. You only had one chance at that first impression.

The vestibule door was suddenly wrenched open, and a little girl, no older than five or six, wearing a cartoonishly pink princess dress and complete with a plastic crown atop her head, didn't even spare Larkin a glance as she ran past and out onto the sidewalk. He automatically put a hand on the heavy vestibule door, holding it as the girl's mother maneuvered a stroller through the tight threshold while calling after her in Spanish. The mother gave Larkin one of those subtle New York nods that indicated appreciation without the need to exchange words, then went out the front door, which her daughter thankfully came back to hold open.

Larkin slipped inside after that.

The building felt a bit like Doyle's—a little worn, a little frayed, but well lived-in. A century of memories, of experiences, of people, all coming and going, hoping and dreaming, existing and loving right up until Death rang the bell and told them it was time but not to worry—he'd be there to see them off. Larkin took the stairs that dipped a little in the middle all the way up to the top floor, the still air markedly warmer. He approached the door to 4D and listened.

Someone was home.

He could hear the squeak of swollen wood—a dresser drawer being yanked open, maybe—followed by the loud ping of something being dropped on the hardwood floor.

"I want you to choose me over this case, but I know you won't."

Larkin winced and jerked his head to one side, like he'd been slapped.

He could walk away.

Right now.

He could turn around, go downstairs, get in the car, and however their investigation played out, Bridget Cohen would not be a central figure.

Except when he *had* chosen Doyle, Doyle told him no, and Larkin's keen insight into the inner mechanics of neurotypical individuals had failed to identify which request was the *real* one.

Maybe it was both.

Or neither.

Larkin put a hand to his stomach as it gave a nauseous flutter.

Time and again, Doyle reminded him that he didn't exist in a binary, that Larkin was as complex and human as the rest of the population, but even if that were true, he seemed to have no idea how to navigate such gray nuance without making Doyle's hurt even more unbearable.

The dead bolt turned, a chain lock disengaged, and the door suddenly swung open, catching Larkin off guard.

She looked to be about sixty hard years, was petite in both build and height, and had to look up at Larkin. She wore a pair of navy slacks and a light blue top with a USPS emblem on the breast. She had a small beauty mark above her lip and thick, dark brown hair with a streak of steel gray along one side, pulled back into a no-nonsense ponytail that showed off split ends in need of trimming. She smelled of one too many spritzes of cheap floral perfume and wore eyeliner on only one eye. She held the pencil and a tube of mascara in her hand. Her brown eyes were devastatingly pretty, but her stare was sharp, dangerous, that of an individual who'd lived through New York's darkest chapter and still bore its scars.

"I knew I heard someone out here. Who're you?" she asked, reaching into the collar of the top and snapping a bra strap into place.

"Are you Bridget Cohen," Larkin asked.

"Yes. *Who're you?*"

He reached for his badge and held it up. "My name is Everett Larkin. I'm a detective with the NYPD—"

Bridget slammed the door.

Larkin tucked the badge away, considered for a long minute, then knocked. He called through the door, "Ms. Cohen, I'm a detective with the Cold Case Squad. I'm investigating a murder from 1982, and I'm here because you're the only lead I have." Larkin waited. He could sense Bridget still standing at the door, listening, and continued. "She worked at the Kitten Klub on Broadway, and on the night of October 2, 1982, she was murdered at the Hotel Cavalier. You might have known her by the name of Esther Haycox."

She was watching him through the peephole now, Larkin knew it. He was quiet, still, his face a carefully composed neutral belying the anxiety swelling inside. He didn't want to come back here, wait in this boiling hallway, knock on this door. Larkin couldn't bear having to tell Doyle his attempt to speak with Bridget was mirroring the difficult experience he'd had with Camila Garcia and would require he return again and again and again.

The door opened a crack.

Bridget studied Larkin critically. "Esther wasn't her name."

"Was it Barbara Fuller."

Bridget stepped back. She held the door open, took Larkin in from head to toe, then inclined her head to one side.

Larkin entered the apartment.

It was a studio, three hundred square feet at best, with two windows overlooking the avenue. The right window, near the foot of the twin-size bed, was open. A sad-looking cardboard box with a Home Depot decal sat in front of it, an off-white box fan propped on top and turned on. It sucked in the hot air from outside, circulating it around the room. The distant sound of the Spanish sports station from the bodega below grew distorted as it filtered through the plastic blades of the fan. To the left of the bed stood a wooden five-drawer dresser that'd seen a tough life. It was covered in scratches and dings, and the top was cluttered with what looked mostly like unfolded laundry—Larkin was uncertain if it was clean or dirty—but there was also a loose pile of drugstore brand makeups, a hairbrush, several black hair ties, a hand mirror, and a few perfume bottles.

He took a brief look at the kitchen nestled into a small alcove just big enough for a sink, about six inches of usable countertop, and a compact stove. A mini fridge sat just outside the nook, a plastic shelving unit precariously balanced on top. It was packed with dry goods—canned beans and vegetables, rice, store-brand cereals. Larkin guessed the one cupboard above the sink was probably for cups and dishes. A short hallway ended with a closed door to what was likely the bathroom, and all of the available wall space along the way was packed with... *stuff*. Not junk, just everyday items and belongings that had no practical home or storage: a jug of laundry detergent, a pair of sneakers, a pair of winter boots, a metal folding chair, an old plug-in vacuum, a plastic take-out bag full of empty Sprite bottles destined for the recycling bin.

"Did you want to sit?" Bridget asked, barely audible over the drone of the fan while motioning to the love seat on Larkin's right. It was a checkered white-and-green monstrosity right out of *Country Living*, and the side closer to the window was faded from years of direct sunlight.

"Thank you." Larkin unbuttoned his suit coat and sat. He watched Bridget resume her position before the dresser, crouched to see her face in the small mirror as she began applying eyeliner again. "Tell me how you knew Barbara."

"It's like you said—she worked at the Kitten Klub."

Although Larkin had Doyle's confirmation that his mother had worked at the club, the fact was, Doyle would have only been a baby, and the statement could be viewed as hearsay. He needed that evidence to come from Bridget's own mouth. "Did you work there as well."

Bridget set the eyeliner pencil aside. She opened the mascara tube and viciously shoved the wand in and out, creating a suction-like sound. "So what?"

"It's not a character judgment, merely a request for clarity."

Bridget stopped and looked over her shoulder. Her eyes were narrowed, her mouth pinched. "Lemme see that badge again."

Larkin stood, removed his wallet a second time, and took a few steps forward, shield extended. Unprompted, he said, "I've been an officer for ten years."

"I've known a lot of cops in my life," she began, pointing the wand at Larkin. "None of 'em look like you or talk like you."

"And I assure you, none ever will."

"You a fag?" Bridget asked next, her tone not exactly cruel, but a sort of critical curiosity, suggesting she'd not experienced any sort of societal enlightenment since the '80s, when that kind of vocabulary was tossed around like no other adjectives were available for use.

In response, Larkin merely snapped his wallet shut and tucked it back into his pocket.

"Just because you're like that don't mean you can't be corrupt like all those other dirt bags."

"May I sit back down."

Bridget huffed, shrugged, and opened the mascara again.

Larkin returned to the love seat. "What were the dates of your employment at the Kitten Klub."

"Let me check my diary," Bridget said sardonically, making a face in the mirror as she brushed the wand over her lashes.

"I understand this was nearly forty years ago, but please be as precise as possible."

"Where were *you* forty years ago?" she countered. "Sucking on a silver spoon and shitting your diaper?"

"I was still in the planning stage."

Bridget set the mascara aside before turning around. "So daddy wasn't even humping mommy when Babs died, but the best cop for the case—" She gestured at Larkin, as if explaining her circumstances to an onlooking and sympathetic audience. "—is a fucking fetus."

Bridget Cohen's rap sheet had been a paint-by-numbers portrait of a time when women turned to the streets in search of freedom, only to find out too late that Times Square was just a prison with bright lights. The neighborhood's boundaries forced its inmates to work live sex shows to survive, to seek drugs to cope, and to turn tricks when rent money was spent on that newly found addiction. Bridget had been chewed up, spit out, and there'd been no system, however flawed, in place to help. She'd carried some kind of childhood trauma into adulthood—feelings and thoughts she avoided at all cost by engaging in increasingly risky, self-harming behaviors—and she'd become so hardened, so deadened over time, that being presented with Barbara Fuller's name and memory was triggering fear, and having to confront such an uncomfortable emotion was making Bridget *angry*.

It was distressing to be able to draw parallels between Bridget and Doyle, but Larkin could see, with naked clarity, the same avoidant behavior, the same unresolved anger. The difference, however, was in their response to emotional vulnerability. Doyle gave. He gave his entire heart and then more. He'd stepped in front of his own generational trauma to protect his daughter, had taken those knives in the back while undoubtably meeting her innocent little smile with one of his own, and even though Abigail was gone now, Doyle didn't know anything but being gentle.

Because vulnerability meant understanding.

Understanding meant acceptance.

And Doyle needed, more than anything, to be wanted.

But Bridget…. She'd lost custody of her child after nine tumultuous years of motherhood, and had never sought him out in the aftermath. Not an inquiry into his well-being, his education, *nothing*. Larkin was confident, even without the proof seen in her bachelor pad living conditions, that Bridget had no healthy relationships. She wasn't intimate with anyone, she likely had no close friends, didn't interact with neighbors, and was probably *that* person on her shift—the one other employees dreaded working with.

Because for Bridget, vulnerability meant danger.

Danger meant fear.

And fear brought back all those terrible, distressing memories of a life lived.

The box fan's tired drone broke the silence.

"Ms. Cohen," Larkin said evenly, "I'm here because I want to know who Barbara Fuller was when she was alive."

"What's it matter?"

"Everyone deserves to be remembered."

Bridget's mouth was twisted to one side, and when she parted her lips, it made a sucking sound. Condescendingly, she said, "I suppose you go to all their funerals too."

—rain and snow and lonely setting suns, pulling overgrown weeds from neglected headstones, wiping debris from abandoned markers, a penny denoting his visitation, paying the passage of the restless dead, speaking their names aloud, remembering all of the city's forgotten—

Larkin answered, "Something like that."

Bridget stared at him with those furious brown eyes, but when Larkin met her stare without blinking, without flinching, she was the first to look away. Bridget picked at a fingernail, as if trying to peel the cheap polish. She said reluctantly, "I knew Babs from the old neighborhood—years before the Kitten." Bridget shook her head and swallowed a few times, like she was struggling to get the words around an unexpected lump. Then she said with forced nonchalance, "She was real sweet."

"Was this Hell's Kitchen."

Bridget looked up. "How'd you know that?"

"I'm a detective, ma'am."

Bridget turned, yanked open the top drawer of the dresser, and retrieved a pair of black socks. "Her fiancé was a fucking piece of work. Slept all day, drank all night. More than once, he put a loaded gun to her head and threatened to pull the trigger—in broad daylight—but no one did nothing to stop him. Whole neighborhood was afraid of him and the thugs he ran with." Bridget crouched and put the socks on. "Babs wanted to leave him but…." She straightened. "Don't know why she didn't buy a bus ticket and just leave, instead of hiding out on the goddamn Deuce."

Because every victim of domestic abuse has a distinct upbringing and set of circumstances that their abuser manipulates and controls, Larkin wanted to say. Because until you can recognize a victim's fear—be it fear of their partner's retaliatory actions or of their own ability to be successfully independent—recognize a victim's shame, and recognize that a lack of resources can stop an escape in its tracks, it's difficult, if not impossible, to comprehend why a victim stays.

Just leave, for many, was a Sisyphean task.

"I told other runaways my name was Sam. I was eight."

And then there were those whose will knew no bounds.

Larkin prompted, "Barbara changed her name to Esther Haycox upon leaving Hell's Kitchen."

Bridget didn't say anything to the contrary as she moved to sit on the edge of the bed, reached underneath, and retrieved a pair of regulation black shoes.

"What year was this."

"It was a lifetime ago."

Larkin took a breath to quell his growing agitation. The apartment was too cluttered, too warm, and Bridget too hostile, too challenging, but he *wasn't* coming back again and again and— "Do you know what Barbara's homicide file says, Ms. Cohen." And when Bridget looked at Larkin, he said, "Nothing. It says nothing. It didn't even have her name. She was a Jane Doe until I was able to track down her identity. This woman died a horrific death, alone but for her killer, and for thirty-eight years, no one has cared. I'm trying to correct that."

"It won't bring Babs back."

"No. But maybe it'll give her peace."

Bridget sat there, one shoe on, unlaced, considering. Half-heartedly, she said, "I think it was '79. I know I was out of high school when she left. Babs was a little older than me."

The date matched Phyllis's story of having met Esther at the burlesque club the same year, and so Larkin asked next, "Tell me more about her fiancé."

"Shithead murdering psychopath…. Look, you wouldn't understand—you're too young and the city's so impersonal now—but back then, everybody knew everybody in Hell's Kitchen. Whose kid got to escape and go to college, whose granny had just passed, who might've owed cash to Spillane."

"But then he was murdered," Larkin said, an echo of Porter's history lesson.

"Got real bad after that," Bridget agreed. She tied her shoe. "Westies took over. They had a real hard-on for all the mafia bullshit going on around the city—wanted to be a part of it. Tony was half Italian, on his mother's side. He gets engaged to Babs, a nice girl from the Irish slums, and *bam*, suddenly the Westies are wining and dining the fucking Gambino crime family."

"What was Tony's last name."

"Vargas."

"*What*?"

Bridget looked up from tying her other shoe. She said again, more curtly, "Vargas. Used to be, he'd force Babs to make business calls for him, so the police wouldn't have his voice on record. By then, they were bugging everything in the neighborhood just to catch Westies in the act of *something*: apartments, diners, phone booths, candy shops…."

Larkin raised a hand, interrupting. "Anthony Vargas worked for the Westies."

"Was I not clear the first two times I said it?" She stood up, grabbed her purse from the dresser, and started checking the contents. "Tony fit right in with those nutjobs—he'd help 'em chop people up, throw 'em in the river. Babs being murdered was only a matter of time."

Larkin almost stood, but Bridget was a hundred and twenty pounds of tension wound so taut, she was about to snap, and he didn't want to pose any sort of threat to this delicate line of communication. He placed his hands on his knees and said coolly, "Barbara was not murdered by Anthony Vargas."

Bridget raised her head. "What do you mean? Isn't that why you're here? To ask me what I know?"

"Barbara was murdered by Matilde Wagner."

"Who the fuck is that?"

"She was a nurse at the New York Infirmary. She and her husband were responsible for the deaths of nearly two dozen sex workers between 1982 and 1989."

Bridget appeared shell-shocked. She glanced at her purse, looked around the apartment as if she'd lost something, then slowly sat back on the bed. She looked at Larkin again. "Really?"

"Why did you believe it had been Vargas."

"Because he was capable of it. He killed at least three people when he was with the Westies. Tony cheated on Babs—which, of course, was fine—but her leaving was public humiliation for him. When I left Hell's Kitchen, he was still saying he'd kill Babs if he ever found her."

"Did Vargas ever do prison time in the '80s or '90s for his Westie-associated crimes."

The inquiry made Bridget laugh—a nasty sort of mockery that bubbled up from deep inside her chest, like she'd been holding on to it for half a lifetime. "Of course he didn't. Ever hear of the Mafia Cops, kiddo? NYPD detectives, like you, on the mob payroll. Why you think it took so long to take down a handful of disorganized Irish boys? Because the same guys investigating them were *protecting* them." Visibly agitated, Bridget stood and pulled the strap of her purse over one shoulder.

The Westies, a gang of disorderly and deadly criminals operating out of one of the last Irish strongholds in New York, had included a half-Italian member so feared by the population that no one dared intervene when he mistreated and threatened his fiancée—a woman known to the neighborhood as one of their own, who'd become notorious for having run away from an abusive mobster—a mobster protected by local law enforcement.

Law enforcement that'd have *surely known* he had a girl.

A girl just like the one found dead in the Hotel Cavalier on the night of October 2, 1982.

And yet, the lead detective didn't know her, didn't recognize her, wasn't able to trace her origins as belonging to a neighborhood just a few blocks west of her final resting place—because if Vargas was suspected, that'd make it hard to keep collecting under-the-table payments. So sure, Detective Noonan didn't know that *poor Jane Doe*, but it was funny how he could identify Bridget Cohen by name. A woman who'd been living as Bridget Doyle, even after the birth of her son a year prior, but—if Phyllis Clark's timeline was still to be believed—had worked with Barbara a month or two before her murder, and would have learned an old friend from the neighborhood had changed her identity entirely to a one Esther Haycox....

"Ghosting was a form of identity theft."

Larkin prompted, before Bridget could not-so-kindly suggest he make himself scarce, *"The Paper Trip."*

"Excuse me?"

"Barbara came into possession of a pamphlet called *The Paper Trip*," Larkin continued. "It taught her how to obtain the certified birth certificate of a deceased child, how to use that documentation to get an out-of-state license in that name, how to request name changes, social security cards—how to live successfully under a stolen identity."

"So what if she did? It kept her alive. Tony never found her, right? And it ain't like the kid was gonna need it."

"Barbara shared the pamphlet with you, when the two of you were briefly reunited at the Kitten," Larkin said as he slowly got to his feet. "That's when you decided to use it, didn't you."

Bridget's brows rose in a blatant display of fear, an intensity stronger than dread but slightly less than panic. Her lower lids were tensed and lips drawn back as her mouth opened but nothing came out.

"Did you know Detective Ralph Noonan."

"Get out."

"Was Detective Noonan the inside man for the Westies."

"Get out now."

"He knew you from before, didn't he," Larkin pressed. "From Hell's Kitchen. And when he interviewed you that night, when he mocked you for identifying yourself as Bridget Cohen, you didn't budge, didn't pretend to be anyone else. He probably made a grandiose gesture of writing your new name down, like an asshole. Bullies target those they perceive as weak, but not always in a traditional sense," Larkin explained. "You were a threat to his social dominance. Because Noonan was a Homicide detective being paid to keep Vargas and other Westies out of handcuffs. He couldn't have a young female sex worker blow the whistle on Barbara's murder. He promised you dismemberment and garbage bags and East River dumps if you talked. And because you'd known the kind of man Vargas was, it never occurred to you anyone else would want to hurt Barbara. You said nothing all these years—"

Bridget was breathing hard from her nose, and she spat, "I didn't say nothing because Vargas is still alive."

"He's been in prison since 2013."

"Yeah? Well, Noonan sure as hell isn't!"

"Bridget," Larkin said firmly, insistently. "I can help, but I need you to—"

"All my fucking life, I've been doing what men've told me to do," she said, and her face grew flushed as all those negative emotions mixed together like a violent chemical reaction. "Men like you, with your fancy suit and expensive watch and posh attitude, treating me like a dumpster you can leave your fuckin' trash in—"

"Please—"

"Get the fuck out of my apartment!" she screamed.

Larkin held one hand up in defense as he reached for his wallet. He removed a business card, turned, and set it on the love seat cushion. "If you want to talk," Larkin said, "I'll listen."

He saw himself to the door without another word, exited, and took the stairs slowly—not because he expected Bridget to change her mind, to run after him, to spill her darkest and dirtiest secrets in the stairwell between the second and third floors, but because he needed to catch his breath. He needed to present a calm and controlled front for Doyle.

Larkin left the vestibule and stepped into an early evening still bright with the summer sun. Nervous sweat had bunched the fabric of his shirt under his arms, and his upper back felt as if it was cooking like a cracked egg on asphalt. He took a deep breath, slid his hands into his pockets, and started for the corner. Larkin wasn't surprised to see Doyle back on the sidewalk, restlessly pacing before the Audi.

And when Doyle turned to cross back in front of the passenger door, catching sight of Larkin as he did, he took to a jog. "What happened?" he asked impatiently. "Was—was it her?"

"Yes."

Doyle took his sunglasses off. "And?"

"Do you want me to tell you about the case or about Bridget."

Doyle's uncertainty played out across his face like a game of tug-of-war. He admitted, "I don't know."

That makes two of us, Larkin thought. He said, "Barbara was a Hell's Kitchen native. She was engaged to a Westie in the late '70s."

"Do you know who?"

"Anthony Vargas, their half-Italian buddy and connection to the Gambino family."

Doyle put his hands on his hips. "I don't understand. He couldn't have possibly murdered Wagner from *inside* prison."

"It's not about Vargas," Larkin explained, "I think it's about those he surrounded himself with. Bridget says he was abusive toward Barbara—that's why she left, why she sought a new identity. Allegedly, Vargas swore he'd kill Barbara if he ever found her. Apparently, he had no qualms with mob killings or keeping mistresses, but it was Barbara's leaving that was the unforgivable sin."

"And despite her caution, Barbara still wound up a victim."

"There's more," Larkin cautioned. "Ralph Noonan, the lead investigator—"

Doyle interrupted, his tone uncharacteristically bitter, as he asked, "Vargas paid him to look the other way, didn't he? Like what happened with Stolle?"

"Arguably worse. Bridget says Noonan was on mob payroll. By day, he investigated the Westies—by night, he protected them."

"Then there's no way on God's green Earth he'd have not known who Barbara was," Doyle said. "Not if she was the fiancée of the guy he was protecting."

"That's my belief as well. And while I couldn't get Bridget to confirm, she didn't deny when I suggested she knew Noonan."

Doyle's brows rose. "Knew him?" he echoed. "Knew him *how*?"

Larkin realized the connotation his choice of words held for someone who wasn't sure of his parentage and said, "I'm sorry. I only meant Bridget was familiar with Noonan from when she still lived in Hell's Kitchen—familiar with his Westie connection. And because she knew Vargas to be a dangerous man, when Noonan confronted her on the night of October 2, 1982, she made the reasonable assumption that Barbara had been murdered by her violent ex. She never said anything because both of those men are still alive, and the system has always been rigged in favor of the predator. And as she pointed out rather emphatically, Vargas might be in prison, but Noonan is enjoying his retirement."

Doyle considered the information for a long moment before he shook his head and studied the ground. He scuffed the sidewalk a few times with the toe of his shoe, almost like he was trying to pull up the black splotches of petrified gum that pockmarked the city. "We've set a precedent for honesty, so I want to tell you what I'm feeling."

"Okay."

"Today has made me want to drink." Doyle raised his head, and the tension in his neck was tight as he swallowed. "But I didn't work on my sobriety for six years, only to start on day one tomorrow."

Larkin reached forward and wrapped his hand around Doyle's nape. He squeezed a little, trying to relax the muscles, but he didn't have a chance to find the right words of encouragement before a nearby door slammed shut. He looked over his shoulder to see Bridget walking in their direction, toward the corner—the bus stop, no doubt. Larkin dropped his hand and said in a voice that left no room for argument, "Ira, stay here." And then he sprinted back the way he'd come. "Ms. Cohen—"

"I got called into work an hour ago to pick up half of the second shift and now you've made me late." She took a step sideways, but Larkin mirrored the motion. She did it again, and he followed. "Fucking *move*," she barked.

"Please allow me to show you a composite sketch," Larkin said, reaching into his pocket.

"A what?"

"A sketch—a drawing. I want to know if you recognize the individual."

Bridget took a big and audible breath, like she was resisting the urge to sucker punch a cop, and then dug into her purse. She retrieved a pack of red Newports and warned, while searching through the bag a second time, "I'm walking away the second I light this."

Larkin brought up the images stored on his Cloud, retrieved the sketch of the Brooklyn shooter, enlarged it, and turned the screen toward Bridget just as she struck the spark wheel of her Bic lighter over and over, to no avail. "Have you seen this man before."

Bridget made an irritated sound in the back of her throat before looking at the phone. She narrowed her eyes and asked, "Is this some kinda game to you?"

"What do you mean."

She motioned to the cell with her unlit cigarette. "You know who that is. That's Ralphie."

Larkin's working theory was that Adam Worth became a contact in the criminal underworld sometime around 1988, just after Alfred Niederman got his first taste for the abuse of children and wanted to capitalize on his own sadistic pleasures. Worth had helped make it happen because they had known each other. Niederman had paid in information. And the sort of information an ex-con-turned-janitor could've had that'd appeal to a man like Worth?

"I got a prison buddy," Niederman might've said. "Helps his old lady kill broads on the Deuce."

"My brother-in-law works at a strip club with connections to the Gambino family," Earl Wagner might've said. "He knows about a guy who useta dump bodies in the East River."

"I had a canary bird," Vargas might've said. "Kept me outta prison. I could do whatever I wanted."

"I'm not the only one who took bribes," Noonan might've said. "I know a guy from Vice who looked the other way for years."

Worth didn't have to know his clients personally. He didn't even need to have been around when their crimes were first committed. He only needed the knowledge of their corruption in order to sufficiently blackmail them. He'd hold that evidence overhead, like a get-out-of-jail-free card, and promise to make it all *disappear*, if only they'd first do him a little favor.

A favor like snuffing out Stolle before he could spill the beans.

A favor like murdering her own husband so she could safely escape.

A favor like hacking up Wagner to reflect the very murders he once covered up.

And all the while, Worth had been there, sowing chaos, little upheavals that, over time, fractured Larkin's very foundation without his realizing, until it was almost too late. Incidents that had been personal, intimate, invasive: the fax that nearly sullied his professional reputation, the church he'd been married in, letters and packages sent to his former home, his current home—once sanctuaries now robbed of their security—the overreaching attempt on Doyle's life, the Honda Civic meant to induce doubt. Even though it had all managed to deprive Larkin of sleep for weeks, had stimulated a sort of death-obsessed psychosis in him that was making decisions and justifying reasons on his behalf, Larkin hadn't broken.

Because he had been through so much more than the sender understood.

But while Larkin was busy being a glutton for psychological punishment, he'd missed realizing that each and every clue had been seemingly marching them toward Ira Doyle's source of guilt and endless torment, that he had unknowingly opened Bridget back up to a near forty-year-old threat upon her life, and that everything was *all his fault.*

Acrid smoke was blown in Larkin's face, and he wrinkled his nose. He looked at the emblem on Bridget's shirt—the modern "sonic" eagle head design.

—standing eagle postal badge and the scent of burning clove—

Abruptly, he asked, "Have you noticed a blue Honda Civic following you at home or work."

Bridget made a face and sucked on the end of her cigarette.

"Anyone new at work—a woman, specifically—fifties, black hair, dyed, she might be wearing a USPS uniform with an outdated patch."

"You touched in the head or something?"

Frustrated, Larkin tried, "Did any of Vargas's mistresses—"

She snorted at the terminology.

"—did any of them run with the Westies."

"Probably, but I wasn't on a name-to-name basis with his harem." Bridget blew smoke at Larkin a second time. "I wanted to stay alive."

"I'm not speaking to hear myself talk, ma'am."

"You sure?"

"I'm asking because there is a chance you're once again in danger."

Bridget faltered as she brought the cigarette to her lips, but then she laughed that same unkind cackle, took a final drag, and crushed the stick underfoot. "If I ever see you again, I'm reporting you and suing this whole goddamn city." She shoved his shoulder with her own before once again walking in the direction of the bus stop.

Larkin remained where he was, his back to Bridget as he stared west at the tree-lined street. A super had dragged the building's trash to the curb before the designated set-out times, and two rats were gnawing a hole into the heavy-duty black plastic bag.

"Bridget!"

Larkin turned the same time Bridget had. She'd walked past Doyle, was perhaps a dozen feet away, when he'd called out to her.

"Bridget Doyle?" he asked.

That same caustic reaction of fear and anger returned to Bridget's face. She reached for the strap of her purse, clutching it tight in her fist as if she was ready to swing it around like a weapon. "Who the hell are you?"

Larkin cautiously approached, putting a hand out to stop Doyle from moving toward her. Out of reflex, Larkin very nearly said his name, but he managed to bite his tongue and keep quiet.

When Doyle didn't say anything, Bridget took a few steps backward, demanded, "Stay away from me—both of you," and then she took off, disappearing around the corner.

Doyle doubled over, his hands on his knees. "She didn't even recognize me."

Larkin moved to stand in front of him. "Ira."

Doyle turned his head to one side and spit. "I feel like I'm gonna be sick again."

Larkin put a hand in the middle of Doyle's back. He was shaking pretty badly. "Breathe," Larkin directed. "In through your nose, out through your mouth." He stroked up and down, more firmly than how he might've touched Doyle otherwise, but he wanted to ground him the way Doyle always did when Larkin needed it. He said, "Did you know that when sound is introduced to the sense of touch, response time in the somatosensory cortex is enhanced, suggesting the brain doesn't process sensory information in parallel, but instead all together, in a sort of symphony. The significance of this find is beneficial in the ongoing research of conditions like autism or anxiety, both of which experience impaired sensory processing, but it also reaffirms early childhood development studies, which suggest rocking and singing to a baby simultaneously not only gives an infant a sense of security and familiarity, but it creates a bond with their caregiver and even promotes early language development."

Larkin felt incredibly self-conscious about doing this, especially on the open street for any passersby to overhear, but he began singing Marilyn Monroe's version of "I Wanna Be Loved By You," and he didn't even skip the scat "boop-boop-a-doop." It was somewhere around not aspiring for anything higher that Doyle straightened his posture, took Larkin's face into his hands, and kissed him with a desperation that Larkin didn't know how to quell other than to kiss back even harder.

Larkin's phone rang.

Doyle broke first. He gently let go, wiping his mouth with the back of his hand.

Larkin collected his phone and looked at the caller ID. "It's Noah."

"Answer it." Doyle's voice was rough.

"What."

"After everything that's been happening…." Doyle replied, rubbing his stubble with a near-steady hand. "Just answer it."

Larkin reluctantly swiped to accept the call and put the phone to his ear. "Noah—"

"*Everett*!" Noah screamed.

The phone jostled, the sound briefly distorted, and then an unfamiliar male voice said, "Everett Larkin, listen very carefully."

"Who the fuck is this," Larkin demanded.

"What's going on?" Doyle asked.

"Greetings from Adam Worth," the man said, almost like he was reading from a script. "They say you're the best detective the NYPD has ever seen. Now you must prove it. Decode the following in thirty seconds, or I shoot Mr. Rider in the head."

And as if on cue, Larkin heard the hammer get cocked on a revolver and Noah's muffled scream, raw and primal and real, echo from farther away.

"Zero, five, three, two, across the grid."

Larkin looked at Doyle. "Zero, five, three, two across the grid. What's it mean."

"I—I've no idea," Doyle stammered.

"Twenty-five seconds," the man said.

"A grid like—like Manhattan?"

Larkin said into the phone, "Manhattan's grid system."

"Are the numbers supposed to be streets?" Doyle continued.

"Are they cross streets," Larkin asked into the phone.

"Twenty seconds."

"No, that doesn't work," Doyle said. "There's no Thirty-Second Avenue in Manhattan."

"It's a permutation," Larkin said suddenly. "*Fuck*. Four times… twelve… twenty—twenty-four. There're twenty-four different combinations."

"Most of those aren't going to be in Manhattan," Doyle countered, and despite being unclear as to what was being said on the other end of the call, he was reacting to Larkin's frantic energy accordingly. "Assuming we're talking street first, avenue second."

"Ralph Noonan is a native New Yorker," Larkin said, speaking into the phone. "He knows how to correctly give cross streets, don't you."

There was a split second of hesitation, before the voice said, "Ten seconds."

Got you, you sonofabitch.

Larkin closed his eyes and laid out the urban map of Manhattan in his mind. His Rolodex brain spun through each cross-street combination at lightning speed, putting mental markers on each location relevant to the island—two each on Fifth, Third, and Second Avenues.

"Five seconds."

"There are six possible addresses in Manhattan," he answered, and the silence that followed was so profound that Larkin could hear a distant and distinct *pop, pop, crack* underfoot as Noonan paced.

"You have thirty minutes to find Mr. Rider. If you use lights, he dies. If you use sirens, he dies. If you call for backup, he dies. Choose wisely."

CHAPTER NINETEEN

"Take the Harlem River Drive," Larkin ordered.

Doyle flicked on the blinker and tore around the corner of Amsterdam Avenue, deftly moving in and out of rush hour traffic as they headed uptown in order to swing back down. Hundred-year-old, six-story multiuses in the distinct "H" shape whizzed by the left side of the road in a blur of sun-faded awnings and colorful graffiti sprayed across rolled-down security gates, while the greenery and rocky outcroppings of Highbridge Park kept pace on the right.

Both of them were compartmentalizing. Doyle had dragged himself free from all his anguish—but it was like a black muck that'd been dredged from the bottom of a lake, so thick and so concentrated that if he stopped struggling against it, he'd be sucked right back in—and Larkin had neatly tucked away the reality of their situation—that thirty minutes was not enough time to traverse Manhattan Island, that this was a hunt for the proverbial needle in a haystack, and that he would not see his ex-husband alive again.

In this moment, *this second*, there was only seeking a solution against the backdrop of a sputtering flame and grains of falling sand.

Twenty-eight minutes left.

"You showed Bridget the composite sketch I made."

"She identified the shooter as Ralph Noonan," Larkin said by way of agreement.

"Is that who you suspected it was?"

"Yes. I spoke with Bailey just before seeing you, and it came up in conversation that the NYPD used revolvers until the early '90s," Larkin explained while busily scrolling on his phone. "That, in and of itself, is not strange, since criminals would have been using similar pistols, but he mentioned the older generation having to get trained in how to use their new 9mms, and that began to suggest—to me, anyway—the shooter's identity might be that of an old-school cop who never got recertified because he'd retired by the time department policy mandated a change to service weapons.

"When Bridget claimed Noonan's mob job was that of cleaning up after Vargas and his fellow Westies, my inkling became more than a mere hunch. I think he's guilty of racketeering, and Worth knows it. He's hanging it over Noonan's head, forced him to rid the world of Wagner in the very method once used by the Westies that he protected. It's rather poetic, in a way. Worth is no hero, but he does seem to be particularly adept at rooting out police corruption."

Doyle turned right onto the Harlem River Drive, speeding up as they got off the surface streets. "Why'd you tell Bridget she was in danger?" he finally asked, like the question had been simmering on the back burner and it'd finally come to a boil.

Larkin didn't look up from his phone. "Olfactory memory."

"What?"

"Bridget smokes Newports. They reminded me of the mail carrier yesterday morning—at the diner. She smelled like Djarum Black, which have a very distinct, clove scent."

"And?"

"And I smelled the same cigarette smoke wafting out of the Honda Civic, when the shooter rolled down the window and shot Joe."

"Why didn't you say anything?"

Larkin huffed and said quickly, almost distractedly, "Because that's how olfactory memory works. It didn't occur to me *what* I was smelling, not until the stink of Bridget's Newports hit me square in the face and I could compare and contrast. Dammit, this isn't working on my phone." He tapped a few buttons before putting it to his ear.

"Unless the next words out of your mouth are 'Help, help, a wild buffalo just bit my dick off,' I don't have time for you, Grim," O'Halloran stated.

"Are you still at work—at your desk," Larkin asked.

"Mentally, I'm sitting on my couch, scratching my nuts, drinking a beer, and watching the game. Physically, I'm sitting in a windowless bullpen, scratching my nuts—"

"Ray, shut up," Larkin cut in. "Yesterday, I asked CO Rodriguez to forward me Anthony Vargas's paperwork from his 2013 arrest and he never got back to me."

"Yeah, I know," O'Halloran snapped. "I mean, I didn't know that, but I've been trying to schedule a time to chat with Tony the fuckin' Tiger, and it's been a whole fiasco with his lawyers and the prison, blah, blah, blah. I got a copy of his file this afternoon—a kinda consolation prize, I guess. What'd you need that has your panties in a twist?"

Larkin said, "Anthony Vargas had a girlfriend at the time of his arrest. She was hiding at the crime scene and later stabbed the OCME driver who was there for the body transport. I never learned her name, and I need to know when she was released from prison. I have less time and even less patience at the moment, so let's perform our usual song and dance at a later date. I'll even let you take the first swing."

"Gosh, my heart's all a flutter," O'Halloran replied, but there was a distinct *click, click, click* of a computer keyboard just underneath his words.

Larkin glanced at Doyle. He had one hand on the wheel, both eyes on the road, and all his attention on the one-sided conversation—and yet he never interrupted, always waited to be kept informed. Larkin lowered the phone and tapped Speaker. He caught a ghost of a smile as it flickered across Doyle's face.

"Her name's Lisa Murray," O'Halloran said. "DOB October 23, 1961. In 2013 she was charged with assault with a deadly weapon in the second degree and sentenced to three years. They let her off at two for good behavior."

"Does she have past charges," Larkin asked. "From the late '70s or early '80s."

"No," O'Halloran said ardently. "Squeaky-clean record, just like Vargas—up until that drug bust, anyway."

Larkin checked his watch a second time.

Twenty-four minutes.

Doyle pressed on the gas and the Audi's engine let out a deep purr as it ate up the asphalt.

"Need anything else?" O'Halloran inquired.

"Find out why Rodriguez never called me back," Larkin answered.

"Oh, yeah, lemme just go tattle to his mommy—"

Larkin promptly tapped End. He pulled up the browser on his phone, did a search of "Lisa Murray NYC 2013" and found articles citing hers and Vargas's arrest, detailed in scummy subway rags as well as *The New York Times* on the first page of results. The *Times* reported that both convicted criminals were long-term residents of Hell's Kitchen while displaying their less-than-glamorous mugshots in full color. She was younger here, of course, and wearing hoop earrings, but Lisa Murray was sporting done-up black hair that looked a little crunchy from hairspray, and wore a hideous shade of blue eyeshadow.

Some folks never left the '80s, it seemed.

"Would you allow me to theorize with only circumstantial evidence," Larkin asked.

"Please do."

"Lisa Murray is from Hell's Kitchen, and although she'd have been young, hardly eighteen, I feel there's a strong likelihood she knew Vargas, Noonan, even your—Bridget, around the time Barbara took off," Larkin began. "Keep in mind, Vargas wasn't the only one to get away with Westie-associated murders."

"You think she might've gotten away with mob murders back then?"

"I think you were correct when you suggested the stalker was more than one person," Larkin answered. "Someone was in the driver's seat when Noonan shot Joe, and I believe it was Murray. In 2013, I never actually saw her face. I was a patrolman. I was on crowd control. But this woman—" He waved his phone, the mugshot still visible on the screen. "—was the mail carrier at the diner. I think I might've seen her again near Joe's apartment. What better way to watch me—*us*—without being noticed. We expect mail carriers in a city, so we become blind to them. Worth blackmailing Noonan makes sense, but if he's involving Murray too, he must have something big on her as well. And what's bigger than murder.

"Here is where I'm forced to theorize, however," Larkin said. "Wagner went to Brooklyn. Whether she knew that home on Carroll Street, knew Phyllis, or had—I don't know—been purposefully misled, that's where she ended up. She was shot, execution-style, with a .38 special that will undoubtably match the bullet used to kill Joe. And Murray, no stranger to knives after having stabbed the driver in 2013, helped dismember

Wagner. Together, they moved the fridge from the basement and drove it to the Hudson."

"I'm still unclear what Murray has to do with Bridget being in danger."

"Bridget works for the post office," Larkin answered. "Murray does not. And while I'm unaware of regulations pertaining to whether or not one is allowed to wear an out-of-date USPS emblem, it seems unlikely an employee today would still be sporting a uniform top from roughly 1990. I suspect the one she had on was acquired online. Vintage thrifting on eBay or something."

"Have they been stalking Bridget as well?"

Larkin said, "When you suggested Worth might be trying to instill distrust or uncertainty in me, I admit I thought it was a bit tinfoil hat."

Doyle spared Larkin a critical glance as they sped past Exit 16 at East 116th Street.

"But you're right. That's exactly what he's been doing," Larkin continued. "He's a spider, spinning a web, and the farther it reaches, the more people who get caught up in it."

"Where does it end?"

"I don't think it does," Larkin said solemnly. "Not until Worth is caught. Everyone who associates with me—and by proxy, who they associate with—might be in danger. Why else would Noah—"

It's all my fault.

Larkin looked at his watch.

Nineteen minutes.

"We need to decide which cross streets soon." There was a heaviness to Doyle's voice, like he'd begun fighting against the squelching muck again in that brief interlude of silence. "We're coming up on Ninety-Sixth Street already."

"Of the six locations, we're looking for one that a fully-grown, *kidnapped* man can be dragged to, and passersby won't take notice."

"None of them," Doyle said dryly.

"Twenty-Third and Fifth is the Flatiron and Madison Square Park," Larkin said. "So that's out. Thirty-Second and Fifth is Koreatown. There're old multiuses and walk-ups, yes, but it's such a busy neighborhood that it's highly unlikely to be the cross streets in question."

"The farther east, generally the quieter the area," Doyle suggested.

"Fifty-Third and Second is still Midtown. A lot of high-rises and office buildings."

"What's the other option?"

"Thirty-Fifth and Second."

"Murray Hill," Doyle said. "Pretty chill neighborhood, finance bros notwithstanding."

Larkin closed his eyes and pulled up his mental map a second time. He placed himself in the middle of Second Avenue, looking uptown with Kips Bay at his back. The basketball and handball courts of St. Vartan Park were to the northeast, and an Armenian cathedral of the same name was to his immediate right. Once luxury condos, now outdated eyesores, loomed several blocks north, but that immediate intersection was still made up of hundred-year-old multiuses—AC units in the apartment windows overhead, and restaurants, office supply stores, and beauty salons on the ground floors, with undoubtably some sort of city maintenance on the sidewalks or roads to inconvenience—

Larkin's eyes snapped open. The exit sign for East Seventy-First whizzed past. He pulled up the browser on his phone and navigated to the webpage for Manhattan Community Board Six. He tapped Work Notices and began scrolling through all of the approved work orders affecting the vicinity of Murray Hill. "My unmitigated obsession—what you lovingly refer to as dedication—introduced me to Community Board websites in April of 2018, when I got home from work one evening to discover Eightieth Street was closed to vehicle traffic without any posted notices explaining the reason I had to park the Audi nearly five blocks away. Turns out, our street needed substantial infrastructure upgrades and it was closed for nearly a year. I followed the progress, or lack thereof, on the Community Board website.

"But to my point: While on that phone call with Noonan, I heard the sound of what I believe to be popping wood—like old joists in a floor needing repair—and there's currently a multiuse on the southwest corner of Thirty-Fifth and Second that's under repair, which required the evacuation of both the storefront and all tenants in the upstairs apartments. Overhead protection and scaffolding has been installed, and construction is underway to both the interior and exterior, weekdays only, weather permitting. Expected completion is October of this year."

Doyle didn't miss a beat when he said, "You're fucking brilliant, Evie."

"Thank you."

Doyle put the gas pedal to the floor as they passed East Forty-Ninth, swerving around the growing traffic like the Audi was trying to show off.

Thirteen minutes.

"Evie."

"What."

"Stop looking at your watch."

Eleven minutes.

Doyle turned off the freeway at East Thirty-Seventh, sped through the green light at First, laid on the horn as he coaxed his way around a moving van and throng of ambulettes parked outside of a multispecialty medical facility, and narrowly missed clipping a minivan that decided to turn for the Queens Midtown tunnel at the last minute.

"*Jesus Christ.*"

"We're fine."

Nine minutes.

Doyle turned left onto Second Avenue, only to be halted by active roadwork. The entire block was being resurfaced and traffic was funneled into a single lane by an NYPD traffic officer. The roar of machinery, the stink of tar and hot asphalt, the shouting of men wearing hardhats and sporting sunburns—

"Pull onto the sidewalk," Larkin said.

"The side—"

"*Do it*!"

Doyle spun the wheel and went up onto the sidewalk, pushing back an orange barrier with the bumper in the process.

Larkin took his seat belt off and climbed out of the car.

Eight minutes.

Upon seeing Doyle's maneuver to get them out of the gridlock, the traffic officer came running toward them. "Sir! *Sir*!" he shouted, waving his hands. "Absolutely not!"

Larkin shut the passenger door, retrieved his badge, and flashed it. "Tow it if you don't like it." He looked back as the trunk was slammed, only to see Doyle had retrieved flashlights from the roadside emergency kit, which was smart, considering an active worksite may or may not have power. Larkin motioned and the two of them took off in an all-out run, sun in their eyes and doomsday clock counting down, down, down.

They reached Thirty-Fifth in no time, crossing the street and glimpsing the Empire State Building as they moved—one hundred and two stories of architectural feet soaring overhead and gleaming in the evening sun like a hundred million diamonds. The work notices for the neighborhood proved to be accurate, and the lot on the southwest corner was indeed blocked off with the usual green plywood and spray-painted with notices reading: POST NO BILLS. A sidewalk shed had been erected and netting surrounded the building, both a means of protecting pedestrians while repairs to the building's façade and roof were ongoing. Larkin rushed into the jungle of scaffolding and found the access door on the street side of the building. The usual lock and chain to keep the curious and the troublemakers out of active sites over the weekend was missing. Larkin and Doyle checked over each other's shoulders for any foot traffic, unholstered their weapons, then slipped inside.

Six minutes.

The temperature dipped in the manmade shade, but the relative darkness forced them to turn on the flashlights and move with caution, so as to avoid banging a shin, knee, or face into an unexpected piece of industrial machinery. To the left was an entrance for what looked like the storefront—a smoothie shop, maybe—and directly ahead was the front door for tenants. Larkin approached, his steps loud as debris popped and cracked underfoot. He tried the knob, not surprised to find this door had been left unlocked.

They were walking straight into the lion's den.

But Noonan and Murray had taken Noah, and what was Larkin *supposed* to do?

He spared a glance over his shoulder and whispered, "We don't split up."

Doyle nodded.

Five minutes.

Larkin pushed open the door onto a pitch-black vestibule. The inner door had been left wide open, and the darkness beyond beckoned him forward like a bad dream. He raised the flashlight in his right hand, rested his gun hand atop for stability, and started forward. He wanted to run up the stairs, take them two at a time, shout and scream for Noah, but there was no telling what Noonan—what Worth—might've planned for.

The air was hot, stagnant, musty, and unbearably still. Sweat rolled down Larkin's spine and prickled his hairline. Every step he and Doyle took sounded amplified, a megaphone announcing their arrival, ruining any chance at an element of surprise.

Four minutes.

There were two apartments on the second floor. Both doors were locked.

The crunching and cracking of debris got worse on the next set of stairs, and the drywall dust was so abundant that Doyle had to stop briefly to stifle a sneeze.

Two more apartments, and two more locked doors.

The fourth-floor landing squeaked loudly underfoot, and—

—*pop, pop, crack*—

—perfectly replicated the noises that'd emanated from Noonan's phone call. Larkin moved toward the door on the left, checked over his shoulder to confirm Doyle had his weapon trained on the staircase and apartment opposite them, then tried the knob.

The door creaked open.

Larkin raised his flashlight and SIG back into firing stance and took in the details as they became available through the tunnel of light: painted pink walls, bulky shapes of furniture hidden under drop cloths, personal belongings boxed and stacked against the far walls—the owner no doubt hoping to avoid any damage done to their possessions during the building's overhaul. Larkin took a step through the doorway, flashed his light to the left, illuminating an open threshold leading deeper into the apartment. He took a step sideways, keeping his back to the wall as Doyle came in and lit up the right side of the apartment.

Someone let out a muffled sob that devolved into a gut-wrenching scream unable to escape his throat.

Larkin knew that voice.

He'd known it for seven years.

He turned and aimed his light in the same direction as Doyle's, finding Noah sitting in a chair in the middle of the open kitchen, ankles duct-taped to either wooden leg, arms behind his back, and more than one strip of duct tape across his mouth. Even from across the room, Larkin could see the black eye, the bloody nose, the tears staining Noah's cheeks.

Two minutes.

Larkin covered Doyle as he moved to the kitchen and then walked backward, SIG still trained on the dark hallway. He reached the tiled floor just as Doyle holstered his weapon, crouched before Noah, and pressed one hand to his cheek as he peeled back the tape from his mouth.

"—*erett!*" Noah cried the moment the tape was pulled from his lips.

Larkin hushed him.

Doyle retrieved his ring of house keys, moved behind Noah, and used the teeth to cut into the tape around his wrists.

Larkin turned at an angle and said, "You're okay. I'm here."

"I—I—"

Doyle tore the tape and Noah flung his arms out and around Larkin's waist.

Larkin stumbled a little and had to twist out of Noah's hold so he could keep a line of sight on the hall. He pocketed the flashlight and reached back to put a hand against Noah's cheek. "You're okay," he said again as Doyle moved to the bindings on Noah's ankles.

"N-No, th-there's—over there." Noah was pointing to the sink.

Larkin turned to follow the gesture.

"Listen," Noah said, and the three of them fell silent.

Tick-tock, tick-tock, tick-tock.

Larkin stepped past Noah, retrieving his flashlight as he moved toward the mechanical sound. He brought the beam across the countertop, empty but for a single sheet of paper that said:

BOOM
—squish
crack—
"Larkin?" Doyle asked.
"Everett?" Noah echoed in a shaky voice.

Larkin leaned forward, shined his light into the kitchen sink, and illuminated a homemade bomb attached to an old windup kitchen timer.

One minute.

"Ira," Larkin said evenly. "Finish up. Quickly." He holstered his weapon, retrieved his phone, and dialed 911. "This is Everett Larkin," he told dispatch. "Shield 928. I need the bomb squad—"

Noah's crying began anew.

"Thirty-Fifth and Second. The building with a sidewalk shed. Tell them there might be an active shooter in the area as well." Larkin ended the call and returned to Noah as Doyle got the tape free from one ankle and swung around to the second. "Noah, are you able to stand."

"I—y-yeah."

Larkin nodded and took Noah's hand, pulling him to his feet.

"Almost there," Doyle said.

"You're on the fourth floor," Larkin explained as he passed Noah his own flashlight. "Go down three flights of stairs. The vestibule door is wide open and the front door is unlocked. Be mindful of machinery outside, but keep going straight. When you get outside, I want you to run uptown. Don't stop."

"Are you not coming?" Noah all but screeched, clutching the flashlight to his chest, its tunnel of light erratic and casting a spooky, campfire glow across his usually model-good looks.

"We'll be right behind you. But we've only got the one light."

Thirty seconds.

"Got it!" Doyle exclaimed.

"*Go*," Larkin ordered, and he pushed Noah toward the apartment door.

Noah stumbled briefly, like he couldn't seem to find his own legs, and then he was off, feet pounding stairs, banister vibrating, debris cracking and scraping with every footfall.

Larkin grabbed Doyle and forced him out the door. He followed the beam of the flashlight that Doyle kept pointed at the ground between them, raced to keep up with Doyle's longer stride, quicker descent, their measured steps now an all-out race. Larkin heard a crash from the ground floor, could hear Noah swearing, but he kept moving. Larkin grabbed the post topper at the second-floor landing, used the momentum to spin him around, nearly fell down the next set of stairs in his rush to reach Doyle, who was already at the bottom, but managed to catch himself by grabbing onto the wall and banister.

Larkin jumped the last two steps and raced through the vestibule and out the front door with Doyle. In the bouncing beam of the light, he saw Noah standing at the construction entrance and shouted, "Out the fucking door!"

"It's *locked*," Noah screamed, and he shoved his body against it, as if to make certain Larkin believed him.

Locked?

Fifteen seconds.

"This way," Doyle ordered, and he ran to their left, where a swath of sunlight came in through a gap in the plywood perimeter. "Larkin, help me." He counted to three, and they both rammed their shoulders against the wall. "Again!"

The plywood cracked, splintered, and Doyle's momentum threw him through the break, and he crashed onto the sidewalk beyond. Larkin turned, grabbed Noah, and shoved him through the hole, passing him to Doyle as his partner scrambled to his feet to take Noah's outstretched hand.

Five seconds.

"Larkin!"

The ground began to shake underfoot and then the building exploded overhead.

CHAPTER TWENTY

It was Friday, July 17, 10:32 a.m., and Larkin stood on the waterfront promenade of Carl Schurz Park, overlooking the dark and choppy waters of the East River. It'd been raining for the last hour, a gentle but constant drizzle that left the bench-lined walkway devoid of its usual hustle and bustle of late-morning joggers, dog walkers, and nannies with strollers. No one sat on the lawns, the nearby dog run was empty, and pigeons huddled together by the dozens along the handrail, their feathered, puffed heads wet, and in general, looking as miserable as the gloom that seemed to have settled over the city.

Larkin held an umbrella in one hand while running his other along the cast-iron rail. He raised his hand and watched the collected water pool to his fingertips and hang suspended like little stars that weren't quite ready to fall.

On August 2, 2019, he'd considered jumping from this spot.

He hadn't, of course, but suicide ideation was a constant in his intrusive thoughts, and it'd have been *so easy*. So easy to climb over, to fall, to take a great big breath of brackish water, and sink into the dark hole he'd been digging for so long. Instead, he'd walked home, filled the tub, submerged himself, and screamed until he came up choking and coughing and gasping for air, and he never told Noah he'd wanted to die that afternoon.

The drop of rain wobbled on the tip of Larkin's finger.

But on March 30, 2020, six months into a habit growing worse by the day and hoping the universe would just pull the goddamn trigger on him because he didn't have the courage to do it himself, Larkin met Ira Doyle. And for the first time in eighteen years, Larkin had wanted to be alive.

He made a fist, catching the raindrop before it could fall. "Everett?"

Larkin turned. Noah was crossing the path toward him, skirting a dip where a puddle had formed. Lingering near the steps that led up to the promenade was a woman their age, her tightly braided hair covered by a gray hoodie. She held a pink umbrella overhead and wore black shorts that showed off her shapely brown legs and thighs. Larkin recognized Steph Coleman as one of Noah's coworkers. She taught first grade as well, and her classroom was across the hall from Noah's. They'd been close friends for years.

She waved politely.

Larkin raised a hand back in response.

"Thanks for coming uptown," Noah said. He came up just short of breaching Larkin's personal bubble meant for one's most intimate circle.

Larkin looked Noah over. He wore linen pants in what Larkin would call *wisteria*, and a white button-down with a little flower pattern in an almost, but not quite matching, purple. Noah's face looked better, but there was still a greenish bruise under one eye, and his right wrist had a bit of a friction burn from the duct tape. "How're you," Larkin asked.

Noah shrugged, nodded, but his eyes welled with sudden tears and his mouth twisted up as he fought back the urge to cry. "I'm okay," he managed to get out. "I, um… I'm still pretty scared. If I think about it, even a little—" He stopped and wiped his eyes. "You look good," he said, trying for an air of lightness that came across as horribly forced.

"I feel like a sidewalk shed fell on me," Larkin said, deadpan.

And just like that, Noah was crying and laughing and Larkin guided him down into a rigid embrace. Noah lowered his umbrella to one side before wrapping his arm a little too tightly around Larkin's neck, yanking him even closer. Larkin grunted in discomfort as his bruised body was jostled, but he didn't want Noah to be more afraid than he already was, so he sucked in a breath and said nothing about the pain.

When the bomb had detonated, the entire fourth floor exploded—glass and brick and splinters of wood three feet long rained down, crashing into the overhead scaffolding put into place to protect against that very sort of debris—but as the domino effect caused each floor to begin collapsing, the temporary structure gave way, and Larkin had gotten buried underneath as he'd been climbing out after Doyle and Noah.

He didn't remember the immediate seconds that followed, after a plywood wall slammed into him from behind and trapped him—saving him from being crushed by the falling wreckage—but he recalled his hearing coming and going among the deafening tinnitus, the roar of fire, the breakage of manmade structures, the howl of sirens, and Doyle calling his name, his voice closer with every anguished scream, and then the darkness had given way to light and Doyle was dragging Larkin to his feet, hauling him to safety.

Noah let go of Larkin. He raised his umbrella, fixed a bit of Larkin's hair that'd fallen from his side part, then asked, "Why'd they have to kill that journalist?"

Larkin hesitated. There was so much he couldn't say, but to leave Noah scrambling in the dark was a cruelty beyond comprehension. So he said, cautiously, "I believe Noonan and Murray were being blackmailed."

"By who?"

"I can't tell you that, not without further endangering you."

"What the hell, Everett?"

Larkin looked down. He was in street clothes, and his bright pink and orange sneakers were wet. He wondered how long he'd been standing in a puddle. Larkin took a step to the side and said, "Joe Sinclair was caught in the crossfire. He was busy following my cases, trying to land an interview, and at the same time, those two were being coerced into—they saw Joe following me, following you, and I believe they thought he was who was blackmailing them. They killed him thinking they were now off scot-free, but they weren't. His murder only escalated the situation."

"And they were forced to kidnap me," Noah whispered.

"Yes."

"The police haven't found them yet, have they?"

"No." But with confidence, Larkin added, "We will."

Rain thrummed over their umbrellas in a low, steady beat.

"This sounds so stupid to say out loud," Noah began, "but… thank you."

"For what."

He laughed again and shook his head. "For answering the phone. For saving my life."

"Oh." Larkin considered the correct response, but what was polite, what was *right*, when someone thanked you for that? He said, "You're welcome."

Noah looked out at the water, at the lighthouse on Roosevelt Island. "When everything—and you were—I couldn't move. I saw that wall *fall* on you and I couldn't… but Ira did. He told me I was okay and he wouldn't leave me alone, but he had to go back for you, and you know how they say mothers become superhuman and lift a car to save a child?" Noah turned back to Larkin and their umbrellas bumped. "It was like that—watching him."

Larkin's heart beat so hard in his chest, it physically hurt.

"He loves you, right?"

Larkin nodded.

"And you're happy?"

Again, Larkin nodded.

"Happier than when we were together?"

"Noah."

"I want you to be honest."

Larkin took a breath. "Yes."

Noah bit his lower lip as his chin quivered, but he only whispered, "Okay."

"Are you staying with Steph."

Noah wiped his face once more. He cleared his throat. "Yeah. She broke up with Michael, actually."

"I'm sorry to hear that."

"No, you're not. You never liked him."

"No, I didn't."

Noah cracked a smile. "He moved out. We're both up the creek without a second income to pay rent, so she asked me to be her roommate."

"I think that'll be good," Larkin agreed.

Noah looked in Steph's direction, and then he said abruptly, "I'm gonna go."

Larkin followed Noah's gaze. Steph was still waiting, but now so was Doyle—a few feet away, umbrella in one hand, a cup of coffee in the other. "All right."

"I'll see you again, won't I? I mean, we have to sign the papers."

"We'll talk," Larkin agreed. "Get home safe." And he watched as Noah slowly made his way back toward Steph, and the two disappeared down the curving stairs.

Larkin turned to the railing one more time.

He touched the wet surface.

But his purpose was to love, and love again.

Over and over.

Forevermore.

Larkin took a breath, and walked away. He fell into step with Doyle as they, too, started down the winding set of stairs and made their way along the green line of trees at the park entrance.

Doyle spoke first. "Is he okay?"

"In some ways."

"Are you?"

Larkin answered, "I have closure."

The Audi was parked across the street, on the corner of Eighty-Sixth and East End. Even from where they stood at the crosswalk, Larkin could see a damn parking ticket stuck under the windshield wiper.

"Let's go home," Doyle stated. "Climb into bed and make love until lunchtime. We can order delivery and then make more love until we either pass out or become severely dehydrated."

Larkin laughed under his breath. "I'd like that."

They reached the car and Larkin grabbed the ticket, collapsed his umbrella, and quickly got in behind the wheel. He dumped the umbrella in the back and started to crumple the ticket to throw too, but stopped.

Because parking tickets were orange.

And this was plain white.

Doyle climbed into the passenger seat and shut the door. "What do you think," he began, while putting a hand to the Mets cap on his head. "Do I wear the hat while—what is it?"

Larkin peeled open the wet, greeting-card-sized envelope. Inside was a folded sheet of white paper, cutout letters so familiar, they made his heart drop to the pit of his stomach.

CLOSER AND CLOSER, LARKIN

The typography of the first letters in each word was reminiscent of the vintage signage that once papered the New York docks, now lost to time.

TO A BAD DEATH

Was it a threat or a warning?

GO NOW TO "THAT COMPANY OF LITTLE ANGELS"

In the crease was what appeared to be a torn portion of a sticker with the letters R E C and half of a skull.

COME FIND ME

Everett Larkin and Ira Doyle return in:

Astor Place Assault

(Memento Mori: Book Five)

C.S. Poe is an author of gay mystery, romance, and speculative fiction. She's a winner of the Next Generation and e-Lit book awards, as well as a finalist of the Lambda Literary award.

She resides in New York City and is a Gilded Age New York historian and board director for the Victorian Society of New York. She loves Romanticism artwork, the films of Buster Keaton, coffee in the morning and whiskey in the evening, true crime, and cats. She's rescued two cats—Milo and Kasper do their best to distract her from work on a daily basis.

C.S. is an alumna of the School of Visual Arts.

Her debut novel, *The Mystery of Nevermore*, was published 2016.

cspoe.com

ALSO BY C.S. POE

SERIES:
Snow & Winter
The Mystery of Nevermore
The Mystery of the Curiosities
The Mystery of the Moving Image
The Mystery of the Bones
The Mystery of the Spirits

Snow & Winter Collection
Interlude

Magic & Steam
The Engineer
The Gangster
The Doctor

A Lancaster Story
Kneading You
Joy
Color of You

The Silver Screen
Lights. Camera. Murder.

Memento Mori
Madison Square Murders
Subway Slayings
Broadway Butchery
Hudson River Homicides

An Auden & O'Callaghan Mystery
(CO-WRITTEN WITH GREGORY ASHE)
A Friend in the Dark
A Friend in the Fire
A Friend in the Glass

NOVELS:
Southernmost Murder

NOVELLAS:
11:59

SHORT STORIES:
Curio
Love in 24 Frames
That Turtle Story
New Game, Start
Love Has No Expiration

Visit cspoe.com for the latest book and audio releases, as well as available translations.

Join C.S. Poe's newsletter for information on upcoming projects, read advance excerpts and free flash fiction, stay up-to-date on sales, conference appearances, and much more!

Follow C.S. Poe on Goodreads to keep your books organized and reviewed and BookBub to be the first notified of new releases and sales!

Check out C.S. Poe's other social media.